VENGEANCE IS MINE

VENGEANCE IS MINE

Mary Burns

Copyright © 2001 by Mary Burns.

ISBN #:   Softcover 0-7388-9911-9

All rights reserved. No part of this book may be reproduced or transmitted in any form or by any means, electronic or mechanical, including photocopying, recording, or by any information storage and retrieval system, without permission in writing from the copyright owner.

This is a work of fiction. Names, characters, places and incidents either are the product of the author's imagination or are used fictitiously, and any resemblance to any actual persons, living or dead, events, or locales is entirely coincidental.

This book was printed in the United States of America.

To order additional copies of this book, contact:
Xlibris Corporation
1-888-7-XLIBRIS
www.Xlibris.com
Orders@Xlibris.com

CONTENTS

CHAPTER 1	9
CHAPTER 2	19
CHAPTER 3	25
CHAPTER 4	33
CHAPTER 5	44
CHAPTER 6	56
CHAPTER 7	70
CHAPTER 8	82
CHAPTER 9	90
CHAPTER 10	97
CHAPTER 11	105
CHAPTER 12	116
CHAPTER 13	122
CHAPTER 14	129
CHAPTER 15	144
CHAPTER 16	153
CHAPTER 17	160
CHAPTER 18	170
CHAPTER 19	179
CHAPTER 20	191
CHAPTER 21	198
CHAPTER 22	206
CHAPTER 23	215
CHAPTER 24	225
CHAPTER 25	231

CHAPTER 1

A ray of early morning sunshine highlighted the blue and white sole of a sneaker lying in the deep shadow of the recessed doorway.

Ramya Nurami frowned, deepening the lines surrounding her eyes and lips. Which member of her staff had allowed a child to leave the day care centre improperly dressed? Perhaps the new girl? Certainly, such carelessness had never happened before her employment began.

Ramya breathed deeply and consciously relaxed her shoulders. She forced her attention to the neighbour's yard where a robin stalked its breakfast. Two black-capped chickadees called as they swooped between shrubs. The scent of apple blossoms tickled her nose and tiny droplets of dew glittered on the dandelion-spotted lawn.

Arriving at the day care centre while the city slept and before the staff and children invaded her solitude, allowed her time to organize her day and keep stress to a minimum. Ramya opened the gate in the chain-link fence, then bent to pull a clump of chickweed from the tiny flowerbed crowding the sidewalk.

Children must learn many things. At her day care centre they learned to respect plants, a small but important lesson. Three tulips were still in bud. She snapped the heads from two that had finished their show, then looked for new growth on the dogwood bushes that formed a second fence around her property.

Satisfied that her yard was immaculate Ramya returned her attention to the house. The shaft of sunlight had continued crawling across the porch and she saw a blue sock growing from the running shoe and merging with a denim-clad leg. She clenched her fists, crushing the weeds she held. Ramya forced herself to step toward the porch.

A child sat slumped against the door, his arms folded across a plush brown bear. The bear smiled inanely. The child's eyes were closed.

For the briefest of moments, Ramya prayed he was one of her charges left by an impatient parent to await the centre's opening. She prayed he simply slept though in her soul she knew the truth and dreaded its meaning.

She searched his delicate lips, his pug nose, and his translucent eyelids for a slight movement, for some sign of life, but found none.

Ramya stepped back then fled down the sidewalk and through the gate to her van. She forced the image of the child's face from her mind as she fumbled with the door and reached inside for her phone to dial 911.

"I've found Tommy."

******

Detective Mike Ceretzke of the Edmonton Police Service pulled his black truck to the curb in front of the day care centre. He looked across at Evan Collins, his partner, who had resembled a zombie since they received the call about the kid being found. Evan's control was tight, but Mike figured the call would defeat it, after all Evan's son wasn't much younger than their latest victim.

Mike scanned the area, systematically spiralling his search inward toward the cordoned-off crime scene. Edmonton was filled with neighbourhoods like this one. Characterless with monotonously similar rectangular bungalows that had been built during one of the city's first boom cycles. Now they were old and worn. The sidewalks were treacherously uneven and the roads potholed. Yards bulged with towering spruce trees that threatened to topple onto curling shingles.

He focused on a black and white house bordering the western edge of the day care, then studied the open field that lay to the east. A five-foot chain-link fence encircled the daycare; neatly trimmed dogwood bushes partially obscured the fence. The deep blue sky contrasted with the green roof of the pink building. Bright orange butterflies and blue swallows decorated the house. A sturdy swing set dominated one side of the yard, a plastic playhouse the other.

Mike drew on his experience, diagramming a scenario that had the killer parking in the field and carrying the child's body through the gate. Sufficient traffic used the road to make such bold action risky, but the entire force knew this offender thrived on surging adrenaline.

The breeze tugged an unruly lock of hair across his forehead. Mike combed it back with his fingers, following the motion with a pensive scratch of his scalp.

He mentally itemized the steps his investigation would follow. Canvas the neighbours to dig up information about strange vehicles. Cast any tire tracks found in the vacant lot. Run a metal detector over the grassed area.

Mike pulled his notebook from his jacket pocket. Should he call for a canine unit? Better give it a try. He pulled out a pen, ready to write, then paused. Hell, who did he think he was fooling? This case would be whisked out of his grasp before he arranged any follow-up. Mike shook off the thought and forced his concentration back to the task of note taking.

In the neighbouring yard, an elderly woman stood beneath the pink and white blossoms of a cherry bush and hugged her sweater close around her chest as she studied each step of the police investigation.

Mike clicked his pen. Was she always this curious? Had she seen anyone last night? Someone better talk to her.

He let his gaze follow the bright crime scene tape encircling the yard. A trail of twisted twigs and crushed flowers lay beneath the boldly coloured ribbon.

From the east corner of the property, near the vacant lot, a cluster of ladies dressed in shorts and slacks stared openly in his direction. They followed his movements as he stepped away from the vehicle then returned their attention to the semicircle of well-dressed parents and clinging children. He circled to join his partner then paused as a woman wearing a pink sari broke away from the group and approached them.

"Are you the detectives they have been expecting," she asked.

"Yes, ma'am," Mike answered. "Detectives Ceretzke and Collins."

"I am Ramya Nurami, the owner of this day care centre. How much longer must we wait for your people to finish? When can we resume our schedule?"

Detective Ceretzke noted the strength and determination visible in the woman's dark eyes. She was a businesswoman concerned with providing a service to her clients. Her call to the police had fulfilled her duty as a citizen, now she expected life to continue smoothly and her business to resume without interruption. The children would be consoled, but no wrinkle could be allowed to disrupt the status quo.

From the corner of his eye, Mike watched members of the Crime Scene Unit taking photos. They were still in the preliminary stages of their investigation. The day care's routine was about to be re-routed.

"You should find an alternate location for a day or even two. We'll complete our investigation without delay, but we need time to be thorough."

"Two days? Who would think a business could be so disrupted for a police investigation? A couple of hours I could understand, but a couple of days? What am I supposed to do with the children? This is going to hurt my business."

The detective forced his lips into a sympathetic smile. "Check with the neighbourhood school or perhaps the library has a room you can use for a couple of days."

"I will make some phone calls." Her voice was calm, but her fingers entwined and twisted, a betrayal of her otherwise businesslike demeanour.

With her hostility directed into a constructive path, Mike asked, "Mrs. Nurami, was it you who found Tommy Jamieson?"

She closed her eyes and nodded. "Why leave him sitting like that? It was the most awful thing I have ever seen. I thought he was sleeping."

"Have you noticed any strange vehicles around lately?"

She shook her head, then clasped her trembling hands. "I come here very early to do the paperwork. I would have noticed. It is something I watch carefully as you cannot be too suspicious of strangers when you run a child care centre. When I drove by the school I saw two police vans watching for the abductor, but no other strange vehicles."

Mike nodded and pushed at the unruly lock of hair. Five police vehicles had been patrolling the schoolyard and its general vicinity for the past two days, hoping to catch the abductor before he could leave Tommy's body and get away, again.

"Get your clients settled, but let an officer know where I can reach you. Also, we need exact details about the location and appearance of the vans you spotted in case one wasn't ours."

She bowed her head, mumbled to herself, and turned toward the group of staff and parents. As Mike walked toward the middle-aged officer guarding the scene, he raised his hand partially in greeting and partially to shade his eyes from the brightness of the morning. He studied the yard as he walked. Why had the killer left Tommy here?

"Hi, Hilda," Mike said as he got closer. "What's the status? Is the victim's identity confirmed? Is he Tommy Jamieson?"

"Yeah, it's him all right."

Mike noted her red, puffy eyes.

Hilda shifted the weight of her heavily laden belt, settling it more comfortably on her ballooning hips, and added, "Ident arrived twenty minutes ago."

He reached toward the gate, then hesitated.

She waved away his concerns. "That was the first surface Pete checked. Too many prints to be useful, but he lifted what he could."

She unlatched the gate and allowed him passage. Evan lingered outside the fence.

Hilda squinted as she studied Mike. "How did you calm Mrs. Nurami down? I figure she would have moved the boy if she knew what an inconvenience we would be."

Mike heard scorn in her tone. His face must have reflected his disapproval because she flushed and kept her eyes focused just beyond his left elbow.

"I suggested a solution."

"Always the problem solver."

Mike stepped into the yard, carefully staying within the corridor created by the Ident team.

"It's the same M.O. as last year," Hilda said, lowering her voice and looking over her shoulder at the cluster of parents and staff. "I was at that crime scene too. It matches right down to the plush bear. Damn it, four years in a row."

"This time he didn't return the kid to the abduction site."

"No, it's the same. He leaves them just outside the surveillance perimeter. How does he know where we set up?"

Mike shrugged his ignorance, then continued toward a hunchbacked officer who was busy inspecting the scene.

"Pete, it's the same as the others?"

Pete Humphries snorted. "That's what we expected, isn't it?" He continued examining a section of porch. "It is the last week of May. The victim is a grade one student abducted from his schoolyard. Four consecutive years suggests a distinct pattern." He turned his head and squinted into the distance. "Still, until we're finished here and the good doctor does her examination, we can't call it identical."

"But he is Tommy Jamieson?"

"He matches the photos."

"So it's Norman's case and the task force will take over," Mike said, speaking as much to himself as to the Ident officer. He flipped his notebook closed. Losing the case to the task force was inevitable. Its leader, Norman Carswell, should already be on the scene. He flipped the notebook open again. What the hell, he would follow procedure until told otherwise. Maybe the good detective wasn't ready to admit he had lost another kid.

Pete raised his arm to shield his eyes from the sunlight, then tilted his head back, and looked Mike in the face.

"You get stuck with informing the parents?"

"Yeah. I'm on my way to their place now. Maybe I can get to them before the media does. Any sign of how our guy brought the kid into the yard?"

"The only access is through the front gate. The back yard is completely fenced with a high, solid board fence to keep the kids in and everyone else out."

"The neighbours . . . ."

"Constables are going door-to-door."

"You'll let me know . . . ."

"When I'm finished. Yes. Now go talk to the parents." Pete looked toward the road and added, "Look after that partner of yours. This kind of crime hits too close to home for the young family men."

Mike looked at Evan Collins who was interviewing a staff member. Outwardly, he looked normal in his charcoal grey business suit, light grey shirt, and subtly patterned tie. Evan never looked rumpled, his wife made sure of that. But closer inspection exposed his clenched jaw and rigid back. Dark circles around his eyes spoke of sleepless nights.

Mike signalled to Evan. "Are you going to be able to handle this," he asked.

Evan breathed deeply and closed his eyes. "Yeah, just part of the job, right?"

"I'll notify the parents on my own. You stay here. Call the station and find out what's keeping Carswell. Keep talking to the day care staff; maybe one of them saw our guy hanging around."

Evan nodded then dabbing at the sheen of moisture on his pale forehead, trudged toward the cluster of spectators.

Mike climbed into his truck and drove the ten blocks to the Jamieson home. Located in a community bordering the day care it was also a bungalow, but the Jamiesons had renovated it with new siding and a sweeping verandah. A large ecoscaped area further distinguished the house from its neighbours.

Two men in their mid-thirties sat on the front step with coffee cups and cigarettes in hand. They watched a pair of toddlers rolling on the grass under the spreading branches of a crab-apple tree.

Mike pulled his vehicle to the curb. As he stepped out of the truck, one of the watchers turned and spoke to the other, who stood and walked into the house. By the time Mike reached down to open the gate in the low picket fence, the man had returned with another man and four women. One woman held a baby; another was very pregnant.

A couple, who Mike recognized as Susan and Howard Jamieson, pushed forward. Mrs. Jamieson's hair hung limp and stringy on her shoulders; her eyes were red smears in her pasty face. Her husband reached out, grasped her hand, and held it. His gaze pleaded for good news.

"Tommy," Susan Jamieson said in a voice husky from crying.

"We'll need you to make a positive identification," Mike said.

They slumped. New tears followed old streaks down Mrs. Jamieson's face. She leaned on her husband's shoulder as his arm snaked around her slim waist.

"I yelled at him that day, you know." Her voice was expressionless. "He'd lost his hat. He was so careless with his belongings, always losing something." The words mingled with sobs. "The last time I saw my baby and I didn't tell him I loved him, just that he had to learn to look after his stuff."

The toddlers stopped playing and ran to their parents, making a wide circle around the stranger who had brought more tears with him.

One of the men put his arms around the pregnant woman. "Was it the same as with our children?" His nod embraced the group on the step.

Mike recognized him as Jim Peterson whose daughter, Sally, had been the first victim.

"The M.O. appears identical, but until we complete our investigation we can't be certain."

Mike heard the formality in his words and his mind screamed at him to say, 'Yes, it's the same bastard'. He breathed deeply, then bit his lower lip. Losing control would be unprofessional and wouldn't help these people cope with their grief.

"We will look after them," the pregnant woman said. She cradled her swollen abdomen and left the protection of her husband's arms to hug the grieving woman.

"Did you catch him this time," Jim Peterson asked. He read the answer in Mike's face. "Four kids. Four years. Damn it, can't you cops do anything right?"

"We thought we had the area covered."

"But he got through anyway, didn't he? Maybe we have to deal with this ourselves." He turned toward the other men as if searching for support.

"Don't talk like that, Mr. Peterson." Mike understood the hatred that hung like sour gas fumes in the early morning chill, but he feared vigilante justice.

"I'll talk however I want and if I ever find out who he is, I'll talk to him with a baseball bat. Talking to you cops isn't doing us any good." He looked toward the street and his shoulders slumped. "Hell, I'd even talk to that slime of a TV reporter if I thought it would help."

Mike looked over his shoulder as a Station Six news van pulled to the curb behind his truck. He held back the curse that threatened to escape his lips. Richard Tanner.

Tanner swaggered toward the house with his lopsided smile and boy-next-door charm turned to maximum. Mike fought to keep his expression neutral. What would it take to wipe that smirk off Tanner's face? He trekked back to the street hoping to head off the reporter and if he couldn't get rid of him, Mike knew he would get out of Tanner's sights as fast as he could.

"Morning Mike. Is it true the score is four-zero?"

"This isn't a sports event. We don't keep score and we won't stop until we catch the murderer."

"Like hell you don't." The reporter motioned with his chin toward the group gathered on the verandah. "What's this, a victim support group? The whole gang is here."

"Lay off them. They're all suffering and it's damned good of them to give the Jamiesons their support considering they must be reliving the agony of their own loss."

"Yeah, okay. I'll get the sob story from them. Any new leads on this creep?"

"Talk to the media liaison officer, Tanner."

"How about telling me who screwed up and let our guy get away?"

"Why don't you go play in traffic?"

"Touchy. How's Beth? Has she dumped you yet?"

Mike shoved the reporter aside and walked toward his vehicle.

Tanner's cameraman flashed him a sympathetic look and Mike grimaced in return.

"How do you stand him, Chuck," he asked the cameraman.

Brown eyes full of an emotion Mike couldn't identify met his gaze. Then Chuck's eyebrows bumped together and his face lit up in a smile. His white teeth contrasted with his heavy beard and mahogany tan.

"We each endure burdens, he's mine."

CHAPTER 2

Officers filled the rows of chairs in the concrete room. Some sat at attention, their faces draped with failure. Others conversed in quiet groups. None of the usual laughter rang out to mark the punch line of an off-colour joke; no curses followed good-natured ribbing.

Associate Superintendent Samantha Weisman stood in front of a white board. News articles and clippings cluttered the other half of the wall behind her.

She surveyed the officers, her gaze stopping at Norman Carswell the leader of the task force. Norman looked all of his fifty-nine years. He had lost at least thirty pounds in the four years since the first murder and he couldn't afford to lose more. She remembered how eagerly he had accepted the challenge of solving that first case. It was to have been a final triumph to savour during his retirement. When the anniversary of the first murder brought a second abduction and each subsequent year another murder, the man's dedication had deepened into compulsion.

Sam let her gaze move over the row of officers to Mike Ceretzke, where she again paused. His record for solving cases was better than good, besides, she liked him. Unfortunately, she couldn't give him the task force. Chief Horban had urged her to give Carswell one more chance.

Male locker room politics had plagued her progress up the hierarchical ladder ever since she signed onto the force, about a century earlier. Still, it had been a rare event for Horban to step in and use his eloquent reasoning to get his way. Should she have told him to get his nose the hell out of her job, consequences be damned? Still, he had made Chief for a reason; partly because he was the best person for the job, but the deciding factor had been his ability to talk a mosquito into donating blood.

She had sat across from Horban listening to his so sensible reasoning. Carswell, he said, was determined to catch the abductor—, but then so was every other officer on the force including Mike. Carswell had an intimate knowledge of all four cases—so did a few others and it wouldn't take long for Mike to get up to speed.

Then Horban struck with an undeniable point—Carswell had the most to lose if he couldn't solve the case. It was his last chance. He knew that if he succeeded his prestige would be restored in the eyes of his fellow officers, but if he failed it meant a retirement relegated to history as a has-been. Horban had argued that if not the carrot, the stick might work. Sam still preferred Mike; she didn't like Carswell.

Two more officers entered the briefing room and she straightened her shoulders out of their perpetual shrug, ready to start the briefing. Remembering to put firmness and conviction into her tone, she spoke into the stillness of the room.

"Now that we're confident this killing is another in the series, Norman's task force takes over the investigation. Cancel your social lives people. Until we solve this case, everyone is working it. Consider overtime approved and expected."

******

Who knew where the surveillance vans waited? Detective Norman Carswell could just about believe the killer had guessed the locations. Just about, but not quite. A guy that lucky had inside information.

One of the cops must have opened his mouth and gave the creep what he needed. Norman knew he would check with every officer again this year. Maybe someone had heard the big mouth spewing details and maybe they would remember who else had overheard.

He shifted in his chair and pretended to focus on what the Super was saying. The leak was probably one of the Super's women, gossiping while nibbling a gourmet bagel at some classy cafe. He would triple-check every woman on the force and every place they frequented. He was due a change of luck; this was his last chance to beat this guy.

Retiring with the biggest case of his career unsolved was a bitch, but Horban said that was the price of failure.

Horban sure had taken to being Chief. They had gone through training together, but Norman had stuck with hands-on investigation. He wasn't a political kiss-ass who stepped on old friends. He had to get this guy and show everyone he still had what it took to put perverts away for good.

He rubbed at the stiffness in his neck. Would that woman ever quit yapping so they could get back to work? Norman's attention wandered away from the Superintendent's voice.

Where had they screwed up? He had personally sent a cop to every grade one class in the city. He had done his job right. His men covered all that crap about who to be on the lookout for, about not getting into cars with strangers.

Tommy Jamieson's school had been near the bottom of the list. Rose Byron had covered it and must have done a lousy job, probably talked all touchy feely, instead of scaring the kids so they'd think twice about letting their own parents walk them home.

Hell, why Tommy? Why no witnesses? Why hadn't the kid yelled his lungs out? Who would a kid trust enough to walk away with after all the warnings?

Two types of people headed his list, cops in uniform and people the kid knew. With each murder, he'd reworked the same ground. But the kids still had no friends, no schools, no classes, and no teachers in common.

Years of his life spent working the same puzzle and he was no further ahead and now the sharks were readying their attack. He'd checked out all the cops involved in the case and all those that weren't. Sure, some of them had worked more than one of the abductions, but what cop could be that sick?

Who else? He had to find the pervert this time; he had to show Horban he could still hunt clues. Samantha Weisman would have passed the case to Ceretzke if he hadn't reminded the Chief of overdue favours and hard-earned loyalties. Ceretzke, her pet detective. That's what you got having a woman in charge. Favouritism. Damn but he was tired of playing this game, especially with the rules forever changing in favour of the perverts.

Norman closed his eyes and stifled a yawn. Who could have known? Who could have spotted the surveillance without being seen?

******

"Beth, unless we get a fast solution to the Jamieson case, I won't get to the River Belle tomorrow evening."

Mike Ceretzke hunched over the phone as he spoke. He hated cancelling their arrangements, but Beth understood. She knew how much catching this guy meant to the morale of every cop and every parent in the city. She had been one of the first citizens to respond to the department's call for searchers when Tommy Jamieson disappeared.

"You can meet my family some other time," she said.

Mike paused, his coffee mug half way to his lips. Was that relief he heard in her voice?

"Is everything all right," he asked.

Mike pictured Beth sitting comfortably in front of the computer in her home office, concentrating on her current project. Her slender fingers prancing over the keys. Her full lips curled into a half smile.

Since they had met six months earlier, not a day passed when he didn't long to kiss those lips and run his hands through her short curly hair. He knew she shared his feelings, so why was she relieved that he had to delay meeting her family? She wasn't worried, was she? He knew he would like them. Beth had told him so much about her parents that he felt he already knew them as well as he knew her.

And he knew her well. Right now, she would have a coffee mug within reach and at least one of her cats curled up in her lap. She spent mornings at her computer tutoring technological illiterates about the intricacies of on-line information management and stock market investing. Sometime around noon she would go to the park for a five-kilometre run, then she would head off for her shift at the public library.

"Jim suggested we tell Mom and Dad about his idea while we're on the boat," she said, interrupting his thoughts.

Mike relaxed. That explained her tone of voice. After all, family business deserved centre stage.

"Well. Okay. Apologize for me if I don't make it tomorrow night, but tell them I am looking forward to meeting them."

"How are the Jamiesons coping?"

"The parents of the other victims are helping."

"What do you do next?"

"Super Sam gave the case to the task force, so it's Norman's responsibility."

"Should he be coordinating the investigation? Is he up to the job?"

"He knows everything about those files, so Sam had no choice but to give it to him. She emphasized that she expected the rest of us to pitch in as needed. I think this is the last bone before she eases him into retirement."

"She shouldn't leave him on this case. Hurting Norman's feelings is less important than getting this guy off the street."

******

Detective Carswell slumped across the staff room table where the remains of a burger and fries, congealed. His tie rested on a tongue of ketchup oozing from a plastic tube. Norman eyed his tie, picked it up, and licked the ketchup off.

The roll of music that announced the evening news started. Norman switched his attention to the screen. Of course, Tommy Jamieson was the lead story. Richard Tanner, that bloodsucking leech, was trying hard to look like he didn't love reporting the sickening details. He should flip the channel and watch that good-looking girl on sixteen, but the remote control was on the counter and he was too tired to get out of his chair and retrieve it.

Damn Tanner, how did the guy manage to look so sleek? He made the kids' parents look like they needed a shower—all the kids' parents. They looked wore out but then, they probably hadn't slept much since Tommy disappeared. Just like him. It had been weeks since he managed even four solid hours.

As the anniversary drew nearer, he'd worried that he hadn't anticipated every possible target. When the kid disappeared, he had stopped trying to sleep; he had dreaded even dozing, because when he did he heard young voices crying out for vengeance.

He listened to Tanner taunt the parents, asking them endless questions. Why had Tommy's mother allowed him out on his own? Hadn't she known the danger? Hadn't they street-proofed their child? Who would Tommy have gone with? Did they realize family members were usually the victimizers of children?

Tanner stopped only when Tommy's mother broke into tears and his father looked as if he was going to smash the camera over the reporter's head.

Norman faintly remembered enjoying that kind of drive, before this endless case took over his life and sucked him dry. Long ago he had asked those same questions.

Endless questions. Hard questions. Tanner asked them all the time, of everyone. He especially pestered cops. Who even noticed reporters anymore? They were everywhere. The maggots of police work, appearing from nowhere whenever something smelled rotten.

Hell, some people knew how to use them to make their point or to publicize their obsession. Some of the guys even admitted they answered questions just to get rid of them.

Norman chewed on a French fry and let his gaze focus on the handsome celebrity in the powerful little box. He felt a light suddenly light up in the fog clouding his mind.

Why hadn't he thought of the media before now? Reporters could weasel surveillance details out of unwary officers. A good-looking phony like Tanner probably had a bunch of the Super's girls panting to talk. A celebrity like him could win a kid's trust.

Besides, Tanner had been tracking Norman's every move for the past two months, nagging for details and ridiculing his every step.

Norman swallowed a final bite of his burger and walked away from the table, leaving the wrappings. He had work to do. Tanner was a good reporter sure, but maybe he was also a pervert checking for weak spots? Maybe it was time to investigate him.

CHAPTER 3

Mike Ceretzke watched as Norman's long-fingered hand came to a rest on top of the file he was reading. Mike looked up, noticing that Norman was still wearing his slightly grubby shirt from the previous day. Bleary eyes and an unshaven face added to his look of exhaustion. What did he want now?

"I'm gone for a while, Ceretzke," Norman said in a husky whisper.

Deciding Carswell was half-crazed with fatigue, Mike decided to cut the guy some slack. "If Sam asks, where will you be?"

"There's a lead I'm checking."

"A lead? Something new came in?" Mike had monitored the night's files and caught nothing relevant.

"It's just an idea. Don't mention it to the Super. I'll tell her majesty myself, if it develops into anything. And don't bug me unless something breaks."

Mike turned in his chair and watched the aging officer drift out of the room. Could Norman have uncovered a lead or was he heading home to sleep? It didn't matter because the investigation would proceed more smoothly without Norman's nagging guidance.

******

"Tanner, you're off the Jamieson kid story. I'll get someone to do a feature on how the families are coping, then we're leaving them alone."

Richard Tanner placed his palms on the desk, leaned forward, and glared at the juvenile hiding behind its oak expanse.

"I get the story back if they catch the guy, right?"

"The way you handled yesterday's interview was cold. We want a sympathetic viewpoint. You practically accused those parents of conspiring to murder their own kids."

"I do a tough interview, that's what my fans expect. But I suppose I can do it as a sob story, if you insist."

Richard bent his elbows, bringing his face closer to the kid. Damn college graduates figured they knew it all. Give him ten years in the business and he wouldn't be so righteous.

"No, you can't. You've got one style of reporting and I find it obnoxious."

"Are you threatening me? Remember my contract is coming up for renewal. Maybe I'll find a station where they'll pay me what I deserve and where I can work without interference from some school kid."

"Don't threaten to quit, Tanner. You might be surprised how fast I take you up on the offer. Now get out of here and find a story you can exploit."

Richard reared back, then plastered a what-the-hell smile on his face, and headed out the door of the office. He ignored his co-worker's smirks and strolled to the building's cafeteria where he bought a coffee and lit a cigarette.

He blew a cloud of smoke toward the no smoking section, smiling at the disapproving faces. Some lawyer must be threatening the station or the kid wouldn't be squawking. Still, being kicked off any story didn't look good. Especially one this big. Especially when his contract was expiring.

Richard added more nicotine to his body. He hated admitting it, even to himself, but that pip-squeak might have the power to kill his contract.

How could he discredit the kid? What he needed was a damn good story, something spectacular to show the board his worth.

******

Jennifer Rivers hesitated in the doorway to the River Belle's office. A slim, dark-haired man stood with his back to the door and watched while Cara, the bookkeeper, photocopied a stack of green registration forms. His straight hair was held back with an elastic band and lay between his shoulder blades. He wore a sleeveless black muscle shirt. Black leather pants hugged his slender hips and slid into the tops of his polished black cowboy boots. A silver chain traced a barely visible line around his neck.

From the family photo sitting on the bookkeeper's desk, Jennifer recognized him as Cara's brother, Lap. He shifted his weight and spoke loudly enough for her to hear his words over the hum and clank of the copy machine.

"Come on Cara, this tub's ready to push off. You should have had this stuff ready, like usual. Doing this now is risky."

Cara placed a green sheet on the screen, pressed a button, and then replaced the sheet with another. "I spent the morning training that new kid, Jennifer. This is the first time I've been able to get rid of her long enough to get at this. But we've gotta talk anyway. Can you slow down on grabbing the cars? You're stealing them too close to people's trips on the Belle, someone's going to connect it."

"Can I sell the credit card numbers right away or do I ask for your permission on that too?"

Cara's thin shoulders stiffened. She cringed as she tilted her head to peer at him; the papers flew less quickly.

"Stick to your part of the business. This is mine," Lap said.

Jennifer shuddered. His tone held a threat of violence.

"We're short on computer parts, so make an effort to get more house keys tonight," he demanded.

Jennifer swayed as the boat fought for freedom, impatient to enter the river's current. She shifted her weight to compensate. She heard the hum of the copy machine, watched the regular flash of light, and listened to the loud laughter of a tourist on the deck above. Her nose twitched at the aroma of coffee drifting from the kitchen.

Her job on this little paddle wheeler was one of the best things that had happened to her since her arrival in Edmonton. She enjoyed relating stories about the history of the river valley to first-time tourists and long-time residents. She especially appreciated having a second pay cheque to supplement her work as an office temp. Jennifer couldn't afford to lose her job and she was afraid that would happen if the two people in the office caught her snooping into whatever they were doing.

She stepped back from the doorway hoping to disappear undetected. Instead, she backed into a stack of plastic cases full of bags of hot dog buns. The cases squealed as they scraped across the tiled floor. Jennifer fought to regain her balance then fled down the hall toward the dining room.

Over her shoulder, she saw Cara race through the doorway, then stop abruptly. Her lips curved into a tight smile but her eyes signalled danger. Lap appeared at her shoulder. Cara extended her arm, stopping his advance. He slipped his hand into the pocket of his leather pants and rocked onto the balls of his feet.

Hearing a burst of talk and laughter, Jennifer spun toward a group of tourists. They demanded her attention, wanting to know all about Edmonton's wonderful river.

Cara and her brother remained outside the doorway, watching her speak to the family group.

She answered the tourists' questions. "Yes, the riverbanks are far steeper than those of the Missouri River."

Cara moved the cases of buns closer to the wall. Lap kicked a second stack toward her though his scrutiny never left Jennifer.

"No, we are not in danger of meeting wild animals during the trip. Well, perhaps we'll see a beaver, or a coyote, and if we're really fortunate a deer feeding along the bank."

With the cases cleared from his path, Lap stepped toward Jennifer.

"Yes, the boat will stop at the Fort Edmonton landing every half-hour until 6:45."

Jennifer moved to her left, one step at a time, slowly circling the family. Finally, they were between her and Cara.

Then the tourists with their curiosity temporarily satisfied continued to the upper deck. She heard their exclamations at the sight of the dangerously swift and swollen river.

Jennifer escaped up the stairs behind them. Cara had guessed that she'd overheard them. What would they do to her? Should she talk to Cara and tell her that she had heard nothing? Or should she run as far and as fast as she could? Not that. She was not running from anything, anymore.

The sun still shone when she reached the upper deck. Somehow, Jennifer thought it might have disappeared in the cloud of calamity that pursued her through life. She clung to the doorframe and searched through the milling passengers for the uniform of a senior staff member. Then she hesitated. If what she'd overheard was true others must be involved. Who could she trust? Maybe she should report their scam to the police?

Jennifer released the doorframe and stepped toward the rail. Report what? A conversation Cara would claim she had misinterpreted. The warm rays of sunshine and the stiff breeze dispersed her gloom. Did she really know anything?

"You'll regret telling anyone what you heard," Cara hissed close to her ear.

Jennifer turned, then froze into stillness at the malice she saw in Lap's dark eyes. The man's face was expressionless, but threat radiated like a fever from his body. Cara squinted her almond-shaped eyes and stood slightly behind her brother's broad shoulder.

"Really, I just didn't want to interrupt you." Jennifer knew she sounded like a fool but kept talking, hoping to find the words that would fix this mess. "I didn't mean to knock over those crates. It must have been the closeness and the motion of the boat, because I desperately needed fresh air. I'll go back and tidy up the hall."

"Forget it. Forget everything," Cara said.

Her brother said nothing.

"Nothing to forget. I didn't see, or hear, anything."

"Keep it that way."

Cara turned away. Lap's gaze held Jennifer captive for another terrifying moment before he spun on his heel and slouched toward the gangway. Cara followed, tugging at the strap of his backpack as if trying to make him stop and listen, but the boat was ready to leave the dock and the attendant held the gate open, waiting for him to disembark. Once on the pier he turned and stared at her until the current caught the boat and pulled it into the middle of the river.

Jennifer felt the darkness of terror descend on her. She began shivering. She had to run. No. Get help. The police could help. No. They had never done anything for her, just hassled her and Eric. She would not go to the cops and she would not run either. There was another way. Richard Tanner would help. If he got a story out of it, he would help.

If he would take her call, but he owed her that much, didn't he? She could phone him and let him expose the scam. First she had to get him to talk to her and he was avoiding her, so that might not be easy. Perhaps if she made an anonymous phone call? Would he recognize her voice?

Jennifer stayed on the upper deck during the cruise. She chatted with passengers, trying to focus on answering their questions about Edmonton and about the River Belle.

She couldn't phone Richard Tanner from the paddle wheeler, someone might see her and she didn't know which members of the crew she could trust. Of course, Lyle was trustworthy, but he wasn't scheduled to work until the supper cruise.

When the boat returned to the landing, Jennifer slipped into the midst of the departing passengers. When the tourists turned right toward the parking lot, she turned left to the park shelter and a pay phone. After she talked to Richard Tanner, she would join another group and be back on board before anyone missed her. Once she'd called Richard, she would be committed. Did she know what she was doing?

Jennifer hesitated, her hand resting on the receiver of the pay phone. Budding trees sheltered the cobbled path, screening her from the boat. Still, Jennifer felt eyes watching her. She looked around at the cyclists, the hikers, and the picnic tables full of families enjoying the first fine weather of the season. She recognized no one.

She rested her head against the plastic bubble protecting the telephone. Either phone or forget it, those were her choices. With a defiant, rapid movement she inserted the coin and punched a number she knew well.

"Tanner."

The distracted tone was supposed to tell her he was busy; however, she had heard him use that tone while reclining, his feet on his desk, with one hand behind his head. He had once told her that he considered it important to always sound besieged.

She put her hand over the mouthpiece and spoke in a husky whisper. "Some members of the crew of the River Belle are stealing credit card information and car keys from the passengers."

"How do you know?"

"I heard them talking. Look I have to make this quick. When can we meet?"

"I'll come to the boat tonight and you can point out the culprits. What's your name?"

"No, we can't meet here. They can't see us together."

"Look, I don't play cloak and dagger. You want my help with the story say so. Otherwise, find another reporter."

Jennifer twisted a strand of hair around her finger. This wasn't how she wanted it, but she would have to take the risk. "I'll find you when it's safe."

"Whatever. Just don't be making this up."

******

Linda Olsson watched from inside the park's rustic shelter. She had been waiting for the boat to return, debating her next step. Now her wait proved worthwhile. The girl at the phone was her Jenny.

Jenny's beautiful mouth turned down in its habitual frown. Linda longed to make that face light up in a smile. A faint hint of tan was the only colour in Jenny's beautiful face. That tinge and the golden highlights in her cloak of hair spoke of sunshine. She did look healthy. Still, she was so slim, almost skinny. Was she too slim?

For once Sheila's gossipy interference had proved right. How Sheila had loved whispering across the kitchen table, "It's her Linda. I swear on my mother's grave that it was your Jenny. We saw her on the boat. She looked too thin and very pale."

Linda hadn't paid attention to the description, because Sheila thought that anyone who was less than forty pounds overweight was stick thin. Linda ran her hands down her own slender hips, feeling hard bone under a thin layer of flesh. No, you could never be too thin.

"What was she doing? Did you talk to her? Was she all right," Linda had demanded, feeling her hope grow, desperate to hear good news. Every time someone swore they had seen her youngest child, she had raced off to follow up their lead, only to be disappointed.

"Of course I didn't talk to her. You told us all not to say a word if we saw her, didn't you? Well anyway, she was wearing a staff uniform. Tight blue slacks, too tight if you ask me. A white blouse, a blue string tie, and a cute little cap, sort of like a beret."

"She was working on the boat?"

"Of course."

Linda remembered the relief that had flooded through her at hearing that Jenny was not walking the streets to survive as Linda had feared. Jenny had been only fifteen when she ran off with Eric, her older brother. He must have protected her while he could.

She swallowed her tears and watched Jenny look around before dialling the phone. At least one of her children was alive and safe. If she rushed over and clasped her in her arms, would all be forgiven?

The words of the police officer echoed in her mind.

"She's safe. She's alive, but she's also old enough to decide she doesn't want you to know where she's living. We have to honour her wishes."

Linda caressed the wooden casing of the shelter's doorway. How could she make it all right? What would it take to win back her daughter's love? She would do anything, but for now she could only watch this lovely girl from a distance. Linda adjusted her purse, straightened her shoulders, and followed Jennifer to the River Belle.

CHAPTER 4

Sam Weisman scanned the room, noted Norman's empty chair and the heaps of file folders on his desk. Sticky notes decorated his lampshade and spotted the back of his chair. The pile of phone messages was a centimetre thick. He hadn't been at his desk in a while.

She diverted her course and walked toward Mike. His attention was focused on the file open on his desk blotter. "Mike, where the hell is Carswell?"

He looked up. "He hasn't been around much today. Asked me to field any calls that came in and to contact him if anything broke."

"Damn, the Chief wants a briefing. What can you tell me? Anything new to pass on?"

"Teams have finished canvassing the area. One of the neighbours thought they saw a suspicious person the night Tommy's body was dumped. It's vague, just a man walking through the field that borders the day care, nothing we can use to distinguish him from any other average looking male in the city. If it was our guy, he wasn't carrying anything when the neighbour saw him. Rose is working with him on a drawing."

Sam felt her shoulders loosen a notch. Norman Carswell might be a concession she had to live with, but Mike was on top of the case.

"The lab is giving us top priority," Mike continued, "but we don't have much for them to work with, except some tire casts from the field."

"I'm sorry I couldn't let you head the case," she said.

"It was your call." Mike flipped the file closed and placed it on top of a tidy stack growing in his out basket. "The important thing is that we catch this creep, not who's in charge."

Sam liked that he never questioned her decisions. He was one of the few officers who hadn't overtly tested her promotion against some yardstick of their own creation. Perhaps his teaching background allowed him to accept her Masters degree in English Literature more easily than did a few other officers she could name. Well, the most important thing now was solving this case.

"When you talk to Norman tell him to get to my office," she said as she continued toward the elevators and the Chief's inquisition.

******

Linda Olsson sat in the shadow of the narrow building that dominated the paddle wheeler's upper deck. The end of the building closest to the stern housed the snack bar. The bridge dominated the bow. A gift shop and washrooms filled the remaining space.

She had purchased a day pass and spent the afternoon on board. Then on a whim she bought a ticket for the evening dinner cruise. It strained her credit card, but what did the money matter if she could spend time watching her lovely daughter.

Her wide-brimmed sun hat shielded her face and she wasn't worried that Jenny would recognize the rest of her. The day before Jenny and Eric disappeared, Jenny had called her a gross, flabby ball of fat.

Linda pulled the brim farther down her forehead. She hadn't always been heavy. At eighteen, she had looked like Jenny did now, thin and young. Then Eric was born and she gained ten pounds. After his father ran off, she gained twenty more. Another fifteen stayed after Jenny's birth and as each lover moved in and out, she added a few more pounds. Ten years ago, the Mounties had chased her last live-in lover out of the province. Then she ate to forget him and his slimy ways.

Jenny was only fifteen when she'd screamed those hateful words and disappeared into the night with her eighteen-year-old brother. Linda's appetite had disappeared that same night and over one hundred fifty pounds had melted from her frame since they were uttered. Linda knew she was unrecognizable to her own daughter.

She watched as Jenny wove her way through the clusters of

passengers. Jenny pointed toward the shore at sights of interest; she talked briefly to each person and moved with ease along the deck. Linda felt pride swell in her chest, somehow her daughter had grown into a calm, mature adult.

She could finally banish the dreams where Jenny, dressed in a leather mini-skirt and stiletto heels, climbed into strange cars. She could laugh at the nightmares that featured Jenny's face bobbing under the surface of a body of murky water her eyes open in a fixed stare. She was here, safe.

Linda leaned against the wooden wall of the building. Damn, Jenny was looking toward her with a professional greeter's smile adorning her beautiful face. Something lurked behind that smile. She was preoccupied, but with so many competing for her attention that could be normal. Linda knew that if she said hello, Jenny would know her voice. Jenny had always shown an amazing talent for recognizing voices, even if she had only heard them once. Unless that had changed too. So many things changed in four years.

But Jenny didn't want to talk to her, the police told her that when they reported Eric's death. Her handsome son, a tall, golden Viking god who resembled his father had died in a single vehicle accident. The way they explained the accident, Linda knew he had aimed his car at the tree.

Linda lowered her chin, sending a signal that she wanted to be left alone.

Would speaking to Jenny be wrong? Should she risk rejection? Her support group facilitator urged reaching out as a positive way to deal with the embedded pain. Others in the group said their children had met their attempts at reconciliation with restraining orders.

Linda rested against the wooden siding. Peering from under her hat, she let her gaze follow the girl through the cooling evening air. Perhaps later, after the dinner cruise, she would try to talk to her. To make a scene and upset her girl during her working day wouldn't be right. She wouldn't start their future with a scene. That was their past.

✶✶✶✶✶✶

"She's blowing the whistle," Cara Poiter said to the tall, blond, well-muscled man who towered over her. She pointed toward the front of the boat where Jennifer stood, anxiously eyeing the arriving groups of passengers.

"See that Channel Six reporter? He does exposés and investigative reports. I bet she tipped him off."

"Cara, she ain't gone anywhere near him."

"Lap will kill her if he finds out."

"His being here is probably a coincidence."

"I promised him that she'd keep her mouth shut."

"She will."

"No, she's going to talk."

"She's too smart for that."

"She likes you, so if you want to keep her healthy keep her away from that reporter. I don't care how you do it. Throw her overboard if that's what it takes."

"That's damned extreme."

"If the police hear about our little scam, you'll be in as deep as the rest of us."

"I ain't going to hurt her."

Cara clutched her clipboard tightly. "If Lap finds out she's talking you won't have to."

✶✶✶✶✶✶

Norman Carswell pulled the beak of his baseball cap farther down his brow, shielding his eyes from the glare reflecting off the river's choppy surface.

It was his first trip on the River Belle. She was bigger than the Edmonton Queen and had more deck space. He chewed and swallowed the last of his hot dog. At least he had managed to get something to eat before the cook closed the snack bar.

The foxy beauty at the ticket booth asked the cook to save it for him, after he'd told her he was hungry now and didn't give a damn if they were eating right after sailing. Hell, he'd been following Tanner around half the night and all day and hadn't eaten anything but donuts.

The cook at the snack bar was cleaning up but she gladly scooped the last dog onto a warmed bun and emptied her cast iron fry pan of onions on top. She winked at him when she told him the dog was better fare than he would get during the evening buffet. Norman figured the old broad was eyeing him, but he wasn't desperate enough to make time for the ugly ones.

He was here for answers and evidence, but he couldn't figure why Tanner was on board. Why bring his cameraman? Did it tie into the murders?

He had followed them from the TV station to the park and watched as they boarded the boat. Tanner bought two tickets. Norman waited until they boarded, then bought a seat on the dinner cruise. He was going to follow this guy until he spotted something or until he got him alone.

His hunch about Tanner was right; he knew that. He also knew he had stopped playing by the rules. No other kid was going to die by this freak's hand.

Tanner turned and looked in his direction; Norman pulled his hat down to shield his face from the reporter's gaze. Then he leaned far over the rail and pondered the choppy current. So far, Tanner hadn't recognized him and he wanted it to stay that way.

A casual look over his shoulder placed the two men in the bow of the boat. The cameraman stood with his feet balanced against the motion of the river. Tanner, tall and thin, showing more teeth than anyone had a right to, lounged against the rail.

His cameraman looked like a slob in this crowd. He hadn't changed from his Reeboks and beer logo T-shirt. He had been fiddling with the eyepiece of his camcorder, but now his teeth barred into a snarl in the midst of his bushy beard. His eyebrows resembled mating woolly caterpillars and his deep voice rose, boiling with anger and disgust.

Norman turned and stared at them, enjoying the scene. What had pissed the guy off?

"You can't be serious! You're going to drag . . . ."

Norman listened to the rising voices.

******

The river of muddy-brown water, swollen with spring runoff from the mountains and littered with tree branches, tugged at the vegetation lining its banks. Another week or two and the North Saskatchewan River would return to its shallow, slow-moving summer personality, but now it matched Beth McKinney's mood.

When she was a child, the tallest building on the riverbank was the MacDonald Hotel. Now glass-fronted towers dwarfed the hotel, like that pink monster Canada Place, bastion of federal government in Edmonton. It stood out like scar tissue against the older, brick buildings.

The Convention Centre, built to resemble a waterfall, was the most creative structure in the downtown core and one of the few that caught the unique atmosphere of the city. Its history included a nightmare of construction with people yelling about horrendous costs and waste of taxpayer money. Others argued the wisdom of building on an unstable riverbank that was honeycombed with abandoned coalmines. But the problems were eventually solved and the structure now stood on firm footings.

So many of the innovative structures and for that matter, ideas around this city had gotten the same rough treatment. Albertans were people who believed in a solid work ethic, conservative policy, and square brick buildings.

Tonight Beth and her brother Jim wanted to rescue their parents from retirement and re-enlist them into the ranks of those hardworking Albertans. Their attempt at breaking the news immediately after boarding was interrupted by a loud argument between Richard Tanner and Chuck Albright.

Whenever Richard passed through her life, Beth prepared herself for disaster. Once it was the death of a dream, the last time it was the murder of a friend. Here he was again, an ominous portent to their evening. Their argument interrupted what should have been a celebration and threatened to sour the occasion.

"Let's go into the dining room. I don't want to listen to them fight," Beth said, trying to guide her family away from the rail.

Jim put his arm around their mother, steering her toward the stairs but she shrugged him off.

"No, I'm not going to let him spoil tonight. It isn't every day we're together as a family," Dorothy McKinney said, her voice artificially bright. "It's unfortunate that your friend had to cancel out at the last minute, Beth. You said it was business that prevented his attending?"

"Yes, Mother. But he did say he was sorry and you will meet him soon."

"What type of work does he do? I don't believe you mentioned it. Of course, you haven't said much about him at all. Have you known him long?"

"What do you think they're yelling about," Jim asked.

Beth blessed his interruption. Soon she would tell her parents all about her relationship with Mike Ceretzke. Soon, but not tonight.

She knew she had put off telling them too long already, but her track record with men was littered with rejected candidates and she didn't want her parents hoping for something that wouldn't happen. Of course, their relief when she broke off her relationship with Richard Tanner had been apparent, but Arthur's decision to join the priesthood had been a disappointment to them. Before Arthur there had been John, who had wanted to settle down on a farm and raise a herd of children. Beth shivered just remembering her close escape that time. She had run all the way to Ontario and graduate school to be rid of him.

Life was sufficiently complicated without a permanent male presence. Still, whenever she thought of Mike Ceretzke and that seemed to be her constant pastime lately . . .

A loud outburst from Chuck pulled her attention back to the scene at the front of the boat. She answered her brother's question.

"Whatever it's about, Richard looks confident he'll win Chuck over."

"Why would Chuck go along with something he obviously opposes," her father asked.

Beth heard his disapproval. Her father distrusted people who could be led against their principles.

"Richard talks people into things that hurt them all the time. He considers it his role in life."

"Not this time, Sis." Jim nodded in the direction of the men. Chuck had walked away. "I don't think Tanner's going to talk him around."

"I'll talk to Chuck later and see if I can help him keep that resolve," Beth promised.

******

Jennifer, along with every other person on the boat, watched Tanner's public arrival. Then, as if his presence hadn't caused enough of a stir, the idiot stood in plain sight and started fighting with his cameraman.

Jennifer slumped into a deck chair. How could she have been so naive? Why had she believed he would keep their meeting secret? He should have left his cameraman at home or told the Captain some story about the station wanting shots of the trip. She would have to find another time to talk to him. A shiver ran between her shoulder blades. If Cara and her brother suspected her betrayal, what would they do?

The men's voices were getting louder. What were they arguing about anyway?

******

Chuck looked at Richard Tanner's smiling face, a face that had conned a thousand innocents into betraying their deepest secrets to the world. With his jaunty smile and boyish good looks, who would suspect Richard had the charm of Eden's serpent?

"You can't be serious!" Chuck bellowed, losing his fight to maintain self-control. "You're going to drag the names of good people, people who help kids, through the mud! If you report this story, enrolment will drop. People will be terrified of putting their kids into any organization. Why do you always have to hurt people?"

"Get off the soap box, Chuck. You might be one of the good guys, but there's a story in this about the jerks who do prey on kids. It's news."

"It's old news. Every paper and magazine has focused on some aspect of it. People have written books about it. Don't you think everyone has heard enough? What makes you think they'll even listen to your drivel? Maybe the story won't sell and you'll fall flat on your face."

"I don't do bad stories. I'll make it work. With your contacts in Little League and in the Scouts, it'll be simple for you to arrange a couple of in-depth interviews. People trust me and more important they answer my questions."

"You want me to play Judas." Chuck's voice rose, echoing across the decks.

A skinny woman wearing a big hat turned her head toward them. Sun glinting from her mirrored glasses blinded him. Something about her seemed familiar. He shook off the feeling. He had to convince Richard to ditch the story.

"You want me to ask my friends, people who give up time with their own families to help kids, you want me to betray them?"

"No, of course not, I don't want you to betray anyone. Just get them to agree to an interview." Richard kept his voice low and reasonable.

Chuck placed the video camera on the deck of the paddle wheeler. He straightened to his full 5'9", five inches shorter than Richard. Richard's air of disdain and his crooked smile never wavered. Chuck knew Richard was confident that he could talk him into doing things his way.

"I thought I knew how low you would stoop to get a story, but I guess I was dreaming that you had a grain of a conscience. Beth was right when she told me I'd regret sticking by you. I quit."

"You can't quit. We're in the middle of a story."

"You run the camera. Just push the little red button and stand in front of the lens. I've had enough years watching you destroy people's lives. Maybe the station will assign me to another reporter, maybe not, but I will not help you sell an exposé on child sexual abuse."

Chuck looked at the staring faces surrounding them and raised his voice. "Child abusers don't get near Edmonton's cornerstone organizations. And, don't try to use my name to meet people because I'll warn everyone I know to avoid you."

The other passengers watched with avid curiosity. Chuck wasn't surprised when someone snickered. A few people turned away when Richard scanned the crowd, but others met his glare. Richard had always made enemies faster than he gathered friends.

"Chuck, you won't work in this city again. No reporter wants a cameraman who doesn't back him on a story as important as this. Don't do this to yourself."

"You try running that story and I swear the station will hear about every dirty trick you've played in the last five years."

Their voices rose and the breeze carried them along the boat's deck. Chuck scanned the small groups of three and four clustered near the waist-high railing that encircled the upper deck of the paddle wheeler. He looked over the rail, watching the banks of the North Saskatchewan River as the boat flowed by hundred-year-old houses and forests that were old when those houses had been built. Fort Edmonton Park was visible in the distance. Kids waved from the banks; he waved back. The trip on the River Belle offered serenity, novelty, and beautiful scenery, but Chuck saw the trip's charm could not compete with bit of gossip.

Chuck noted the vertical crease in the middle of Richard's broad forehead. It ran down to his arrow straight nose, a sure sign of his discomfort. In fact, the only sign of stress Chuck had ever seen him betray. He felt a touch of satisfaction and played for the audience. He raised his voice and turned toward the crowd so that all the observers could hear.

"Pedophiles don't get into Edmonton's organizations. We screen our people; we protect our kids."

Chuck turned his back on the gleam he detected deep in Richard's dark eyes and walked toward the stern of the boat.

A voice coming through the loudspeaker announced seating for the dinner theatre and asked all passengers without dinner tickets to leave when the boat docked at Fort Edmonton Park. The audience gathered their jackets and bags ready to partake of the evening's more conventional entertainment.

Chuck jabbed his shaking hands into the pockets of his baggy jeans and hunched over the rail near the snack bar. He had to prevent Richard from doing this story. He would let Richard sweat a while and then he would go back and try to reason with him, without an audience.

Maybe he'd listen, for once.

CHAPTER 5

Long trails of scum surrounded pieces of debris, then broke into chunks for the river to reabsorb. During its passage through the Rocky Mountains, the water ran clear. Then a winter's worth of detritus from towns and farms polluted it as it journeyed to Edmonton. An occasional chunk of dirty, nearly melted ice floated by, long overdue to return to its liquid state.

Chuck smelled the rotting vegetation that formed the base of Edmonton's spring perfume. The sharp slap of a beaver tail sent a warning and drew his attention to a spot near the shore. He studied the swirling water and leaned over the rail to watch a branch navigate the body of the boat.

He imagined himself floating among those branches, just another piece of society's cast-off garbage.

Chuck knew he wouldn't fight Richard's threat to have him fired. Mudslinging wasn't his style. He would leave Edmonton, find another job, another city. It was time to move on anyway. He had lived in Edmonton longer than he had ever stayed in one place before.

Just thinking of Richard writing his exposé on those helping organizations, made Chuck shiver in the night air. He couldn't calculate the damage Richard would do with that kind of story. All kids needed the support and camaraderie provided by those clubs and the sad little ones, the ones whose parents ignored their pain, needed them more than most. Parents didn't have time to love their kids anymore; sometimes they needed reminding. He had devoted his life to making people understand how precious their children were.

The sun dipped behind a dark fringe of trees leaving only the May twilight lingering over the river valley. Soon the captain would switch on the deck lights and take away his camouflage.

Not that it mattered. He had finally placed the thin woman with the big hat. She looked different than when he'd last seen her, but if she had recognized him, well it was time to get out of town anyway.

******

Beth looked around the dining room hoping to spot Chuck, but the dinner theatre began without him appearing. Several of Beth's co-workers had assured her the boat ride was a great way to spend an evening and she agreed that it provided an air of charm and elegance that Richard's presence had only partially ruined.

The large windows in the dining room provided a panoramic view of the river valley. Round, wooden, pedestal tables were randomly arranged inside the spacious area. With its white linen, gleaming glasses, and shiny silver, the room rivaled the best of the city's restaurants.

B.C. salmon, wild rice, and Saskatoon pie were featured on the menu along with the more generic fare of fried chicken, roast beef, and parsley potatoes. Tonight's entertainment was a melodrama performed by one of the many local theatre groups. The actors encouraged the audience to participate by booing the villain and cheering for the hero.

It had sounded like a fun evening. Maybe not the ideal place to present Jim's plan for starting another fitness club, but a way to divert attention in case their parents hated the idea. The plan had evolved from Jim's MBA project. Beth had studied it and agreed to invest her time, money, and expertise in helping their parents get the project running.

This time she would kill Richard Tanner before letting his faulty reporting hurt them. He still claimed that naming their facility in an exposé of fraud and irregularities, had been an honest mistake. She didn't believe him because the report aired soon after she ended their two-year relationship. Beth knew the incidents were tied together. She knew that if Tanner kept his nose out of their business her parents would succeed.

Jim laid out his plan during the second intermission, just after the villain had tied the innocent maiden to the railway tracks in the hope of forcing her to consent to his indecent proposal of marriage. Beth's Dad sat back in his chair and watched his wife. His own pleasure was obvious in his gentle smile, but he awaited her mother's reaction. It was her dream Richard had destroyed.

She started crying, at first wiping at the tears welling in her eyes, then giving up any attempt to stem them.

"I need air. You stay and enjoy the show. I'll be back soon," she said as she rose and fled the room as the curtain went up on the third act.

Ten minutes later Jim whispered, "I'm going to go find Mom. This plan has really shaken her up. Do you think it's the right thing to do?"

"Just talk to her, Jim," his dad said. "Our last catastrophe nearly destroyed her. She's overwhelmed, but your idea is a good one and she'll come around. Go convince her that with the expertise you two have, we'll be in good hands."

Beth watched her brother weave his way between the tables, then stretched her arm across the white linen, and squeezed her father's hand. She answered his encouraging smile with one of her own.

******

Sanctimonious do-gooders made him crazy. How had he missed recognizing that quality in Chuck?

Hell, Richard knew his cameraman had a conscience. He could forgive Chuck that one fault, but threatening to expose his methods for digging up stories was downright perverted. The station didn't really want him playing by the rules. That kid in charge of the news wouldn't know what to do without him, but he would love acting morally outraged if Chuck went public with some of the techniques he'd used over the years. But that just meant the wise-ass kid would make Richard the story, while he gloated over increasing the station's ratings and ruining a stellar career.

Richard knew his scoop on the Mounties had saved his job from the station moralists. Still station moguls weren't interested in last year's triumphs just in audience share and in ensuring scapegoats were handy.

He was in trouble. If Chuck so much as hinted he had stolen those leaked party documents he would be unemployed in a minute. There were too many politicos among the station brass for him to survive.

He should never have told Chuck about his deal with that native kid. How could he have known the kid exaggerated the story like that? Besides no one really got hurt and the kid overdosed without recanting. Damn it, that one alone could get him fired. It might cost him a few hours of grilling by the cops, too. It wasn't as if he had actually broken the law, just twisted a few facts. Of course, the guy in jail might be interested. He could appeal his conviction and be back on the street within a week. Was he the kind to look for revenge?

Damn Chuck for making trouble. Still, trouble was what being a reporter was all about, if there was a story in it. If he didn't turn out to be the story. He had to stop Chuck before his career was guillotined.

******

By the time Dorothy McKinney slid back into her chair, the hero had rescued the maiden and the play was over except for the bows. Her face was flushed, but Beth felt relieved that the relentless desperation that had haunted her eyes for the past few years was gone.

"I feel better now. Where's Jim," Dorothy asked.

"He went looking for you."

"I'm sorry to spoil your evening, but I couldn't stop crying."

"It doesn't matter, Mom. We just want to help you and Dad. Perhaps we should have waited to tell you our idea."

"No, you picked just the right time."

"You're willing to give it a chance?"

"I don't know yet, but I'll think about it. I'm sure any business plan you and Jim develop has an excellent chance of success."

******

Jennifer panicked as the icy water filled her mouth and covered her ears. She struggled for air and fought as the water rushed over her head. Sputtering, she cleared her mouth and gasped. The river water rushed in, threatening her life.

She grabbed at the dark silhouette of a tree branch as it swung within her reach and held tight to its slick bark. The water tasted like dirt. Her clothes ballooned around her. Her runners tugged her feet downward, until they bumped against rocks and dragged through loose stones. The fast flowing water wrestled the branch from her grip and again she fought the current, but the brief reprieve had given her the strength to force her feet toward shore.

Jennifer stumbled against a bulky mass and grabbed at it, pulling herself forward. At the touch of denim-covered flesh, she jerked her hand away. She scrambled around the body and felt it dislodge from the rock that had held it captive. It fled into the current and disappeared.

Jennifer shivered, then crossed her arms over her thin chest, hugging herself to retain what warmth remained in her shivering body. The current deposited her on a broad strip of gravel, upstream of the ship's dock.

Exhausted and fighting for breath, she struggled toward the shore across gravel that bit into her hands and knees and through branches that collided with her thighs and shoulders. Once out of the icy flow she stumbled uphill toward the bike path, cursing as the tangled undergrowth grabbed at her.

The path would be deserted at this hour. She had to get to her bike; she had to reach the safety of her home. Jennifer pulled a clinging tendril of hair from her cheek. She shouldn't have called Richard Tanner.

An animal scurried across the trail in front of her, just a dark shadow in the dim light of the waxing quarter moon. Jennifer rubbed her arms to restore the circulation. Then she pulled the cold, wet cloth of her shirt away from her breasts. It was not far now. She had locked her jacket in the storage shed with her bike. She fumbled through her pockets, but couldn't find her keys. They must have fallen into the river.

The night was dark. Her legs shaking with fatigue, Jennifer stumbled along until a burst of laughter sent her crashing through the brush to take shelter behind a fallen tree. She crouched, then peered toward the trail as a group of teenage boys pushed and shoved their way into sight. A couple of them carried cases of beer, others drank from smaller bottles.

Jennifer huddled against the tree trunk, pulling her arms close to her shivering body. She waited for the last of their loud cries to fade and for the night noises to resume before moving back to the trail. Now she listened carefully, aware that she was close to the parking lot and fearful of discovery.

Jennifer cast a furtive look over her shoulder and continued in silence. "It will be all right," she whispered into the night. "I will leave town. No one will miss me." Her words vanished into the dark night.

Minutes later she spotted the lights of the parking lot gleaming through the trees. The storage shed stood to one side of the well-lit area. An attendant watched over the cars, continuously scanning the parking area without interrupting his conversation with the driver of a van that idled near the kiosk.

As Jennifer focused on the locksmith logo painted on the side of the van, Cara's words came to mind. Was this how they stole cars? She didn't want to know. From now on, she minded her own business.

The attendant scanned the woods near her hiding place. Jennifer froze as he pointed toward a flashy sports car parked twenty feet from where she hid. She would have to skirt the edge of the clearing because he would spot her if she dared cross the opening to reach the shed.

Her legs shook as exhaustion overtook her and she stumbled over a fallen branch. She winced as the rough bark of an overhanging branch scratched her face.

Jennifer wiped away the dirt and blood. She examined her scraped knuckles and broken fingernails, then peered toward the attendant who was again looking in her direction. Had he seen her? She watched until his gaze moved on.

Careful to keep her movements slow, she pushed herself into a sitting position, rested her back against a maple, and then pulled her knees close. She wrapped her arms around her knees to conserve what little warmth remained in her body and hoped for a few minutes of rest.

******

Richard stood at the rail watching the last gleam of sunset spread color across the horizon. The sky turned red, then purple, and finally, black. He inhaled deeply, then flicked the butt of his cigarette overboard. It hit an island of tangled branches. He heard laughter drift from the dining room as the evening's entertainment wound to a close. The cruise seemed to have been a success.

Though not for him. His contact hadn't shown up and he could see the dock lights in the distance. If that call had born fruit, it would have been a good story. Maybe he could have sunk the paddle boat business single-handedly. More likely, he would have aroused people's interest enough to make the idea of taking a boat trip irresistible.

He shook his head. It had been a long time since he had read a tip wrong, but this time he'd wasted an entire evening. Still, he had bigger problems now.

Why had Chuck chosen to complicate his life? And that remark about Beth was out of line. She'd forgiven him, a little anyway. After all, she had given him the biggest story of the year after he saved her life last fall.

What was so wrong with doing this story? With Tommy Jamieson dead, stories about freaks would be on every station. If that pipsqueak of a boss wanted a personal, tear-jerking angle he could provide it. Chuck's connections would have made life easier but what the hell, he would get the story without him.

God, Chuck must really be deluding himself if he thought Edmonton was immune to freaks. Everyone knew pedophiles gravitated to places where kids were found. When he thought about all the articles and books that exposed the big organizations—the Catholic Church, the Boy Scouts, and Little League—damn that Chuck. He knew everyone important in at least two of those organizations. Richard didn't think Chuck was Catholic. He didn't remember Chuck mentioning going to church at all, but then they never talked about personal things, just business.

A gentle bump heralded the boat's arrival at the dock. Richard watched the first passengers depart, seeming as anxious to leave as they'd been to get on board.

Beth and her family gravitated toward the pier. She made a point of glaring at him. Richard smiled at her and shrugged. Damn, she was mad again. Beth always did take anyone's side but his. She turned away, missing his best look of remorse.

By now, a steady stream of people flowed down the gangplank. Snatches of conversation drifted within hearing.

"Great show...."

"The fried chicken was good...."

"Let's hit an after hour's club, it's too early...."

"God, it's that late. I've got a seven-thirty meeting...."

"But why go with a melodrama, why not...."

"What do you think the fight was about...."

Richard winced. He'd hoped people would forget Chuck's pre-dinner entertainment.

"Damn," he muttered in a voice loud enough to be heard by those close to him. "If he's deserted me it really will mean his job."

The flow of people faded to a trickle and eventually stopped. A big blond kid, dressed like a sailor, approached.

"The boat is closing now sir, you'll have to leave."

Richard caught the slow twang of a Newfoundlander accent in the young man's voice. "Have you seen my cameraman?" The boy's puzzled look prompted him to add. "About 5'9", big jaw, long, curly, black hair and a beard—pouchy eyes. He was wearing a tee-shirt and denim jacket."

"The guy you were fighting with?"

"It was a professional disagreement. We do it all the time. It's kind of like brainstorming."

"Yeah, sure. No, I ain't seen him."

"Is anyone left inside?"

"Just the crew. Look, he probably got off already. You gotta leave now cause we're closing up."

"If he shows up . . . no, don't bother, I'll tell him myself."

Richard debated leaving the camera on the deck, but it was station property and it would be his head if it went missing. He lifted it by the handle, grunting slightly as he hefted it onto his shoulder and headed to the dock.

The van was still parked at the side of the lot nearest the river. Richard pulled a spare set of keys from his pocket. He stored the camera behind the driver's seat and hopped behind the wheel.

******

Jennifer shivered and tightened her arms around her chest as a horn blared in the night jolting her back to awareness. She stretched. It wasn't late if the Belle was just now docking. Her head hurt; she put her hand against the sore spot and felt a lump. How had she hurt herself? She tried standing, then slumped back to the ground. She couldn't get to her bike unseen yet; she would be safer if she stayed hidden until everyone was gone.

Music drifted from the river and voices approached. People straggled by no more than ten feet from where she crouched. They sounded happy, tired, disgruntled, and relaxed. Their faces were hidden until they stepped into the pool of light generated by the overhead lamp and turned toward their vehicles.

Car engines flared to life, beams of light blinded her and the pounding in her head grew louder. She raised her hand to touch her head. Why did it hurt?

******

Linda Olsson was among the first passengers to leave the boat. She followed the path until she reached the point where it branched, then stepped into the trees. One branch led to the parking lot, the other to the walking trails and eventually to the park building where she had seen Jenny that afternoon.

She rubbed her hands over her hips, squeezing the loose cotton of her skirt. Where had that girl gone? She had watched for her throughout the first act of the play while forcing down a wilted, bitter-tasting salad, but Jenny hadn't appeared. When she asked the waiter where Jenny was, he went to look, then returned claiming he couldn't find her.

Unable to concentrate on the melodrama, Linda had slipped from the room soon after the second act began. She prowled the ship finding the office deserted and the kitchen busy. The stairwell leading to the upper deck had beckoned and she retreated there to sit in the darkness and quiet solitude.

The crowd of people leaving the boat thinned. Linda waited until the crew disembarked and locked the gate behind them.

She approached the group of staff members. "Pardon me," she said , startling them when she stepped out of the shadows.

"Was Jenny Rivers on the boat tonight?"

The dark-haired woman who had sold her the ticket for the dinner cruise, answered, "Jennifer? She left early. She's scheduled to work tomorrow if you want to talk to her."

"Are you sure she left?"

"Can we help you?"

"No." Linda dragged the word out. Then in a more confident tone she added, "No, it's personal. I'll stay in town and talk to her tomorrow."

The quiet of the night closed around her as the group continued toward the parking lot. A gentle evening breeze carried their words back to her.

"Cara, why did you say that? We don't know where Jennifer is."

"Well, she wasn't on the boat when we docked, was she? Therefore, she must have got off, if not before we sailed, then when we stopped at the Fort Edmonton dock. Did any of you see her after that? Besides, you don't know who that woman is, maybe Jennifer disappeared because she didn't want to talk to her."

******

Jennifer opened her eyes to find the night had grown quiet. The lot was vacant and the overhead lights were dark. Only a string of solar beams lining the walkway to the river's edge, cast a glow into the night.

Stiff joints made standing a struggle, but she stretched each limb and used the tree trunk to pull herself erect. She winced as she bumped a tender spot on her leg. She was cold. Her clothes were dried to the point of dampness, but the breeze drove a chill through her inner being. She needed her jacket.

The lock on the shed door was fastened. Could nothing go right? Dim light shone on a piece of wood that lay just off the path. She grabbed it, raised it over her head, and brought it down on the lock. The wood splintered. The lock remained fastened.

A rock. That was what she needed, but a soft covering of rotting leaves hid the ground. She pushed the leaves around with the end of the stick until she uncovered the bone white of a softball-sized stone. She scratched at the earth with her fingers, then with the end of the splintered stick. By the time she freed the rock from its resting spot, the stick and several of her nails were broken. With the stone clutched tight, she looked around. All was still. Even the animals waited for her next move. A sharp blow to the padlock. Then another and a third before it broke.

Jennifer removed the lock and pulled the door open. She sucked the knuckle she'd skinned on the door's rough wood exterior as she contemplated her bike resting against the back wall of the windowless room. Only a faint glow from the moon allowed her to see its streamlined shape. She hesitated, then straightened her shoulders, and stepped inside.

The door would not close locking her into the total darkness that crowded around her. She had to overcome that silly fear. Jennifer's breathing quickened and became shallow. She grabbed the bike and dragged it outside into the pale moonlight and the clean air. Resting her forehead on the handlebars, she breathed deeply, and waited as her heartbeat slowed.

Her cold fingers fumbled as she opened the bike's saddlebags. Jennifer pulled her jacket from one compartment, slipped into it, and zipped it up to her neck. She could do nothing about her soggy shoes or the slacks that clung to her legs until she got home. She anticipated the warmth of a hot shower and felt a shiver race through her. A few minutes peddling her bike and she would warm up.

CHAPTER 6

Detective Ceretzke looked down at Chuck Albright. His long, dark hair floated in the tiny stream running through the gravel bed beneath the Capilano Bridge. His jeans clung to his pudgy thighs and his tee shirt lay loose around his middle. One sneaker was gone and his big toe poked through a hole in his sock. The river was at its seasonal peak, shrinking the shoreline to a quarter of its normal width and Mike was surprised the body had washed ashore.

Dr. Elizabeth Smythe, one of Edmonton's medical examiners, placed her hand on the small of her back as she straightened her knees. She stripped off her gloves, then shielded her eyes against the glare of the early morning sun dancing on the swollen river.

"See the dent behind his right ear? I doubt it was something that happened in the river; the blow that made it was hard enough to stun, if not kill him."

"Maybe he was hit by a log," Detective Evan Collins pointed out.

Mike hoped he was right.

"I doubt it," the doctor said.

She might not like her opinion being questioned, but Mike disliked the idea of a good guy being killed.

"I'll get an Ident unit out here. He probably went into the water ten to twelve hours ago, between eight and eleven last evening." Her cool glance floated over the detectives. "I'm betting it's a homicide, so treat it accordingly."

Mike turned to climb the hill to his truck. "Let's go talk to Tanner and see if he knows what Chuck was doing last night."

They had already lost valuable time if Dr. Smythe was correct about it being murder. Mike hoped she was wrong.

✶✶✶✶✶✶

"What the hell do you want," Richard Tanner asked, glaring at the men standing in the doorway of his apartment. He looked at his watch. Six o'clock. Two hours sleep was not enough when he had to deal with cops.

"Well, what?"

Detective Ceretzke asked, "Can we come in?"

"Got a warrant?"

Richard shoved his shirt into his pants and zipped the fly. Who did they think they were barging into a guy's home at six in the morning? He glared at Ceretzke. Being half-asleep, half-naked, and in bare feet put him at a disadvantage and he didn't like it.

"Look Tanner, we're being civil. We want to talk to you about Chuck Albright. Your cameraman, you remember him? Is that his van parked outside?"

"Hey, he wasn't around. What was I supposed to do? If he says I stole it, he's full of shit." Richard stepped backward. What was Chuck trying to pull? Was he starting his smear campaign already?

"He's not saying anything." Ceretzke brushed his arm aside and walked through the doorway. "Am I correct in understanding the van is his?"

"Yes, the van is his or at least it's the one assigned to him by the station. No, it isn't. He quit last night, so it's not his any more. Look what's this about?" Richard felt a tingle of electricity surge up the back of his neck. That tingle was a signal from his subconscious that something was going on.

"He worked with you for a long time, didn't he?"

"Yeah. Come on, what's the punch line."

"He's dead."

"What! Don't give me that kind of . . . . Are you serious? April Fool's day was last month."

"It's no joke."

"He was all right last night, or at least early last night."

"So you were together?"

Richard noted the detective's rigid mouth and his cold eyes. Whatever was going on was serious. Chuck dead, he couldn't believe it, but he would make a story out of it. Looked like the kid at the station was going to get a weepy-eyed tribute whether he liked it or not. "I had a tip. We were on the River Belle checking it out."

"When did you last see him?"

"Just before the boat sailed. He wasn't around when we docked."

"You left without him?"

"We had a small disagreement and Chuck left. At least, I thought he left."

"What was the disagreement about?"

"It was nothing. Just a story I'm gonna do. What happened to Chuck? I'd have waited for him but I thought he left without me."

"Without his van?"

"He wasn't around. I waited until the crew kicked me off the boat. I even asked them if they'd seen him. You can't say I deserted him."

"What happened after the fight?"

"He took off to watch the show I guess and left me outside waiting for a source. The person I was supposed to meet didn't show." Richard turned toward his kitchen nook. "I need coffee."

He tripped on a shoe that he'd kicked off when he got home early in the morning and cursed as he danced his way to the sink. Damn cops, how did they look awake at six a.m.? He should have stayed home and got some sleep last night. He felt adrenaline flowing to his brain as he scooped the aromatic coffee grounds into a paper filter. Chuck would understand what a good story this would make. He pulled a cigarette from the pack on the counter.

"Did you see him after your argument?"

"No. He was ticked-off, said he quit, walked away leaving his camera on the deck. I figured I better give him time to cool down."

"What story was so controversial?"

Richard shook his head and a lock of hair fell into his line of vision. Should he tell them or make them work for their supper? What the hell, half the passengers would fill them in. Better to get his version on record first. "I wanted to do pedophiles-in-the-city. You know the stuff about how organizations screen their people; any cases of abuse reported in the past few years; maybe a few interviews with victims. The usual sob-story/scare piece, an aside to the Jamieson kid's murder. Chuck freaked."

"That was at what time?"

"Hey, Ceretzke, don't make this so formal."

Richard plucked a stained coffee cup from the sink. He had known these guys for years; heck he'd interviewed Ceretzke about the Jamieson abduction and murder just a couple of days ago. Of course, Ceretzke had referred him to Community Relations, but he always did that. Richard knew it was nothing personal.

"What time, Tanner?"

"Maybe seven. The dinner theatre was announced, then the boat stopped at Fort Edmonton. After that the decks were nearly deserted."

"What happened then?"

"Nothing. I just stood there waiting for this guy to show."

"The guy about the story?"

"Yes."

"Did you talk to Chuck again?"

"No. I was waiting until he cooled down. Look, what happened to him? How did he die?"

"He drowned. Had he been drinking heavily?"

"Chuck didn't believe that drinking was a socially acceptable practice. Hell, he only smoked if he was under pressure. You think he fell in the river?"

"We don't know what happened."

"Did someone see him fall?"

"You get to answer the questions, Tanner, not ask them."

Richard recognized Ceretzke's look as the one he usually reserved for felons. He lit a cigarette and inhaled; his brain kicked into overdrive. He had to do something fast.

"Look, we fought, he stalked off, I stayed put, I didn't see him leave the boat, I asked the steward if anyone was still on board, he said no, I left and took the van. End of story."

"What time did you get home?"

"About four. I'd missed supper waiting for that creep to show, so after I left the boat I went to Paddy's Place, had a couple of drinks and something to eat."

The detective wrote more notes. Richard tried reading them, but the cop held the notebook out of his line of sight.

"Is that all?"

"Can anyone verify your story?"

"Sure, probably lots of people saw me on the boat and at Paddy's, too. Ask Beth, she was there with her oh so righteous family."

******

Richard downed his coffee as he butted out his cigarette and phoned the station's news desk for more information. Chuck's body had been found on the south bank of the North Saskatchewan River, just past the Capilano Freeway Bridge. It was a shallow spot where bodies often washed ashore, even in years of high water and fast currents. It was just bad luck for Chuck that he went over the side this time of year, later in the summer the river would have been so shallow he could have walked to shore.

Richard asked the desk to send another cameraman. Then he set about deciding where he could get some background data. First, he wanted to get to Beth McKinney before she talked to Ceretzke. He hadn't seen much of her since last fall, but he had heard she was very busy dating the good detective. No accounting for taste.

He would give her a year before she dumped Ceretzke the same way she had dumped him. Richard had never understood what their break-up was about. Beth just got hysterical one day and started yelling that he was a heartless user and walked out the door.

Richard grabbed his cell phone and punched her number. As usual, she was awake. By the gods, he hated morning people.

"Richard, what do you want?"

She didn't sound her usual cheery self.

"What's the matter love, Mikey had to leave early this morning?"

The receiver went dead in his hand. He hit the redial button.

"You've got three seconds to convince me not to charge you with harassment."

Beth must have lost her sense of humour.

"Chuck's dead."

This time she didn't hang up.

"Richard, is this some kind of game? He was all right last night."

"When did you last see him?"

"After your fight. He went to the back of the boat."

"Not during dinner?"

"No, I watched for him, but he never came into the dining room. What happened?"

"Cops say he drowned. He must have been livid because no one in his right mind would have tried to swim it. I didn't think he was that mad at me."

"Hold it, you think he jumped?"

"What else?"

"He could have got off at Fort Edmonton."

"That makes no sense. He drowned, though you'd think that if he fell overboard he would have called for help. I didn't hear anything and I was on deck the entire evening."

"Why are you calling me, Richard," Beth asked in that distinctive, cautious tone of voice that Richard remembered had always preceded their worst arguments.

"I just didn't want you hearing about him on the news. I know you liked the guy."

"And?"

"Did he ever mention his family to you? We never got around to the subject."

"Your station should have his next of kin listed on his employment form."

Richard paced, thinking hard. That touch of steel in her voice wasn't good; she didn't want to help him. He knew her so well, how had he ever let her get away?

"It's Sunday. The personnel office isn't open Sunday. Besides,

I want to get to the family before the cops do. You know, to sort of break the news gently."

"You want to interview them, don't you?"

He heard hysteria creeping into her voice. She would hang up again if he didn't backtrack a bit.

"No, no of course not. I'm not that callous. I just want to inform them, gently."

The receiver went dead.

The door buzzer sounded. Tanner flipped his phone closed and grabbed a suit jacket and tie and rushed out of the apartment. When he saw the six-foot vision of long legs and luscious hair waiting beside the station van, he cursed. Damn, who had assigned Christy to him? She had a big mouth and showed no respect; besides, she had rebuffed every advance that he'd sent in her direction.

He had to live with her for now, but he would get someone else assigned on a permanent basis. Now, he had to check the records, then get to the family. His neck was tingling. Chuck's death was more than an accident. It was the kind of story he was destined to report. That kid at the station could keep the Jamieson drivel.

******

Beth McKinney released the button and gently replaced the telephone receiver. Richard still made her crazy. She stroked Splatter's fury head, evoking a hungry purr. Her temper subsided. She wondered if Richard could be right. The morning news had reported that a body had been found, but had given no names or details. What had happened after that fight on the River Belle? Had Chuck confronted Richard again? Had they fought? She should have found Chuck and insisted he sit with her family.

Now Chuck was dead and if Richard's theory was right, maybe he had jumped into the river. If she had talked to him, she could have stopped him from taking such suicidal action. Magpie joined Splatter in a chorus, pacing in front of the fridge, then rubbing against her leg. She relented and opened a can of food.

No. Wait. Chuck wasn't suicidal and a fight with Richard wouldn't have sent him jumping into that river. He must have fallen over by accident.

Still, Richard said he hadn't heard him call out. The railings on the boat were waist-high, not easy to trip over. Unless he had gone to the back of the paddle wheeler and somehow slipped and hit his head, then fell into the river unconscious.

She would ask Mike about that possibility when she saw him. Maybe tonight, if he got a break from the Jamieson case. No more procrastinating, she would tell her parents all about him right after breakfast. After all, who could not like Mike?

Beth's computer beeped, alerting her to an incoming call. She checked the kitchen clock. Six-thirty sharp. Time to start Debbie's lesson.

******

Richard looked at the form and cursed. The spot for next-of-kin read 'N/A', as did the 'to be notified' box. He slammed out of the deserted office leaving the lights on and the file drawers open. He tossed Chuck's personnel file onto his desk and stomped toward the locker room.

Then he paced, anxiously waiting for the custodian to open Chuck's locker. It took only moments to rummage through the contents. There was a pair of gloves and a heavy coat, probably left over from before he took holidays in April. A spare set of apartment keys; a toiletry kit with a disposable razor, shaving cream and soap; a stack of file folders and two library books on pedophilia.

Richard grabbed the books from the locker. What the hell. Chuck said he wouldn't help on a story about pedophiles. Was he researching the story himself? Maybe Chuck wanted to be in front of the camera instead of behind it? You couldn't trust anyone.

Richard flipped through one of the folders. It was full of stuff on the Jamieson case and had photocopies of articles on the older cases. More stuff on pedophilia and abuse and . . . . Damn, the guy was a traitor.

He nonchalantly picked up the books and the folders and walked out of the room to his office where he deposited them in his desk drawer. There was no point in letting quality research material go to waste. This stuff looked as good as what Beth used to gather for him, before their alliance and their affair ended. He would do almost anything to get her back, at least as a research assistant, because she was much better than the ones the station employed.

Time was moving onward and he knew if he didn't hurry, the cops would search Chuck's apartment before he could. The apartment keys jingled as he tossed them into the air, then grasped them tightly, and put them into his pocket. He located Christy in the coffee room and signalled her to follow. She grabbed her bagel and her camera and strode after him.

******

Jennifer's left ankle throbbed. She shivered and moved to rub away the chill, but stopped when a thousand shards of glass grated, cut, and gnawed at the inside of her skull. She sank back onto the damp earth and looked through newly burst leaves toward the pale blue sky.

With tiny movements, she tested her extremities. Did she have other injuries? Her left wrist wouldn't move.

"Help."

The word came out sounding more like a croak than a plea. With her head planted on the ground to avoid further explosions of pain, Jennifer rolled onto her side and tried to figure out where she was. The spokes of her bike wheel were visible and through them, she saw the dirt of the biking trail. Relief flooded through her; help would soon arrive. She moved her shoulder and turned further to the left, toward the path.

Her left wrist was swollen, the skin pulled tight and shiny.

She couldn't make it bend. The dull throb in her left ankle changed to a sharp pain as she swung her right leg over it and rested her foot on the ground. The pain and the movement exhausted her.

A cyclist came into view. She raised her right arm but he whizzed by. Minutes passed and Jennifer gritted her teeth, fighting through the pain that filled her body. A long time later a jogger approached. Headphones covered his ears. She held her breath against an onrush of nausea. Then resting on her left elbow, she raised her right hand. It wasn't much, but with the spring undergrowth so sparse, it was enough.

The sight of his surprised face as he knelt over her was the last thing she saw before blackness engulfed her.

******

"Christy, check out this room, look for anything relating to Chuck's family."

"Look through this junk." She motioned toward the coffee table crowded with dirty dishes, crumpled paper bags and pop tins. "You've got to be kidding. I ain't had my shots lately. Besides, I'm just here to take pictures, you're the reporter."

Richard looked at the mess. An open carton of duty-free cigarettes sat on top the portable television, crowded by a plastic ashtray with what looked like Chinese characters plastered around its rim.

The same character was embroidered on the lapel of the terry housecoat spilling out of an open suitcase. To one side, a pile of crumpled clothes waited for wash day. Richard caught the musty, salty smell of the tropics. It clashed with the stale smoke and moldy pizza aroma that permeated the room.

He picked his way through the clutter until he reached the window and opened the drapes. The room seemed grey, its walls were naked, and nothing personal jumped to his attention.

Who would have thought Chuck lived like a slob? His workspace was always meticulously tidy.

"The bookcase should be safe to touch." He couldn't have her pulling that union garbage on him, not when time was short.

Christy shrugged her football player shoulders and met his stare with a glare. It was a weak show of outrage. Beth had always done disgust and rage better.

"Say please."

Richard plucked a pack of cigarettes from the carton and stuffed it into his jacket pocket. "Not likely," he answered, wondering how to enlist her help without pleading. He knew from experience that ordering her around could prove disastrous.

She crossed her arms and leaned against the doorframe.

"Oh, what the hell. I don't have time to play kid's games, please check out that bookcase."

Richard pulled the robe from the suitcase. A dead cockroach fell to the floor. What kind of cheap hotel did the guy stay at? He looked at Christy prancing toward the bookcase. Chuck had always done what he asked and rarely argued. He was going to miss the guy. With that thought, Richard strode down the narrow hall. He passed the kitchen on his left and at the end of the hall, he entered the single bedroom.

The night table had no drawers and its surface held only a reading lamp and a stack of magazines. Richard sorted through them but found nothing to his taste. It was all world news stuff. He straightened the pile and crossed the carpet, mindful of scattered shoes and an open bag of generic gingersnaps.

The closet contained a few tee shirts and three immaculate uniforms that looked like scouts or maybe naval cadets. Chuck had kept some secrets. He was a more selfless volunteer than Richard had figured. Well, it would add to the story. He tackled the dresser where baseball caps, even some in kid sizes, filled one drawer. They seemed to represent every team in the league. Most of the hats were new, though a few were dirty and tired looking.

He would have Christy take some shots of the hats and the uniforms. Play up the community volunteer and sports fan angle. In the other drawers, he found a surplus of jeans and underwear.

Richard pulled a mangled manila envelope from under a heap of socks. A peek inside revealed official looking correspondence, plastic cards, and a passport. Richard folded the envelope and tucked it into his inside jacket pocket. No time to go through it now.

"No albums, but he was a reader." Christy spoke from the doorway. "Mainly a true crime and biography fan."

"Yeah, he was always reading. Take a pan of the place, especially the closet and that top drawer—please. It'll have to do for background on the human-interest angle for now. I'll fill in the commentary later."

He located no other pictures or letters, but maybe the envelope contained something about his family. Richard examined the key chain he'd taken from Chuck's locker. The van keys he recognized and the brass one had opened the apartment door, but another remained. It was blue, probably a duplicate Chuck had cut at a mall kiosk. Did it open the door of a lady friend's apartment? Richard couldn't envision the possibility, but maybe Christy would know. That kind of gossip usually thrived among the station's hired help.

"Did Chuck have a girlfriend?"

"You mean a woman friend?"

"Yeah, that's what I mean." Richard bit back a vicious retort. His need for the information outweighed his desire to strike back.

"Why ask me? He was your shadow."

"I don't need your attitude, just tell me if any rumours were circulating."

"Not about Chuck. Now if you want to hear what people say about you, I'd be glad to oblige."

"Just hurry up with your shots. I want to get down to the river; maybe his body's still there. If not we'll check out the boat, talk to the staff, and find out who saw him jump. Then, I've got to talk to Beth McKinney again. I know they used to have long soulful conversations."

He left Christy to finish the video and join him in the van.

******

"Tanner, what the hell do you think you're doing! This is a criminal investigation. You can't go around stealing personnel files and rummaging through the victim's belongings. Were you in his apartment?"

Mike Ceretzke leaned into the van window, his hand clenching and unclenching as it neared Tanner's collar. He badly wanted to squeeze Tanner's neck until it resembled a tiny dead twig.

"Mike," Evan's warning was quiet and controlled.

"Hey guys, keep cool. I know better than to disturb evidence." Tanner paused for a fraction of a second, then asked, "Exactly when did this change from an accident to a crime?"

"When the M.E. said she suspected foul play," Mike snapped, regretting his slip because now Tanner knew in what direction the investigation was moving.

"What! Chuck might have jumped, but foul play—like murder you mean?"

"Like maybe you'd better talk to a lawyer, Tanner. You're the only person we know of who fought with Chuck lately, or for that matter, ever. He was a nice guy, just unfortunate in the company he kept."

Mike spotted Christy Sommers striding toward the parked vehicle. She raised her free hand in a salutation.

"Hey Mike, Evan. You here to arrest us both or just Richard?"

"Christy, get this on tape."

Tanner stepped into the street. He straightened his tie and grinned. "Okay, Mike, for the camera this time."

With a shake of his head, Mike turned toward the apartment building.

******

A blinding pinpoint of light penetrated the darkness behind Jennifer's eyes. The pain in her head was bearable, but she felt her heartbeat in the pulsing of her wrist and ankle.

"Banged yourself up pretty good, Miss. Very bad concussion. How did it happen?"

She raised her hand to her eyes. The noise! So many people talking, phones ringing and that incessant intercom.

"Miss, can you please tell me your name?"

Jennifer focused her eyes on the chocolate brown nose that loomed over her. It was a patrician nose, long and slender. She followed it to finely sculpted lips and then to a firm jaw. "Jennifer. Jennifer Rivers," she said.

"Well, Ms. Rivers, how did this happen?"

"It was dark. I remember the bike skidding. Falling. I put my foot out but landed wrong. I must have been riding the trails last night." She tried shaking her head to let him know she couldn't remember more, but the pain was relentless.

"Who can we call to come for you?"

"No one."

"Your family, a friend?"

"No."

"Then you just rest, miss. All the details will return soon; you're going to be just fine. No permanent damage, just a sprained ankle and a broken wrist. We'll get a cast on that wrist right quickly. Tomorrow I will find you a crutch so you'll be able to walk, but only with difficulty."

Jennifer relaxed into the mattress, her mind searching for answers. She remembered being terrified. Had she really escaped into the river? Would she never be left in peace? For now, she was safe. Who would believe how fast the current was; she could have drowned. Should she have drowned? It would have been better if she had.

******

Dr. Rajaratanam held the curtain open and looked at the young woman. Her long brown hair lay in disarray around her bandaged head. The bruises on her flesh would grow grotesque, but they would fade in time. He felt certain she had been in a bike accident but there was more to the tale. She had an excess of bruises, almost as if she had suffered a beating. It seemed obvious that someone had hurt her badly so until she could defend herself, perhaps he could keep her close.

He would be pressured to discharge her, still she could not manage without someone to care for her. Besides, that concussion needed watching and she was practically incapable of movement. He would keep her here for a few days.

CHAPTER 7

"Kenny's going through the terrible twos," Evan Collins said. "He'll outgrow it. You don't know what you're missing not having kids."

"Sure I do. I'm missing a lot of sticky fingers and tantrums. I saw my niece and nephew as little kids. Still, maybe one of these days my opinion will change."

"If you're thinking of having kids, you and Beth should start pretty soon. Neither of you is exactly young."

"Neither of us is ready for that kind of commitment. Just drop it, Evan."

Mike stopped the truck at a traffic light and drummed his fingers against the steering wheel. It was no one's business when, or if, he and Beth took their relationship further. Was something wrong with what they had? They didn't think so. Sure he'd thought of kids lately, but why risk something good by pushing for more?

The detectives pulled into the narrow side road leading to the dock of the River Belle. Mud holes and deep ruts filled shady spots hidden from the spring sunshine. This wasn't a road passengers used, it was strictly for the caterers and crew members and it ended in a tiny lot sheltered from the river by a stand of poplar and spruce.

They picked their way over the rutted ground toward the boat dock, then across the walkway to the paddle wheeler. The gate that led to the ticket booth and the boat itself was unlocked, and no one was around to question their presence. The sound of voices drew the detectives toward a cluster of crewmembers who fell silent as they approached.

"Boat is closed to the public. We open at noon," said a blond kid, who Mike figured was around twenty. Mike judged the boy's height to be near his own 6'3".

"We're police," Mike said. "What's so interesting?"

He stepped around the kid and into the midst of the crew. Then he followed their stares downward to a mop and pail. The water in the pail was tinged pink. Beside the pail a puddle shone on the wooden deck.

The young man spoke again. "Max was washing the deck and didn't notice that until it rinsed out red in the bucket. We think it might be blood."

Evan pulled his phone from his jacket pocket and called for a team from the Crime Scene Investigation Unit.

"Wait in the lounge, we'll want to question each of you. Just leave everything the way it is," Mike ordered the crewmembers, then turned to the young man again. "What's your name?"

"Lyle Lamont. I'm the head steward. Should I call the captain?"

"Sure, just a couple of questions first. Any idea how the blood got here? Anything out of the ordinary happen on yesterday's cruise?"

"No." Then Lyle paused. "Well, last night a couple of men had a loud argument, a real blow-up."

"Do you know their names?"

"It was that reporter on Channel Six and his cameraman. Me, I don't know them from Adam, but that's what the passengers was saying."

"Did one of them get hurt?"

"Nah. It was only yelling, not hitting."

"Do you know what the fight was about?"

"Can't say I was paying much mind to them. Too busy making sure things was done right in the dining room. But later, when everyone's gone, the guy with the camera asks me if I seen the other one get off the boat."

"The guy with the camera," Mike asked.

"Yeah, tall, skinny, kinda good-looking, I guess. I told him no one but him was left on board. I figured the other guy had just gone off in a group and the first guy missed him. You think maybe not?"

Mike turned to Evan and said, "Find out what the others saw." Then turning back to Lyle, he said, "We'll need a list of the crew and passengers who were on the cruise last night."

Lyle rubbed his large, square hand across his flat top. "Best I talk to my boss first." He turned his head, looking around the boat. "It's too early for him to be here. I'll have to give him a phone call at home."

******

Cara watched Lyle hand the computer printout to Detective Ceretzke.

"It's a list of all the passenger reservations from the office and this," he offered a second sheet, "is the staff schedule for the week."

The detective thanked Lyle, then turned toward Cara. She recognized his puzzled expression as he analyzed her oval eyes, high cheekbones, and tiny frame. People always tried, but rarely guessed her heritage correctly.

"Can you tell me if all the people on the list actually showed up?"

"Yes, of course." She planned to be very helpful. No reason to provoke his suspicions. "One tick mark in front of the name tells me a credit card secured payment, a second pencil mark shows that the party arrived."

"You have only the number of people in each party, not a complete list of names?"

"That's right, but you can phone the people who made the reservations and get the other names." Cara caressed the keyboard. Their snooping wouldn't matter. When she had finally managed to find sufficient privacy to phone Lap about the murder, he had reacted wisely and was even now making sure no one on that list was robbed.

The officer scanned the names. "This list provides a lot of information."

Cara smiled before she could stop herself. She had made sure the list provided the name, address, phone number, license plate number and credit card details of every customer. Cara had been careful to give the detective the copy with the card numbers blackened out.

"Why do you list license plate numbers?"

She pressed a key and a line of underscoring sped through the letter she was typing. Why did he have to notice that bit of information?

"The management decided to record the license plates and include parking in the price of the evening. We have limited space and people who aren't our customers were parking here. It's a liability of locating near the river trails and the bridge to the convention centre. Restricting parking was the only way we could assure our patrons a parking spot."

Cara hit the delete button and erased the underscoring. Recording license plate numbers was also one way to match patrons' addresses with their cars, in case they got an order for that model of vehicle.

The detective pointed to an entry that held a dollar amount, but no name.

"He paid cash." She answered the detective's implied question.

"Did you see him?"

"Yes. I check-in all the passengers for the dinner cruise. We have a cashier during the day for the other trips, but because of the prepayment and whatnot, I like to handle that one myself. Yesterday two people bought last minute tickets at the dock. They were really taking a risk because we're often fully booked for the dinner cruise."

"Tell me about those people. Were they together?"

"No." She pulled the computer printout closer and skipped her finger down the page. "He paid cash. The other one, a woman, was also alone but she charged the ticket." Her roaming finger came to an abrupt stop. "Here she is. Her name is Linda Olsson."

"What about the man? Can you describe him?"

"He was old. Not very polite and hungry."

"Hungry?"

"He asked about the snack bar. Said he hadn't had lunch. I assured him that we served the soup and salad soon after sailing, but he insisted he wanted a hot dog. I phoned and the cook was cleaning up, but she saved him a dog."

"How old was he?"

"Sixties would be my guess. He wore a dark baseball cap and dressed casually."

"Was he tall, short?"

"Everyone's tall to me, Detective." She smiled up at him from her 4'10" viewpoint.

"Okay, how about the woman? What do you remember about her?"

"Wrinkled skin and age spots. She looked about sixty. Really thin and wearing a floppy hat."

"Are you certain they weren't together?"

"He came late, right after that reporter. She'd been on the boat for half the afternoon."

"Do people usually sail that long?"

"Some people do. They buy a day ticket. Maybe they're pretending that they're on an ocean cruise. I've never asked them why they do it."

"Is it common for people to go on the dinner cruise alone?"

"Not common. Common here is a group. Still, some people do things on their own."

"Who served them?"

"Table twenty? Tommy Wong." She consulted the staff schedule. "He will be working tomorrow."

The detective jotted a few last notes and took the printout with him when he left.

******

Beth checked her security monitor and frowned in annoyance. Why was Richard standing there wearing the pleading look of a suppliant?

"Beth, we've got to talk," he said, speaking toward the security camera. After their early morning telephone conversation, she was far from ready to listen to him, but her parents were sleeping upstairs and the doorbell threatened to disturb their rest. Jim, used to a two-hour time difference, was already out of the house on his morning jog.

She looked at his hands when she opened the door, half expecting to see him twisting a cap in nervous anticipation of her answer. He always had played his part to the fullest.

"Why do we have to talk," she asked.

"Let me in, just for a minute."

Against the advice of the little voice in her head, Beth stood back, allowing him into her front hall. He looked around, no doubt appraising the value of each item.

"Still collecting soapstone carvings, I see. If I remember correctly, this room used to resemble a grey morning. Couldn't live with the memories? Well, the cream and peach suit you better anyway."

"I don't want to talk about my decorating scheme or why it's changed. That's history."

She also didn't like to think about how easily the house she had once considered an impregnable fortress, had been invaded. A complete redecoration of the living room and front hall was the minimum action necessary to restore her peace of mind. She'd been tempted to sell and start over in an apartment that boasted full security, except she now knew that such a thing didn't exist.

"What do you want?"

"The police say Chuck was murdered."

"They're wrong. It was an accident. It had to be. Who would kill Chuck?"

"Someone who was on the boat last night and who had a motive."

"They're suggesting you killed him?"

Beth discounted the idea as soon as she voiced it. Richard didn't have a passionate soul, and by the time his calculating mind decided it might be a good idea, his dominating, self-interest would have him talking some innocent into doing the deed in front of him. Then he would broadcast an eyewitness account.

"What is it with you women, can't you stop being flippant? You and your family were on the boat too—maybe one of you pushed him over."

"Our grudge is against you and it's a valid complaint."

"Yeah, I know, I know, but listen to me. We have to figure out who killed Chuck or it could mean cop trouble for any of us."

"What?"

"Personally, I think it was a case of mistaken identity. Try this scenario. We were on the boat to investigate a story about a crime ring. I think the person who runs this ring of crooks figured that out. My source sounded spooked and said we shouldn't meet on board, that it was dangerous. Anyway, the ringleader spots us, puts two and two together and decides to get rid of me before I can expose his game. However, unlikely as it seems, he doesn't recognize me and when he sees I have the camera, he figures I'm Chuck and goes after Chuck thinking he's me."

Beth felt her jaw drop open.

"You think even a murder has to have you in the middle of it?"

"You think someone would kill Chuck on purpose? Get off it. You need a reason to murder someone, what reason could anyone have for killing Chuck? Did he ever mention even arguing with anyone? Can you believe he had enemies?"

"I don't know. In fact, I've been thinking about him and I have no recollection of him talking about his past. It's as though his life started when he arrived in Edmonton five years ago."

"You think he's in a witness protection program or maybe wanted by the police?"

Richard's voice rose, his eyes gleamed, and he licked his lips.

Beth recognized the symptoms as Richard formulating some wild story.

"Don't even think about exploiting him!"

"Those quiet guys are always hiding something."

"I was thinking that maybe something personal had happened to him, something he didn't want to talk about. I wasn't speculating that he was hiding a dark secret, just a hurt soul."

Beth rubbed the back of her neck. She hated the way Richard thought the worst about everyone and focused his stories so they would cause maximum distress. Worst yet, he claimed to do it in the name of truth in reporting. It was exactly that kind of behaviour that had made breaking off their relationship easy.

"Beth," Richard held her by the shoulders and looked into her eyes. "Let's be a team again. Let's find out why Chuck was killed."

She heard excitement growing in his voice and felt an answering tingle shoot up her spine. The days when she had joined Chuck and Richard in researching stories had been exhilarating. She shook her head. That part of her life had ended when she'd kicked Richard out.

"No. Let the police do their job. It has to turn out to be an accident."

"Beth, I miss you."

Those damn puppy dog eyes came closer. She felt his arm slip around her shoulders, his breath warmed her cheek. His lips caressed hers.

"What's going on?"

They jumped apart like teenagers caught by an outraged parent.

"Jim, long-time no see." Richard extended his hand toward Beth's brother, but continued holding her close.

Jim's breathing was heavy and his face flushed. Beth hoped the colour was a result of his morning run, but his next words dispelled that illusion.

"Get out of here and stay away from my sister."

Richard's mouth turned up at one corner. "Cool down puppy. Beth can run her own life."

Beth pulled out of Richard's embrace. "Jim, stay out of this." Then she looked up at Richard. "I can't help you, leave it to the police."

With a shrug and an ironic grin he turned and as he pulled the door closed said, "The offer is always open."

A shudder ran through Beth. How could she have let him get to her like that?

"How could you let him do that?" Jim echoed her thoughts.

"Butt out, Jim."

She headed for her den and slammed the door. Watching the

hypnotic lines moving slowly and rhythmically across her computer screen calmed her.

Richard could still get to her. How could she have let that kiss happen? He was totally wrong for her. The thought of Mike's calm smile soothed her. How could she betray him?

Beth covered her face with her hands, then refusing to give in to embarrassment and self-condemnation she straightened and stared at her computer screen. Richard had great instincts. Was he right this time? Was Richard the intended victim? That theory would make more sense than trying to believe someone wanted Chuck dead.

Damn, why did Richard have to be so sexy? She had Mike now. They'd been friends for months and their relationship was moving smoothly into something more.

She pulled her office chair out from the desk. Splatter, her speckle-faced, grey cat was keeping the chair warm knowing she would eventually reappear. Beth took the ball of fur in her arms and stroked her as she stared out of the office window.

In the park across from her house, lilac blooms covered the dwarf bushes. Crocuses and tulips swayed in the breeze. Bright green leaves peeked from their winter casings. Splatter's body tensed as a robin hopped from a branch onto the grass and turned its head to track an earthworm. Another hop and then a quick stab of its beak and the resulting tug-of-war ended unhappily for the worm.

Beth stroked the cat. Who would believe such a beautiful, fresh spring day could have started so badly?

A truck pulled to a stop, blocking her view of the park. Mike. She must have conjured him with her thoughts. Or Richard was right and they were all suspects. Her stomach fluttered in anticipation. She left her office and intercepted him at the door.

"Let's walk," she said, heading down the front sidewalk, forcing Mike to match his long stride to her shorter steps.

He spoke first. "Did you see Chuck Albright on the River Belle last night?"

"Richard told me that Chuck is dead. He's trying to change the story-line to one where he was the intended victim."

Mike's eyebrows shot upward. "Not a bad idea, but how did he get around to that conclusion?"

"They had a fight in front of everyone on the boat. Chuck left the camera with Richard and walked away. Richard says they were checking out a tip about a crime ring and he thinks the people they were investigating thought Chuck was the reporter."

"That's a far-fetched idea, still if Tanner was the intended victim we would have a few dozen suspects and as many motives. Right now, we have nothing on either count."

"So Richard is right? Chuck was murdered? It wasn't just an accident?"

"The autopsy is scheduled for tomorrow afternoon so we will know more then. Dr. Smythe has Tommy Jamieson in the morning. Evan will be observing."

"Why the wait? Why wasn't it done on Friday?"

"The Doc is in Hawaii, back today. The Chief wants the best to do it."

"That poor little boy, how his parents must be suffering. But Evan's son isn't much younger than Tommy, how could anyone ask him to watch the autopsy?"

"We all feel it when a kid is victimized. It's hard to deal with, but having Evan attend was Norman Carswell's idea. He requested that all officers working with the task force be there to boost their incentive to catch the freak."

Mike reached out and held her hand as they walked. "The M.E. suggested we investigate this like a homicide, so I've got to question you and your family."

"Oh."

"We'll be questioning everyone who was on board last night."

"This isn't the way I expected you to meet them."

Beth squeezed his hand, wanting to hold it forever. Her procrastination had returned to haunt her. There was no hope of easing into an introduction now.

"Let's get it over with." She turned toward the house. "I'll have to wake them."

When they walked across her patio and into her lemon yellow and white kitchen, they found her family already gathered for breakfast. Jim looked up as they entered, lines of anger still etched his face, but they faded rapidly when he saw a stranger standing beside her.

Beth surveyed the questioning faces before her, then with a mental shrug she said, "I'd like you to meet Detective Mike Ceretzke. He works with the police and needs to ask us some questions about last night."

Ron McKinney was the first to collect his wits and stood with his hand extended.

"The Mike Ceretzke who was supposed to be with us on the riverboat? Beth never mentioned you were a police officer. Glad to finally meet you, though why so formal?"

"Chuck Albright was found dead this morning and we will be questioning everyone who was on board."

"Is that why Tanner was here? To tell you about Chuck?" Jim's voice held an unusually bitter, angry note.

"Yes, that's why," Beth said, watching Mike pull a notebook from his pocket, but knowing he had heard Jim's hostility.

"Did any of you see Tanner or Chuck after their fight," Mike asked.

His answer was a general shaking of heads.

"Their fight, how serious was it?"

"Tanner probably killed him," Jim blurted out.

"I didn't say anyone killed him."

"Well, a cop wouldn't be asking questions if he'd had a heart attack."

"Jim, that's no way to talk," his mother spoke up. "I don't think the fight was serious. Beth, didn't you say they often fought?"

"Richard could usually talk Chuck into going along with his ideas. Once Chuck calmed down. Really, Mike, I don't think that argument ended with Richard killing Chuck. Richard's theory is more plausible than that."

Beth then explained Richard's theory to her family. It was greeted with a thoughtful look from her dad, a nod of agreement from her mom, and a snort of disbelief from Jim.

"What's your opinion Mr. McKinney," Mike asked Ron.

"I never liked Tanner, especially when it came to being part of our family." He looked at Beth, then Jim. "But I don't think he would kill anyone."

"Right." Jim pushed back his chair and stomped to the sink. "If he thought he could get a story out of it and live, he'd have sunk the boat."

"That's enough, Jim. Remember a man is dead," Dorothy McKinney said.

"Yeah, the wrong one."

"Really Mike, we don't have any more to tell you. After the argument, dinner was announced and we followed the crowd to the dining room," Dorothy said.

"Well, I guess that's all I have to ask you now. I might have to follow up later if other questions arise."

"No problem," Ron said, pulling out a chair. "Now why don't you sit down and have a cup of coffee."

Beth poured Mike a cup and sat it on the table, noting the gleam in her father's eyes. It was Mike's turn to answer a few questions of the father-to-suitor variety.

Mike's face lost its official look as he smiled and said, "Beth has told me all about you."

Beth felt a flush move up her face. Why had she put off telling her family about him? She hoped he wouldn't be offended when her procrastination became obvious.

CHAPTER 8

"How did your hunch work out, Norman," Mike asked as the grey-haired detective walked by with a coffee mug gripped tightly in his shaky hand.

"It was just another false lead," he mumbled and kept walking.

"Did you hear about Chuck Albright?"

Drops of coffee slopped from the full cup as the older detective turned toward Mike. He wore a perplexed expression, the same one he'd exhibited every day since they'd met years before.

"Who?"

"Richard Tanner's cameraman, Chuck Albright."

"Oh. I don't think I ever knew his name. What about him?"

"He drowned Saturday night. The M.E. is betting it was murder. That's why I was out of here all day yesterday."

"So now you have your own case and can stop poaching mine?"

Norman pushed his way between two officers as he walked toward his desk. Mike turned back to his reports. Norman got touchier every day. They better catch the guy who was killing kids this year or the police chief might toss him out of the force for having a lousy attitude.

******

Mike scanned the cafeteria. Dr. Elizabeth Smythe seemed to be meditating in the bright sunlight streaming through the window. A cup of coffee and a donut sat on the table in front of her clenched fists. He headed toward her.

"May I join you?"

"Sure, Mike. Carswell didn't manage to goad you into attending the autopsy?"

"I had a more pressing matter to attend to. Did you find anything new?"

"I gave it all to Carswell, but here we go again. I found no surprises such as old bruises. Also, there was no new evidence. The last thing the kid ate was macaroni and that was a couple of hours before that creep killed him. Damn sicko."

She stared at her coffee mug.

Mike watched her for a long minute, then exhaled a deep breath. "Anything that can help us identify the killer?"

"The murderer strangled him with a covered cord, maybe an electrical cord, something like that. We took scrapings from under his nails, picked tiny remnants of duct tape from near his mouth, and got all the necessary swabs. Lab techs took everything but I doubt they'll find anything for a DNA match. This killer is so careful about leaving evidence that he shampooed Tommy's hair and washed his clothes. Same story as the others."

"Tommy died soon after being abducted?"

Mike hated his job some days, almost as much as he hated the people who could do things like this. Damn, the kid was only six, what was his mother thinking to send him off to school on his own! Hadn't she heard the warnings? Four victims and the creep's M.O. remained the same to the smallest detail. The profiler said he should have changed something during that time.

Elizabeth used both hands to raise her cup to her lips. She replaced it on the table without drinking. "The files are nearly interchangeable. The kid is sexually abused and strangled, then several hours or days later his body is dumped near the site of the abduction and with all of our knowledge we don't have anything to match against a suspect, if we ever catch one."

Mike knew the lab wasn't the only place to suffer a shortage of evidence. All the task force seemed to learn were negatives. They had investigated each individual case and discounted the theory that a family member was involved. To date no witness had provided a description, no footprint waited matching, no DNA sample lingered on the body, and no motive became apparent. Hell, they couldn't even be certain they were looking for a man. That was just what the profiler said was the most likely possibility. Whoever did kill them didn't even take a souvenir.

******

Samantha Weisman looked down the length of the table studying each officer.

"Norman, give us an update on the task force's progress," she said.

"Dr. Smythe has confirmed the abductor used the same M.O. as in the cases of Sally Paterson, Johnny Wu, and Belinda Ortiz. We have officers canvassing the neighbourhood near the day care centre and the school looking for anybody who saw something. We'll review each case looking for similarities. Then we will re-interview the school staff and the families of all the victims. Maybe we will find the connection this year."

Sam nodded. Norman sounded bored with the whole investigation. Where had his drive, his compulsion to catch the murderer gone? Obviously, Norman running the task force was a mistake. She would talk to the Chief about Mike taking over, even if it meant shifting him off the other current murder investigation.

"Mike, what do you have on the Albright case?"

"I'm attending the autopsy in twenty minutes, but unless someone suggests a motive or we find a witness, it will be tough going."

"He argued with Richard Tanner."

"Witnesses don't think that amounted to much, just threats of getting each other fired. I've started a background check on Chuck, but until the autopsy results are in I'm inclined to think his death was accidental."

"We can't hang this on Tanner and get him off our backs about the crime rate?" Sam smiled to let the officers know she was just kidding.

******

Dr. Smythe bent over the body. She pointed to an oblong mark running along the side of Chuck's neck. It was just centimetres away from the protection of his skull.

"That's the mark I pointed out yesterday."

"The river is full of debris from the spring runoff," Mike said.

"This was caused by something harder, metal of some kind. See here." She pointed to something Mike couldn't quite see. "The edges of the wound are straight, but slightly rounded. It might have been a pipe. Also, there was a lot of force behind the blow."

"You're saying someone killed him before he went in the river?"

"He was unconscious, if not dead when he went in. See this cut." She touched his skin near a gaping wound on his forehead. "I would speculate that he was hit from behind, then as he fell forward he hit his head a second time. The other bruises and cuts on the face and hands are what I would expect to find on a body dragged face down by the current."

She continued talking as she worked. "Look here, there is no water in his lungs, so your boy was dead before he went in the river."

The remainder of the autopsy uncovered no other anomalies but made it official. He had a homicide on his hands. Mike decided to stop in at the Ident unit to see what Pete Humphreys could add to the doctor's findings.

Pete was peering at a computer screen when Mike walked in. Mike gave him a brief summary of the autopsy results.

"Elizabeth is right about the blow," Pete said. "Take a look at the pictures I took on the boat." He opened a folder containing blow-ups. "The blood splatters show where his head impacted the rail as he fell forward. He was on the deck long enough for his blood to start pooling. See these drag marks and streaks? That pattern was messed up by the kid with the mop, but enough is intact to tell me he was pulled a few feet toward the railing, then heaved over."

Mike pointed to the clear print of a running shoe in the blood. "Any chance that print belongs to the murderer?"

Pete looked over his hunched shoulder and up at the detective towering above him.

"It's a perfect fifteen point match to the runners of the kid who mopped up the blood. If he's a suspect you're all set."

"Anything else," Mike asked.

"There was little drying of the blood before his body was dragged, so I would guess he was hit and pushed over fairly quickly."

"Any hope of finding trace evidence on Chuck's clothes?"

Pete grunted. "After being in that river? Don't worry, we'll look at what comes from the autopsy, but I doubt anything from the crime scene survived prolonged immersion. What we will have to process is a lot of river garbage caught on the body. I do have one little gem for you though." Pete paused as if waiting for Mike to ask what that gem might be.

"What?" Mike relented, hoping for something major like a neon arrow pointing to a suspect and flashing the word 'guilty'.

"I found a key pushed under the bench near the snack bar. It belongs to an equipment shed near the parking lot and the attendant said someone broke into it Saturday night, late."

"Who has keys?"

"Must I do all your work for you?"

"Do you think it's related?"

"I just find the evidence. You get to interpret it."

******

Mike and Evan split the riverboat's passenger list between them, hoping to cut interview time in half. Still, Mike had interviewed barely a quarter of the people on his list, so after talking to Pete he decided to tackle a few more.

Today his list started with G. Azzara, a party of four. He had barely raised his fist to knock when the apartment door opened, revealing a tall, slender woman with dark brown hair, dark eyes, and an impatient frown.

"It's about time you got here. I called two hours ago and I have to leave in twenty minutes."

She crossed her arms over her linen suit jacket, a two-piece red and black ensemble.

Mike hesitated, disconcerted because she seemed to be expecting him. He introduced himself, "Detective Ceretzke, city police. I would like to speak to you about a homicide. Are you G. Azzara?"

"Gloria Azzara, yes."

"Were you expecting me?"

"Yes, no. A homicide, not a robbery?" Her hands rested on her hips; her eyes bore into his.

"A homicide. I have a few questions to ask about last Saturday evening. I understand you were onboard the River Belle with some friends."

"Damn, can you take a robbery report too? I suppose you can't." She pointed into the apartment. "Let me make a call. I have to cancel a meeting."

He watched her stride across the room to the phone where she punched a coded number and spoke in a crisp tone to the person who answered. Mike glanced around the living room while he waited. A white leather sofa and shiny black end tables sat on a white carpet. Several crystal sculptures added to the cold ambience. One wall was covered in black and white pictures. The wall behind the sofa displayed a winter landscape painted in several shades of snowy grey. No need to ask if she had children. Even the bulky briefcase propped near the sofa was shiny black leather.

But a robbery? He probed the room, but nothing appeared disturbed. Then, his gaze settled on the entertainment centre, empty of its equipment. Faint outlines in the dust showed where objects had recently sat.

"Okay, Saturday night," she said as she walked toward him, her hands waving in a bizarre sign language as she spoke. "Sara and Philip Weaver, and Reggie and I were on the River Belle celebrating their tenth anniversary. I made that booking because I like riverboats. Wherever I travel I search them out, the big ones," she said, swinging her arms wide for emphasis, "on the Mississippi are the best, but the ones here aren't bad either. The casino nights are my favorites, but Sara and Philip enjoy dinner theatres."

"Did you notice anything unusual during the trip?"

She tapped her finger against her chin. "I noticed lots of unusual things, a tree floating by with a bird's nest still intact in its branches, a truly awful dress on a woman who should have known better, a group of kids under the bridge playing with fireworks . . . ."

The detective broke into her recital. "Did you notice an argument between two men?"

"Tanner and his cameraman? Sure, everyone noticed that. You would have had to be deaf and blind not to. Is that all?"

"Have you heard that the cameraman was later found dead?"

"It's been all over the news. Some reports say it was an accident, some say murder. You're here so I assume it was murder." Her hands rested briefly on her hips before taking flight again.

"Did you see Chuck Albright, the cameraman, after the fight?"

"Nope. They announced dinner just then and asked everyone to go to the dining room and that's what we did. I did see Tanner as I was leaving the boat, though. He was muttering about being deserted."

"Did you see anyone leave the dining room during the performance?"

"A few smokers in need of a nicotine fix. A skinny woman with a big hat only stayed for the first act. And Dorothy McKinney and her son left for a while during the third act."

"You know Mrs. McKinney?"

"She was my personal trainer some years ago. I heard she set up her own place and it went bankrupt. Chalk one up to the power of the media. Tanner should be shot for what he did to Dorothy's dream."

"What time did they leave the room?"

"She left at the end of the second intermission. Her son followed, maybe ten minutes later. She was gone about twenty minutes. Him, maybe fifteen."

"So they didn't leave together?"

Ms. Azzara shook her head. Her hair was bound in a twist at the back of her neck, but thin tendrils escaped and curled near her ears, swinging as her long neck moved emphatically from side to side. "Didn't return together either." She motioned to the white leather sofa. "Look, why don't you sit, maybe you could take the information you need about this burglary."

"Just a couple more questions. Do you have any idea why she left?"

She twisted her large gold earring. "I was going to stop by to say hi during the intermission, but they were having a really serious conversation. I didn't feel right interrupting."

"Did the others in your party notice her leaving?"

"Maybe, but as I said, the play had started again, so I couldn't say what they saw."

"What was stolen, Ms. Azzara?"

"Today? I came home to copy a file from my laptop. I walked over to turn on the stereo and noticed it was gone." She demonstrated by walking to the wall unit and pointing to the empty shelves. "The whole entertainment system snatched. Also, some cash I keep on hand and my laptop. That's what I really need to find."

"How did they get in?"

"That's the creepiest thing. I don't know. The door lock isn't standard apartment issue. I replaced that piece of junk with a good dead bolt the day I moved in, but I had to give the building manager a key. Do you think he did it?"

"No windows were forced?"

"I was hoping you'd tell me. How much longer before a constable gets out here?"

"Not long, I'll phone before I leave. Can you give me the full names and addresses of your companions?"

"If you're interviewing everyone on that boat, you've got a lot of legwork ahead of you."

CHAPTER 9

"Drop dead. I heard what you did to Chuck and I have no intention of talking to you."

The door to the bungalow slammed in Richard's face.

"That's three, Tanner. Maybe it's time to give up and let someone else handle this story."

Richard heard her mocking tone. Christy Sommers, camera operator! Who was she to tell him how to get a story?

She raised her hands when he turned toward her.

"Don't bite, I'm just stating the obvious. No one is going to talk to you about Chuck. It's funny how they believe you killed him after he refused to introduce you to the same people you're now harassing. Our competition is getting pretty good mileage circulating the story of your fight."

"I'll get the story, it's just time to change my tactics and maybe recruit a little assistance. Phone the head office of the Scouts and ask when the next meeting of the troop Chuck was helping takes place. Tell them your kid wants to join."

"Why me?"

"I already asked them for a membership list."

"Which they refused to give you," she said in a cheerful voice.

Richard ignored her interruption. "So, they might recognize my voice."

"What are you going to do while I'm phoning?"

"Just drop me at my car. I'll call later to see what you have."

Richard saw Christy's frown, but chose to ignore it. Let her get her back up, he intended to keep her in the dark about his methods. Chuck's threat of exposure had taught him the price of indiscretion. You would think you could trust a partner and that's the way he had always treated Chuck, as a partner, still the guy had turned on him.

Christy pulled to a stop in the parking lot behind the station and Richard hurried into the building, stopping briefly to grab Chuck's books and files. He wanted to review them in private, though the abuse story could wait until he completed researching his tribute to Chuck.

The envelope of stuff he'd borrowed from Chuck's apartment had been no help. Just the birth certificate and driver's license of someone named Carl Aimsworth. A quick check of records dug up four people by that name. One was a senior citizen, two were kids, and the other had died in infancy. The living ones claimed they had never heard of Chuck.

He didn't like unsolved mysteries, but now his priority was convincing people in the know to co-operate. If he could get them to talk about Chuck's volunteer activities he could combine his interviews, getting the usual 'he was a great guy' story, plus quotes about agency screening procedures. If he worded his questions carefully, he knew he could uncover hints of any problems they wanted kept secret.

He drove through the downtown traffic, catching every light before it turned red. He had decided not to phone the Little League office because warning them was the mistake he had made with the Scouts. He never made the same mistake twice. A large dose of charm would get him a list of the kids on last year's team then he would go directly to the kids for interviews. He would show that management-infant he could do good human interest.

Richard pulled into the parking lot of a generic office tower on a busy bus route. The directory listed accountants, lawyers, a podiatrist, and a computer-dating agency. The Little League office was located on the fifth floor. Richard passed several doors as he made his way down the narrow, grey hall. All were closed and showed no signs of life.

The sixth door wore the label he hunted. It opened into a small reception area. A metal desk and a half dozen uncomfortable chairs that looked like government surplus rejects filled the waiting room. Two doors led off the reception area, one was open, but no one was inside.

A middle-aged woman sat behind the desk. Richard refrained from rubbing his hands in glee. These old bags might put on an iron front but they melted under the fire of flattery. Getting a team list wouldn't be a challenge to a person of his talent.

"Good afternoon." Richard smiled his most endearing smile and looked straight into her eyes. "I hope you can help me on a very important story."

She looked away, refusing to smile back. "You're a reporter." She shoved an index card under a pile of paper.

"Yes, with Channel Six. I'm working on a tribute to a great community volunteer who suffered an untimely and tragic death. Interviews with some of the fine young children he coached would add much to my tribute."

She scowled. "I can't give you personal information."

"I'm sure you can supply a team list. It must be right there on your computer."

"Our policy is to give lists only to coaches or parents of team members who agree to act as volunteers."

"I want last year's team list, how can that information be sensitive?"

Richard studied the dowdy little woman. Was he losing his touch? She should have been falling over herself to pull the data for him.

"Is there some way you can bend the procedures? I don't think you told me your name," he said, then waited expecting to hear a name that was as ordinary as the woman herself.

"Anita Phillips like the sign says." She pointed to a nameplate hidden behind a ceramic baseball batter. A group of similar figures turned the corner of her desk into a showcase of tacky workmanship and sick humor.

"Well, Anita," he said, pleased to note that at least some part of his intuition was working. "That's such a strong name. It was my mother's name and one day I hope I have a daughter I can name Anita."

"Personally, I've never liked it." She looked up at him, frowned, and turned her computer screen farther from his line of vision.

Reading computer screens, even when they held something as useless as a recipe for a caramel pudding as did hers, was a reflex Richard had cultivated. The ability to read upside-down and backwards was another of his invaluable skills. Combining these talents, he had learned vast amounts of information without the owner's knowledge.

Today his skill again paid off. A file folder, peaking out of a large stack on the far side of her computer, sported Chuck's name. Richard pulled his attention away from the file and tried his puppy-dog look. She was a surprisingly hard sell, but hard won victories made the best war stories. He turned away from her and scanned the office, hoping to discover a way to get her out of the room. He spotted the closed door.

"Would you ask your supervisor if this situation could be considered an exception? I do want to present a touching tribute to Chuck."

Richard held his expression to casual concern and friendliness. He detected no trace of humour or kindness in Anita's stern glare. Finally, she sighed and pushed back her chair.

"I'll go talk to Mr. Barkly, but he's a busy man so don't count on him agreeing to see you."

She stomped off in the direction of the closed door, entered the room, and shut the door behind her.

Richard circled her desk. He pulled Chuck's file from the pile, stowed it in his briefcase, and was back in his original spot before Ms. Philips opened the door.

A stocky man followed her into the room. His clothes were casual, a sweater over a shirt, cotton twill slacks that bagged at the knees and sagged where they hung under his basketball stomach.

"Mr. Tanner, it is against League policy to discuss our coaches or to give out team data. That goes double for releasing information to the media," Mr. Barkly said.

"Even when the man's dead? He volunteers his time with your organization and you don't have a word to say about him."

Richard wished he'd brought Christy along, but unable to use the threat of an on air refusal he pulled a notebook from his pocket. A touch of righteous anger sometimes helped. "How do you spell your name. I want to get the facts straight when you tell me why I am getting the silent treatment."

Hesitation appeared on the man's face. Richard waited. He knew he had won. He would get his quote.

"You may inform your audience that Chuck Albright had been a coach for the past three years, but that he was not currently affiliated with Edmonton's Little League organization."

"Whoa." The man's words were cold water on Richard's anger.

"He never said he wasn't coaching this year. He loved being with kids, he even enjoyed the out-of-town tournaments and it takes a saint to relish travelling with a dozen ten-year-old kids."

"Many of our coaches leave after a few years. They find the pressures of life, family responsibilities, or other commitments require additional time and feel they can no longer help us."

Richard looked down. Why was Barkly staring at his tie?

"What reason did he give for quitting?"

"I believe he was heavily committed to other organizations. If that's all, Mr. Tanner."

Richard, stunned by the revelation, could think of nothing to ask. As Richard watched the office door close behind Barkly's broad hips, a stray thought tugged at his mind. Had Chuck withdrawn from the Boy Scouts too? Was that why they had cut his request off so abruptly?

Out of habit, Richard smiled at Ms. Philips. She met his smile with a smug grin. Was she feeling triumphant that the revelation surprised him? Well, he had the last laugh. Without a twinge of conscience, he sailed from the office. With the pile of work on her desk, she might not miss the file for days and might never connect its disappearance with his visit.

Once back in his car, Richard opened the file folder and skimmed the top page. It was a parent's testimonial to the best coach that their kid had ever had. The next was more of the same. He quickly flipped through the rest of the pages and near the back of the pile found the team lists. He plucked out the most recent sheet of names then dropped the file onto the stack of research that he had removed from Chuck's locker. He would go through the rest of the letters after he talked to some of the kids. Maybe he could cull a few quotes for the segment.

He phoned the station and talked to Christy, hoping she had discovered when the next Scout meeting was being held.

"I hate lying to nice people and I'm not good at it."

Richard pulled into traffic, his cell phone in one hand, his other hand on the wheel. She was always complaining. He was definitely requesting a different camera operator.

"The next time, do it yourself," she continued in a bitchy tone of voice.

"But you got the info?"

"Seven o'clock Wednesday night in the community hall basement. You want the leader's name and phone number?"

"Keep it for now. I'll be by to pick you up and we can start talking to the kids on Chuck's Little League team."

"They gave you the kids' names?"

"All I had to do was ask nicely."

******

The schoolyard was nearly empty when they arrived, but a couple of questions to the kids still hanging around sent Richard to the local arcade. After assuring the wary arcade owner they were not doing a feature on kids who spent their lunch money and afternoons in his establishment, he pointed to a group of boys wearing all-star jackets.

Some disappeared when they spotted the camera perhaps afraid their parents would see them on TV and swat them for being at the arcade. After a lot of jostling and daring, three of the remaining kids agreed to speak to him on camera.

"Mr. Albright was an okay coach," said the first youth. He was a red-haired kid whose wide eyes and awed smirk told Richard he was drooling over Christy. Not that he could blame the kid.

"Was he fair?"

"Yeah, sometimes he had favourites, but mostly he played the best kids."

"What position do you play?"

Their answers came in rapid succession. "Back catcher."—"Third base."—"Short stop."

"So you went to the tournaments with Mr. Albright?" Richard addressed the question to the group, but again the redhead acted as spokesman.

This time he tore his gaze away from Christy's legs and looked directly at Richard. "Yeah, I went, but my Mom and Dad came with me and we stayed in a motel."

The others nodded.

"Didn't you want to camp with the rest of the team?"

"It was no big deal."

"Did you know that Mr. Albright wasn't planning to coach this year?"

The boys shrugged in unison.

"We gotta go," the redhead said as he slouched away. His friends followed his lead but their nudges and quick backward glances made Richard wonder what they were hiding. Perhaps it was adolescent hormones, but his gut said it had to do with Chuck not Christy.

"Another glowing testimonial. What's with these kids, don't they know a good thing when they see it?"

"You're just upset because your story isn't going the way you want."

"Let's get out of here. It's time to try a different tactic."

CHAPTER 10

"Mrs. McKinney." Mike cleared his throat, wishing he had asked Evan to do the interview.

"Call me Dorothy, after all you are Beth's friend."

Mike shifted on the sofa, feeling uncomfortable facing Beth's mother in a room where he and Beth had spent many pleasant hours.

Would questioning her story affect that relationship? He definitely should have asked Evan to do this. Well, it was too late now. "You were hurt financially when Richard Tanner aired that story about your fitness centre," he said, then paused, hoping for a voluntary response.

"That two-second mistake destroyed a dream I'd savoured for twenty years. I think we had a right to sue and I'm glad the court gave us a decent settlement."

"So the court decision satisfied you?"

"You want to know if I forgave Richard?"

Mike found himself studying Dorothy, pleased that Beth had inherited her mother's fine physique. The firm muscles revealed by her sleeveless blouse and walking shorts, subtracted years from her age. Her hair held only a touch of grey and her face was virtually unlined. She could be taken for Beth's older sister except for the air of maturity emanating from her every word and action.

"I'm not a forgiving person, Detective. Ron is better that way, he tells me it was an honest mistake and that I shouldn't hold grudges."

"Nevertheless, you felt . . . ." He let the sentence dangle.

"I believed, and still do, that Richard Tanner used the power of television to seek revenge for Beth dumping him. For the life of me, I don't know what she ever saw in that preening phony. He is self-centred, demanding, and worst of all he doesn't realize that he hurts people with his stories."

"Were you also angry with the station?"

"They should have fired Richard immediately. A person like him should be banned from any job where he can influence what people think."

"Chuck was part of the news team, did you hold him responsible too?"

Dorothy McKinney didn't answer, but instead asked, "Why?"

"A witness says you left the dining room at the end of the second intermission and that you were gone for several minutes. Where did you go?"

"You think I pushed Chuck off the boat? He was bigger than I am."

She sipped her tea as she watched him over the rim of her mug. Mike saw the wariness in her that Beth had displayed during the first weeks of their relationship.

"He was dead when he was dumped in the river. Please Mrs. McKinney . . . ." She smiled a rebuff and Mike corrected himself. "Dorothy. Just tell me where you went when you left the dining room."

Mike had caught her alone in the house. Beth was working an extra shift at the library. Jim and Ron were at a tree nursery looking for an apple tree to plant in Beth's backyard.

Dorothy McKinney had welcomed his arrival with obvious pleasure but directed him to the living room, not the bright, friendly kitchen that Beth preferred for casual entertaining. Before he could speak, she had set out fresh home-baked cookies and herbal tea. Another difference between the women, because Beth would have stuck with coffee and commercial bakery products. Was her hospitality normal or was Dorothy delaying his questioning?

Mike ran his fingers through his hair. Evan should be doing this.

The seconds passed as Dorothy McKinney hesitated. She put her mug on the coffee table and leaned against the sofa back. Then she picked up a peach-tone toss cushion and twisted its corner. Finally, she looked at him and asked, "You like Beth, don't you?"

"Our relationship has nothing to do with this investigation." When she said no more, he added, "Beth means a great deal to me."

Dorothy smiled, then continued as if somehow his answer had relieved her concerns.

"I went out on deck to get some air. During the intermission, Beth and Jim told us they had developed a business plan for a new fitness centre. They want to form a partnership where they provide start-up funding and business expertise and Ron and I do the hands-on management.

"Jim believes we can take over a warehouse, install small studios and lease them to groups or individuals. That way we won't be pressured to sell memberships, just to keep the place running. In fact, signing up members need not fall on us at all. We could be nothing more than the management.

"The kids are keen on the idea and they sprang it on us. I was overwhelmed by their generosity and the faith they showed after my dream failed so dismally the last time."

She placed the cushion on the sofa and Magpie settled onto it. Then she reached for her teacup. Mike waited for her to continue.

"I am afraid that something will go wrong and I don't want to fail again. Our nomadic lifestyle is an easy way to live and I don't know if going back into business is the best thing for us. That's why I wondered about your relationship with Beth. Has she discussed this plan with you?"

"She wants you to be happy and believes you will have a longer, fuller life if you have a reason to get up in the morning."

"I'm fifty-four; Ron is fifty-six. Isn't it time we stopped working?"

"That's up to you, but three years ago you wanted to start this business, a twenty-year dream didn't you say? What's changed?"

"Fear." She bit into a chocolate-iced brownie and took a moment to savour it. "Why should I risk failing again? We manage on Ron's pension."

"Beth believes the centre might add a challenge to your life. I don't think money is a consideration to her."

"She has always had a knack for making money. Still, that's beside the point. Sometimes I'm so tired I can hardly move. I've suffered from bouts of fatigue ever since the gym failed. The idea of finding the energy necessary to establish and run a new business scares me."

"Maybe your fatigue is caused by depression resulting from the gym's failure?" Mike watched a light begin glowing in her eyes and he added, "And perhaps a bit of boredom with your current lifestyle?"

She smiled for the first time since he arrived and he noted Beth's laugh lines emphasizing her eyes.

"Beth has chosen well this time," she said.

Mike let the comfortable silence continue for a few minutes, then repeated his question about her activities on the paddle wheeler. This time she answered him directly.

"I left the dining room and went up to the deck. Richard was looking north over the rail. He watched me walk up the stairs but turned away when he recognized me. If it were anyone else, I would say he felt too guilty to face me but Richard was just showing his contempt. I walked to the rail on the south side of the boat. The river was hypnotizing, full of violence and turmoil. For a long time, I watched the shoreline glide past. I wasn't thinking or anything, just absorbing the night and sorting my feelings. Then the deck lights flickered on and I felt exposed, so I returned to the dining room."

"Did you see Chuck?"

"Richard was the only person I saw on the deck, other than a couple of crew members."

"Can you describe them?"

"One was a tall, blond fellow. The captain was at the bridge with another, smaller young man. There could have been others, but as I said, I wasn't paying attention."

"Did you hear anything?"

"Like a splash? The music was so loud I couldn't even hear the night sounds."

"Your son went looking for you, did you see him?"

"You can't think Jim had anything to do with Chuck's death. He was angry with Richard, not Chuck."

"I'll want to talk to him anyway. I have to find out if he saw anything."

She nodded, then added, "I didn't blame Chuck, either. He was a quiet, self-contained man who I believe would never intentionally hurt anyone. He sent us a huge bouquet of daisies and daffodils when the gym opened and a card expressing his regret when we finally admitted defeat and shut the doors. Have you seen the album he made of the opening ceremony?" She jumped to her feet and strode toward the end table where a photo album lay. Mike hadn't seen it before. "Surely Beth showed you? Well, she should have. Chuck put it together for us even though Beth and Richard had split up by then."

By the time Mike finished examining the photo album, Jim and Ron had returned. Dorothy put on a pot of coffee and they moved to the back deck where the conversation turned to the best placement of the new tree.

It took some effort, but Mike managed to question Jim about the night on the boat. He said he had stayed on the deck, soothed into inactivity watching the moonlight glitter on the mini-waterfalls created as the boat cut through the current. And no, he emphasized, he would not hurt Chuck, but Tanner might not be so lucky if he were offered an even chance of getting away with murder or at least grievous bodily harm.

******

Sam Weisman looked from one detective to the other. Her gaze came to a rest on Evan Collins.

"What do we know," she asked.

"During the intermission between the second and third acts several people saw Chuck standing at the rail on the upper deck. He was at one end of the boat and Richard was at the other. One passenger said she tried talking to Chuck. He bummed a cigarette from her, then ignored her."

"Mrs. McKinney went to the upper deck just after the third act began and didn't see Chuck," Mike interjected.

"So how much time are we looking at," Super Sam asked.

Evan looked at Mike for confirmation. "No one was certain of the exact time the intermission ended, but I would estimate a ten minute window of opportunity."

"And no one but the McKinney's and Tanner were outside the dining room?"

"Some crew members were legitimately elsewhere. And we do have one missing person, a Jennifer Rivers, who should have been working as a hostess Saturday evening." Evan checked his notes. "She worked for most of the day but never signed out. We haven't been able to locate her and no one remembers seeing her during the evening cruise. She could have left the boat before it sailed or disembarked at the Fort Edmonton landing, but we haven't confirmed either possibility."

"Does she tie into the case?"

"Not that we've discovered."

"What else do you have?"

"A man bought a single ticket for the dinner theatre but he never showed up in the dining room so we have little on him."

"Little?"

"He paid cash, he was in his fifties, and liked hot dogs."

"Mike, you're convinced the McKinneys weren't involved," Sam asked.

"I never thought Mrs. McKinney held a grudge against Chuck. Jim McKinney is more hostile than his mother is, but again toward Richard. If Tanner was dead, Jim McKinney would be high on my list."

"This isn't some convoluted way to punish Tanner? They aren't trying to frame him for Chuck's death?"

"Do you want us to check out that theory?"

"Check out everything. Now what about the tip Tanner supposedly received? Have you found anything to substantiate his claim that a crime ring is operating on the boat?"

"None of the passengers I checked with was robbed, but if we check farther back than Saturday we might find a pattern," Evan replied.

"One of the people I interviewed had her apartment burglarized with no obvious signs of forced entry," Mike said.

Sam pondered briefly. "Check the customer lists back a month, that should give us a picture of what's happening, if anything. If you can't establish a pattern, we'll assume it was a con to get Tanner on board. If something shows up, we might have to figure Chuck got close to some dangerous people.

"Mike why don't you tackle Tanner again, see if he knows more than he's telling. He could be holding back information to spring as an exclusive, hoping to make us look stupid."

"If I can get him away from his camera. I don't want the interview showing up on the six o'clock news."

******

Lyle wished he could stretch his arms wide and push the walls away. Unlike Cara who was sized for the tiny office, Newfoundland's endless ocean views had programmed him for open air and vast horizons.

"You looked after it," she asked, glancing up from her computer.

"Lap tried calling off the crews, but he couldn't stop all the robberies and he's already sent the registration forms to the overseas buyers. I've passed word to our people to take a vacation until the cops go away."

Cara fiddled with her pencil, tapping the lead gently on her desk blotter then sliding the smooth shaft through her fingers and tapping the eraser end. "Has Jennifer turned up yet?"

Lyle felt the hypnotic power of her repetitive action and longed for escape. "I've checked her apartment, but the landlady hasn't seen her since Saturday and she didn't visit the gym today. Maybe she packed up and left town? She isn't a snitch. She didn't go near Tanner on Saturday and we watched him all evening. Why do you think she's dumb enough to meet him right under our noses?"

Lyle felt the room closing in on him and moved toward the door. He liked Jennifer and sensed a deep wound under the independence she wore like armour. He hoped to understand and eventually help her heal.

"Maybe she's not so dumb." Cara laid the pencil on the desk and looked at him. Her eyes narrowed and her lips flickered as she attempted a smile. "You say she didn't talk to Tanner, but she could have known we were watching and decided to wait, or she might have had an accomplice."

Lyle caught the speculative way Cara was looking at him. Could she doubt his loyalty? "Do you have spies watching me too? The only time he talked to me was just before he got off the boat."

Cara shrugged her delicate shoulders as if accepting his statement, but her expression remained skeptical. "If Jennifer turns up, get her out of town. Once the police stop snooping, I want to be able to get back to business without worrying about her talking to them."

"Cara, we should stop now. Why risk getting caught?"

Her look increased his nervousness.

"Lap says we continue."

"Think of your family. How will they feel if they learn you're robbing people."

"You're thinking of yourself, not of my family. However, my family will survive and surmount these difficulties as we have so many others. It is too late for us to get out."

Her sad tone encouraged Lyle to say more, but before he could her miniature shoulders pushed to attention and her expression hardened. Lyle followed her gaze to the photo on her desk. Lap stood in the position traditionally occupied by the male head of the household. A worn, middle-aged woman sat next to him, her heritage obvious in her dark hair and tiny frame. Cara and two younger children clustered around their mother.

"It's too late for us," she said.

CHAPTER 11

Richard pulled to the curb in front of the ugly, five-storey apartment building. It was tall and pink and flaunted Doric columns over the front entrance. Ordinarily the gaudy building would have amused him; today it added to his premonition of doom. He hadn't felt this fearful of continuing a story since the—actually he had never had to push himself so hard to continue researching.

It was all Chuck's doing. Somehow, he'd hid everything about his life before he arrived in Edmonton. How could he do a piece on a guy and give no details about his childhood? He needed trivia. He needed to know if Chuck was the teacher's pet, an honour student, the Boy Scout of the Year. That was the drivel viewers wanted and the kind of thing the kid running the station thought he couldn't do. Damn, he'd worked with Chuck for years, what had they talked about?

Richard thought back to their investigation of fraud and misuse in the Employment Insurance system. Chuck had been particularly sympathetic to the Atlantic fishermen. Did that mean he was a Maritimer? Of course, he also sympathized with Saskatchewan's farmers when their crops blew away during three consecutive years of drought. And with the fight of the B.C. environmentalists against clear-cutting. And damn it, every other bleeding heart, underdog group in the country. All that proved was that Chuck had been gullible.

Richard stared out his car window at Chuck's apartment building. If he had to search the place from baseboard to light fixture, he was going to get a handle on Chuck's family. Had he ever gone home for the Christmas holidays or for a summer vacation or even a funeral? Not that Richard recalled and he would have remembered because Chuck was a drone who never in his life committed an unplanned action. At least as much of his life as Richard knew about. He even went on the same holiday year after year. Always during the last two weeks in April and always to Hawaii. How could you visit the same place year, after year, after year?

At least Chuck didn't flash a bunch of pictures when he got back. He'd probably taken them all the first year and never bothered again because the places were so boring. Still, why would a photographer not take pictures? Wasn't it a compulsive thing? Like writing postcards? Wish you were here, ha, ha. Sorry you couldn't go on vacation but I'm willing to torture you with stories of all the sun and fun you missed.

Of course, Richard would have refused to look at them anyway. Few things in life bored him more than looking at someone else's vacation photos. Still, even when Chuck was just roaming the streets he carried a couple of cameras and seemed driven to snap random shots.

Chuck must have boxes of pictures stashed somewhere. Christy hadn't found them, but then she had only searched the bookcase for albums. Richard got out of the car and started up the walkway. He stopped and turned around at the beep of a horn. Mike Ceretzke had pulled his truck to the curb.

"Tanner, just the man I wanted. Hop in. You can buy me a cup of coffee."

"Sure," Richard muttered under his breath as he climbed into Ceretzke's thug mobile. Maybe he would use the opportunity to learn a few things from the cop. "What have you found out about the tip I gave you?"

"It doesn't look good for your theory. Only one woman from Saturday's cruise was robbed and that's well within the range of coincidence. Evan is checking passengers from the past month to see if a pattern exists."

"Any more on Chuck's death?"

"The M.E. is listing it as a homicide. Tell me about Saturday evening. Who did you see? Who saw you and when?"

Richard was fast discovering he didn't enjoy being on the answering end of questions. Nevertheless, he told of the smokers and fresh air fiends who had migrated from the dining room during each intermission. They were the desperate ones who ignored the management's best efforts to keep them seated and buying fresh drinks. He mentioned seeing Dorothy McKinney.

"The old bag ignored me. Still holding a grudge, I guess. Some people never let go. From the way she acts you'd think I won the big settlement and they were left standing in hot water up to their necks, instead of the other way round. A few minutes later, her self-righteous son hurried by me as if I wasn't there. They should have met somewhere on the deck because they were headed in opposite directions, maybe five or ten minutes apart."

"Did you notice anyone talking to Chuck?"

"I stayed put hoping my source would show. I figured I'd find Chuck later and talk to him because I thought he was in the dining room sobbing on Beth's shoulder."

"Was anyone else around?"

"Some crew members wandered by and the captain asked if I was doing a feature on the boat. What a joke. One young guy did seem to hang around, in fact I was beginning to wonder if he was my contact, but he never approached me, just watched."

"No sound of a struggle?"

"You think I'd miss investigating that?" He countered with his own question.

"But your informant, who you don't know, agreed to risk meeting you in front of his or her co-workers."

"I told you that he sounded scared."

"So it was a man's voice. You weren't sure before."

"It was a disguised voice. It could have been either.

"I'll let that observation slide for now, but we'll get back to it after you go over the crew roster for names you recognize. Right now, I want to talk about your theory that the caller used a scam to lure you on board so he could kill you. That's what you told Beth isn't it? That you were the intended victim."

Richard was still formulating an answer when Ceretzke changed the topic.

"Why were you going to Chuck's just now?"

"Look, Ceretzke, I don't understand what's going on here, but I'll level with you. I didn't kill Chuck and I was asked to be on that boat, for what reason I don't know. Bring on the thumbscrews if you must, but I don't know anything more. Look, I've played nice and answered your questions so maybe you can reciprocate. I'm planning a 'touching-farewell-to-a-comrade' segment but I can't find a damn thing about Chuck's background. Have you found anything?"

Ceretzke sat back with a 'no more, thanks' to the waitress' offer of a coffee refill. His amusement was so damned obvious Richard was tempted to walk, but Ceretzke had access to information that his own sources couldn't risk checking.

"He had a driver's license that was issued in Saskatchewan. He renewed it when he arrived in Alberta about five years ago."

"So he's from our neighbouring province to the east. Have you found his family? What city are they in?"

"We have nothing more, yet. Now it's your turn. What were you hoping to find?"

"Probably nothing. With this Saskatchewan lead I probably won't even bother looking again." Richard looked straight at Ceretzke and smiled, knowing he couldn't search until Ceretzke stopped watching him.

When they rose to leave, Richard dropped a couple of bills on the table. Ceretzke did the same.

"Forget it, Ceretzke. I'll put it on my expense claim."

The detective continued toward the door without picking up the money. Richard shrugged and pocketed the extra bills and the receipt. No point wasting a good expense claim.

They rode through the quiet streets in silence until they were again parked in front of Chuck's apartment building.

"How serious was your argument? People from the boat said he threatened to get you fired by telling tales."

"Hey, you know Chuck. He wouldn't turn on a friend." Richard flashed his most sincere smile. "Even if I had anything to hide."

Ceretzke unfastened his seat belt and opened the driver side door.

"Let's go through Chuck's apartment together. That way I won't have to wonder if you're hiding evidence."

"Hey, I don't like what you're implying." Richard scrambled from the truck and hurried after Ceretzke. Damn, he'd wanted to look on his own.

"Come on Tanner, this is your big chance to help the police."

They walked toward the apartment building where the manager, Mr. Simpson, let them into Chuck's suite. Then he stood in the doorway, as if uncertain whether to leave the men alone. He shuffled from foot to foot and jingled his key chain as he watched their movements.

Ceretzke looked back at him and asked, "What kind of tenant was he?"

"Quiet. He never had parties or complained about his neighbours. Sometimes he helped new people move in. He even helped me shovel snow in the winter."

"What about hobbies? We know he volunteered with Little League and Scouts. Were there any other activities he was involved with or friends who dropped by?"

The manager leaned against the doorframe.

"No, he didn't have much company. Some of his scouts hung around but I never noticed anyone else. Course his hobby was photography, he was always taking pictures."

"We didn't find any pictures when we searched his apartment."

Richard listened carefully as he perused the bookcase.

"He might keep them in his basement studio. He's got a bunch of boxes and other stuff down there."

Richard looked up quickly. Damn, a studio. He should have guessed. He looked around the bare apartment and felt absolutely convinced they would find Chuck's photo collection in his studio. The last key on the key chain probably opened the studio door.

"Why didn't you tell us about the studio when we searched the apartment," Ceretzke demanded.

"Didn't seem important, it's just photography stuff, nothing personal. Besides no one asked."

"I'm asking now."

"If it's so important I'll take you when you're done here."

He turned to leave, but Ceretzke stopped him.

"Let's look at the studio first then come back here. That way we won't take up more of your time."

They followed the stocky man, in his neatly patched jeans and droopy tee shirt, along the carpeted hall to the elevator.

"Did he mention his family to you," Richard asked.

"Told me once they was long dead and good riddance. That was all."

"Do you know where he was raised? Was it Saskatchewan?"

"Told me he'd lived on the East Coast. What am I supposed to do with his stuff? I'll be wanting to rent the place out again."

"Hold off until the end of the month."

"I want his photos, if the police department doesn't mind," Richard said. Chuck had done good work. Arranging a memorial showing might help his image with that snot-nosed kid.

After a shaky trip and a jolting stop, the elevator doors opened revealing a grey concrete wall. Turning to the left, the manager pointed out the boiler room, laundry area, and the door to the underground parking garage. The smell of oil and stale exhaust greeted them when he opened the garage door. More doors lined the outside walls of the garage.

"We rent these out. Some are just for storage. Others are workshops. Chuck rented the biggest one."

He clutched his key ring and flipped through half a dozen until he found one that he inserted into the lock and opened the door.

Richard stepped inside. The room was about sixteen feet square. The walls and ceiling were white and a piece of white carpeting covered the centre of the grey concrete floor. One corner of the room was set up with a folding table. A mirror, surrounded by light bulbs hung on the wall above it. Tripods holding lights and cameras faced a bed covered with a green and purple plaid blanket.

Cables ran across the floor to a heavy-duty power pack and from the power pack to the wall socket. A worn recliner hugged one corner of the room. Sheets of coloured gels, reflector boards, and background paper were crowded between stacks of cardboard tote boxes.

"Where does that door lead?" Ceretzke pointed toward the left wall.

"A dark room. It has a water hook-up. That's one reason he took this area. Originally it was supposed to be a hobby room for the entire complex but no one used it much so when he asked to rent it, I agreed."

Richard strode across the thick pile carpet and opened the door. The room ran the length of the studio, but was only about five feet wide. It was divided into three work areas, one for processing stills, one for printing them, and a final area equipped with a computer and video equipment. Richard turned back to the studio and noticed an empty tripod that was strong enough to hold the station's full size camcorder.

"He didn't stint on his equipment." Richard directed his comment to the air somewhere between himself and the two men rooted in the doorway.

"Was he running a business out of here," Richard asked the building superintendent.

"I think it was mostly just his friends and kids from his teams. I don't pry into my tenants' affairs."

"You saw people coming here though," Ceretzke asked as he headed toward the tote boxes.

"Not really."

At Ceretzke's sharp look, he added, "If they come through the parking garage, I don't see them."

The detective lifted the lid of the first box. A faint sound, almost a groan, pushed through his lips. Richard turned away from the manager and walked back to the interior of the room where Ceretzke stared intently into the box.

Over the detective's shoulder, Richard spotted the cover of a magazine. Maybe Chuck wasn't a monk after all. Damn, if he didn't smell a story.

He grabbed another box and lifted the lid. It was half full of photos, the kind with a big market. Chuck had a sideline all right. No wonder he could afford this set-up.

"What are you finding in there?"

The manager moved into the room but Richard intercepted him and turned him toward the door. This was too good to share.

"We'll finish here, then check the apartment later. We might take some of these boxes to search for clues to the next of kin. Don't worry, we'll make sure to lock the door when we leave."

He didn't look happy, but Mr. Simpson shuffled out of the room looking back twice before he was out of sight. Richard pulled the door shut and turned back to Ceretzke.

"What the hell!"

"They're kiddie porn magazines." The detective's usual melodic baritone had changed to a monotone.

"It can't be his. He was the good-guy pin-up of the decade."

Richard read the horrified expression on Ceretzke's face. How could he use this information? It obviously wouldn't fit into the all-round-great-guy scenario he had planned. Could it be the opening volley in his original pervert-on-the-loose story?

Richard flipped open a third box and found crudely labelled videocassettes. Another held neatly piled magazines.

"You think you know a guy until something like this happens," Ceretzke said.

"That must be why he dropped Little League. They must have discovered his hobby." He turned toward Ceretzke for confirmation. A photo Ceretzke held seemed to have him mesmerized and he didn't react to Richard's outburst.

Ceretzke held the photo by its edges, shuddered, and then placed it back in the box face down. Then he straightened. "Time to leave Tanner. This is now police business."

"Hey, I thought this was a partner thing—we search and share whatever we find."

The grim look on Ceretzke's face told him the rules had changed.

"I'm going to call for a crime scene unit and I want you out of here, now."

Ceretzke pulled his phone from his pocket and started punching keys while blocking Richard from looking further into the room's contents.

The cryptic request for a CSU gave the reporter no further information.

"What did you find," he asked again when the detective finally punched the disconnect button. "I won't release any details until you give the okay, but I worked with the guy. Tell me what got to you. What's it evidence of?"

He watched a flicker of indecision move across Ceretzke's face and decided another plea would do the trick.

"You found something that ties into his death, didn't you? Maybe a picture of his boyfriend. Was he gay too? Was he killed because of a lover's quarrel?"

The lines on Ceretzke's face hardened and his hands clenched into fists. He stepped toward Richard. "Get out. Now."

Richard didn't stop to think but opened the door. Ceretzke pushed him out and then shut the door in his face. He stood for a moment taking stock of the situation, then hurried to his car. He got in and moved it closer to the driveway leading into the underground garage. Then he called the station asking that Christy be sent out.

Richard sat in the car, motionless, staring into the distance, his mind wildly active. After a few moments, he snapped his fingers and pulled his briefcase onto his knees.

What he needed was halfway through the League file, buried among the glowing tributes to coach Chuck Albright. It was printed on plain white paper and requested a meeting of the executive committee be convened to deal with the problem of a child who no longer wanted to be on Mr. Albright's team. It seemed he was scared of the coach. The letter was vaguely worded, but Richard deciphered it to mean that during an out-of-town tournament Chuck Albright had approached the boy in a way that had sexual overtones.

Richard let the paper slip from his hand. Was the kid lying? No, the boxes in the studio told their own story.

Police cars started arriving. Whatever Ceretzke had found must be important because he had enough cops here to take the place apart. Richard watched the officers piling out of vehicles.

Christy knocked on the side window. "Big happenings? What's going on?"

Richard ignored her and watched the faces of the police officers. Excitement hid behind their masks. They were not headed for bad news. They covered the sidewalk in powerful ground-eating strides. Their words were few, but their tone spoke loudly of hope, of resolution, of the irony of life. Those determined faces belonged not only to the police service, but were those most closely involved in the Jamieson case, including Norman Carswell, the team leader himself.

Ceretzke must have found something that related to that little boy. Richard slid the letter back into the file folder. He had been so close. If he'd opened that particular box instead of the cop, he would have had award-winning material.

"Christy, I've got a big story by the tail. Wait here, I'm going to check out Chuck's apartment."

"The building's crawling with cops." Christy slid into the passenger seat of the low slung car. "They won't let you in."

"They're in the basement. This could be my last chance to look around."

He returned the folders to his briefcase and lifted it out of the car.

"What am I supposed to do?" The pout in her voice was audible.

"Get some background shots of the building and of the cops arriving," he said, as he walked to the rear of the vehicle and tossed the case into the trunk. "With good luck I'll be quick, with bad I'll be quicker. Notify the station to be ready to air a breaking news story and if the competition shows up, buzz me. I won't be scooped on this one."

Trying to look inconspicuous, Richard hurried toward a side door, skirting the front entrance where a cop stood guard. The key to Chuck's suite fit smoothly into the outside lock and he opted for climbing the stairs. His regular trips to the gym helped, but still his breathing was laboured by the time he reached the fifth floor.

He peered through the crack between the stairwell door and its casing. The hallway was empty. He slipped through the door and walked to Chuck's apartment.

No sounds came through the door so Richard inserted and turned the key. Inside, he headed for the bedroom and the drawer containing the baseball caps. A kid's grubby Blue Jay's cap had caught his attention earlier, but he hadn't understood why. Now he remembered that it looked like the one in the picture of the Jamieson kid. The one he had lost the day before he was abducted. His mother was nearly as upset about yelling at him for losing the hat as she had been about her son's abduction and death.

"Give me the key, Tanner, and the hat."

Richard looked up, meeting Ceretzke's cold stare in the dresser mirror.

"This is all about Tommy Jamieson, isn't it?"

The detective shrugged. "We'll let the lab decide, but yeah, that's the way the evidence is pointing."

"The picture you were staring at was of the kid?"

"Yeah," he said again.

He extended his hand and Richard gave him the keys and the grubby little cap. Then, in a voice that sounded about a hundred years older than it had earlier in the day, Ceretzke added, "Down play it, in case we're wrong."

CHAPTER 12

Norman stood in the doorway of the white room and watched the crime scene crew dust fingerprint powder over the pristine surfaces. He was certain they would find Tommy's prints. Maybe some prints from the other kids too. Why had Chuck Albright killed them? To keep them from telling about the pictures? For kicks? People like that made him sick.

Albright had gotten off easy, because according to the M.E., he was dead before hitting the water. Norman shrugged away his regret. At least he wouldn't be spending a few years in some comfy mental home only to be released on a technicality.

"We would have caught him eventually, though I don't know why we never checked the media more thoroughly," Ceretzke said.

Norman turned to face Ceretzke. Little did he know that some of them had suspected the media, but that war story was private and Norman wasn't about to repeat it. "Yeah. We should have thought of the media."

Norman stared at the plaid spread covering the bed. It was wrinkled where someone had sat on it. Albright or the Jamieson kid?

"We'll have to find a link between him and the other kids, something other than the photos," Ceretzke said.

"Guys like him make me sick." Norman turned away, then feeling ill, fled to the stairwell and the back entrance of the apartment building. He needed air. He needed to forget. The solution had been so obvious. He could have ended the case and retired on full pension three years ago if his inspiration had arrived sooner.

Winters in Arizona, summers golfing. Oh yes, he would take golf lessons now that he could finally retire.

Energy surged into his mind like a bright shaft of light in a dark cave. He was free and he wouldn't be spending the rest of his life sitting in some courtroom trying to make the creep pay for the lives he had taken.

******

Beth stepped onto the plank floor of the deck and stood behind her mother's chair. She rested her hands on its high wooden back hoping to catch a few minutes of her mom's favourite talk show. Today's visitor was discussing exotic summer travel destinations.

He was cut off mid-sentence by a shot of Richard Tanner standing in front of an apartment building. A banner running along the bottom of the screen announced a breaking news story.

"Police are investigating new information regarding the Jamieson murder. Behind me is the building where recently murdered Chuck Albright lived. While searching for evidence this reporter and a police officer, uncovered information that leads us to believe that Chuck Albright abducted and murdered all four children. I will continue investigating and promise to break in with further details as I uncover them."

The talk show resumed. Beth squeezed her mother's shoulder. "Don't believe him. What would Chuck have to do with that kind of crime?" Beth knew Richard would go to great lengths to report a story, but slandering Chuck was beyond even him.

Her mother reached up, took her hand, and held it tight. Beth tried to decipher what she'd just seen. Richard had been unusually careful with what he said. He had made no statements that brought condemnation without proof. His expression was one she had never seen him wear before. It seemed more serious than the expression he reserved for natural disasters and terrorist attacks. A shiver of dread raced through her as she recognized it as a look of concern.

******

Mike found Super Sam's demand for an explanation on his desk when he returned to the station. He met Evan on the way into her office and hauled him along.

"I heard the news. There's no mistake," Evan asked.

Sam echoed the question when the detectives entered her office. Again, Mike shook his head.

"I had hoped it was a coincidence but he had pictures of the other kids too." Mike plopped into the visitor chair, extended his legs, crossed his ankles, and forced his hands to release their grip on the arms of the chair.

"We found a file containing negatives with information about which magazines had bought them. He was a regular contributor. It's possible he recruited kids from his Scout troop and Little League teams to act as models."

"Congratulations on solving the case. It's a feather in your cap." Sam leaned toward him, looking closely at his expression. "You don't look happy. Does something about this—other than the obvious—bother you?"

"I'm happy. The families will be happy. We're all happy the case is solved. I'd just like to understand it. How could I have been so wrong about him?" Mike's voice died away.

He ran his fingers through his hair. A grimace full of irony spread across his face as he added, "I sound like the friend of every killer we've ever caught. I guess nice guys do make the best murderers."

"You'll have to talk to the families," Sam said, her voice breaking the echoing silence.

Mike caught a distant murmur of voices coming through the office door. The families. He recalled Mrs. Jamieson's shattered look. How would she react to the announcement? Pleased of course, that they would finally have closure, but to learn it was someone the police already knew. Someone they considered a wonderful person and a friend. Well, no one had suspected Chuck. No one ever could. He wouldn't have believed it himself, if he hadn't found that damning evidence.

"Of course. I'll try to notify them before they hear the news reports, but Tanner's already started that wheel turning."

"Mike, get on track here."

Super Sam's sharp command drew his attention.

"You're investigating a murder and you've just come up with one hell of a motive. Notify the families, sure, but find out where they were Saturday night and search for anything that connects them to Chuck Albright."

Her voice rang with the satisfaction of knowing a difficult job was successfully completed. Mike stared out her window at feather clouds in the pale blue sky. Of course, Sam hadn't known Chuck. To her he was just a name, not a real person. A jet stream wrote across the sky, connecting the clouds. How had he missed seeing some sign that Chuck was an abuser?

"Can you tell the families why he did it," Sam asked.

"We didn't find an explanation. Without the pictures and the hat, I don't know if we could make a case against him. We can prove he rented the room and had regular access because he had a key to the studio. It was on the key chain I took from Tanner."

"Just make sure he's guilty. The last thing I want is some creep laughing until next spring when he kills another kid. I want this to stick like epoxy. And, I expect you to find the evidence to make it do just that. But while you're investigating his crimes don't forget to find his killer. Pull all the paper on similar crimes, follow his movements, and track his history. I want this put in a file marked solved."

******

Jennifer Rivers wanted out of the hospital. She hated the continuous noise and the smell of sickness, but mostly she hated the lack of privacy. She felt uncomfortable with that doctor with his so precise, so cultured British accent. He asked too many questions. Why did he want to know if she had someone to look after her?

He even had the nerve to ask if she was frightened of something, just because she'd had that dream again and woke up crying and screaming.

The dream always came when she was scared and it made her

crazy. The psychiatrist said reviewing it would desensitize her to its power. She knew the technique didn't work for her, but started the routine anyway. She visualized walking down a dark, narrow tunnel crowded with the hot, cloying smell of a recently vacated den. Then felt rough fur scrape her skin, peeling away her flesh until she was naked right down to her skeleton. That was when she woke up, screaming. Jennifer let the remembered fear and pain wash over her. She breathed deeply and opened her eyes.

She knew what the dream meant. That psychiatrist had helped her figure it out. It should have gone away once she deciphered the imagery thus striking down its power, but when conditions were right, when the memories reawakened, she dreamed and woke screaming.

Last night her screams had scared the old woman with a bandage covering half her head who shared her room.

This morning, the nurses started asking if they could contact someone who would look after her for a few days. She wasn't sure. Could they call Lyle? He had always seemed ready to lend a helping hand. He was big and friendly like Eric had been. Maybe she could trust him, but why should she burden him with her problems? She had looked after herself since Eric died and that's how it should stay even if she had to spend another twenty-four hours in hospital.

"Maybe I'll just leave," she muttered, ignoring the dull thud of her pulse as her blood pounded through the veins in her ankle. When she lay quietly, the pain was nearly bearable. Sure getting home would be uncomfortable, but she knew how to handle physical pain.

"What did you say, dear?"

The sugar-coated voice came from the old woman in the bed next to her.

Jennifer shot a look in her direction hoping the old woman would realize that she was intruding and shut up. It didn't work.

"I don't think leaving without the doctor's approval would be wise. You might make matters worse. If they are letting you stay with all the bed shortages and cutbacks these days, there must be a very good reason."

Jennifer ignored her and struggled into a sitting position. With only one arm working properly it wasn't easy, but she managed. She swung her good leg to the floor. A hop off the bed sent her careening until she grasped the curtain surrounding her bed. Breathing hard, she swayed as she tried to regain her balance. The pain in her head thumped viciously and she almost returned to the safety of the bed. With her right hand she clutched the curtain, then tested her sprained foot on the cool tile floor.

"Perhaps you will need this, miss?" The doctor stood in the doorway holding a crutch. "You must practice walking before you leave. Getting around with a crutch will be difficult, but any real progress is definitely impossible without it."

The elderly woman chuckled, making Jennifer want to lash out at both smug faces, but she knew if she released the curtain, she would fall on her nose. She continued her precarious balancing act until the doctor approached and extended the crutch.

He took her hand in his, releasing her tight grip on the curtain. She felt herself flinch as his brown, finely boned fingers touched hers. The doctor hesitated, then took a firmer grip as he transferred her hand to the crutch.

"I have adjusted the length so you shouldn't find it too uncomfortable."

She heard the hurt deep in his voice. Hell, he probably thought she didn't like his colour. Well, being emotionally weak and allowing others to hurt him was his problem and he had better learn to deal with it.

Fifteen minutes and three near disasters later, she collapsed onto the bed, panting, sweating, and hurting. She had navigated the hall to the nurse's station, miles away, then collapsed into a wheelchair for the short ride back to her room.

"You did very well and you must try again later, but tomorrow will be soon enough for you to try looking after yourself."

Jennifer managed to summon only a tiny, pathetic glare to focus on his chiseled face.

CHAPTER 13

Mike boarded the River Belle an hour before it sailed on the evening's casino trip. When Tommy Wong signed in, Mike led him to a quiet section of the deck. It was his job to find Chuck's murderer and he planned on following every available lead until the mystery unraveled. Currently, he had two last minute passengers in his sights.

"A group of four and a woman on her own, for a total of five," Tommy said, answering his question about the occupants of the table.

"The bookkeeper said she assigned another man to your table."

The youth coughed on Mike, then drew a tissue from his jacket pocket, and blew his nose.

"Sorry, I can't shake this bug but I can't afford to miss work either. That guy never showed up."

"What about the woman?"

"She only ate the salad. Must have been dieting."

Mike pulled a handkerchief from his pocket and tried to look casual about wiping his cheek to eradicate the germs before they burrowed into his system. If Tommy's cold had been as bad then, she might have thought starvation the preferred alternative.

"Did she leave the dining room during the performance?"

"After the first act though I don't think she saw much of that either. All she did was stare around the room. She did ask me once about Jennifer."

"Jennifer?"

"Rivers. I thought she was working that night, but I never did find her to pass on the message."

"The woman was preoccupied with finding this Jennifer Rivers? Do you think that's why she was on board?"

He sneezed, barely getting the tissue to his nose in time to smother the explosion.

"Hey, man, I don't know. She just asked. Said she wanted to talk to Jennifer. I didn't act like a cop and ask why."

******

The motel was depressing in a grubby, shabby way. Linda Olsson stretched out under the patched spread and picked up the remote control. Maybe the six o'clock news would have more coverage of the murder.

Linda had planned to spend Sunday watching for Jenny to return to the riverboat, but she arrived at the dock to find the area cordoned off and people being turned away. She watched for hours, but Jenny never appeared so she walked the trails near the river hoping for inspiration to guide her next move. When the boat reopened Monday morning and Jenny still hadn't shown up, the words of the staff member returned to haunt her.

Could Jenny have recognized her, as changed as she was, and gone into hiding? Tears tracked down her cheeks, tickled her ears, and plopped onto the pillow. Hadn't she paid a high enough price to get her daughter back?

The news broadcast switched to a reporter giving an update on the riverboat murder. He said the victim was tied into the murders of a bunch of kids. She studied the pictures of Chuck Albright and his four victims. Linda wiped at the tears that wouldn't stop. He still looked like a wonderful person. If she'd known he lived here sooner, would any of those kids still be alive?

The reporter was asking for anyone with knowledge of Chuck's death or activities to come forward. She picked up the phone and dialled, prepared to lie to her boss about being home sick. She couldn't help the other parents, but she had to find Jenny.

✶✶✶✶✶✶

"Beth."

"Richard," Beth said, ignoring a familiar tug at her heart.

"I've hit a wall and have only you to turn to for help. Who but you would . . . ."

"Cut the line, Richard. Just tell me what you want now." Beth marked her place in the book with an information request card. Richard had a lot of nerve if he thought he could still con her into doing things for him.

It was late and Beth's shift at the reference desk was finishing. The library was quiet for the first time in months because university and college classes were finally over for the year. There seemed to be no escaping Richard, until a patron looked in her direction. Beth smiled at her potential saviour but he turned toward the business reference section.

"Can we talk after this place closes," Richard asked. "I truly do need your help."

"Why? So you can stab another friend in the back?"

One side of Richard's mouth turned downward, giving his open, guileless smile a touch of remorse.

"It's a hard story to report, but Chuck was a newsman, he understood the necessity of beating out the competition."

"Why are you tying him into the murders of those kids? That's not Chuck. Don't you feel how wrong it is?"

"The evidence was there. I saw some of it myself. You better talk to Mikey if you don't believe me."

Beth knew he was baiting her and ignored his ploy. "I'm not talking about evidence. Don't you have faith in the innocence of a good man? If he were alive, Chuck could defend himself. We have to defend him in his absence, not pronounce him guilty to the world."

The other side of Richard's mouth dropped and his lips formed a straight line. A crease ran down the centre of his forehead to his nose. Beth clenched the pencil in her hand.

Richard reached out and caressed her hand. In a soft voice he said, "He did it, Beth. We found boxes of kiddy porn at his place."

"There's probably an excellent explanation for what you found and even if there isn't owning that stuff doesn't make him a murderer."

"Chuck had Tommy's hat. The one that went missing the day before the kid did. Mike found a picture of Tommy in those boxes."

"A hat like Tommy's. It's circumstantial evidence. You can't convict him on flimsy circumstantial evidence."

She pulled her hand out of his grip and turned her back to him as she closed several books and returned them to their place on the reference desk.

She had to convince Richard of Chuck's innocence and that would be difficult because he never admitted making mistakes. After she convinced Richard, she would present her case to Mike. Then the police could announce his innocence and stop this slur campaign. First though, she had to devise a plan that would prove Chuck innocent of all suspicion.

"I'll meet you outside in ten minutes," she said through clenched teeth.

When Beth stepped out of the air-conditioned library, the evening sunlight was beginning its gradual fade into twilight. The heat of a perfect spring day radiated from the sidewalk. Street sweepers had just finished washing the road in front of the library and the smell of wet dust greeted her. The city always delayed the task, hoping to miss the traditional May snowfall.

Richard was waiting for her and they walked across the quiet street to the park. Kids wearing ragged black outfits and multi-coloured hair occupied a few of the benches. Their faces changed, as did their look, but Beth recognized their gathering as the millennia old spring mating ritual.

"They make you feel ancient, don't they?" She nodded at the youngsters lounging around the square.

"Speak for yourself, I'm never getting old and if it ever happens, I won't admit to feeling it."

They sat on a bench facing city hall, a white stone building with trapezoid windows that stood as a monolith to the ego of a past city council.

Beth watched the traffic glide by. "How do I prove Chuck is innocent?"

"You're asking the wrong guy. I've already said he's guilty, can't go back on that without losing credibility. Besides, he is guilty."

Beth felt her heartbeat quicken and her breath grow shallow. She inhaled deeply, shut her eyes, and tried to make Richard's earnest face disappear. How could she convince him of his error?

"Think of all the good things Chuck has done. All the people he helped. All the kids . . . ." Beth caught his triumphant smile and held her hand up. "Okay forget the kids, but you know he was there for anyone who needed him. Can you really believe such a person would hurt a child?

"Remember how he lectured us on being responsible parents? He hated hearing stories about parents neglecting their kids. A couple of years ago he said that every parent needed to be taught the importance of their child's life, the importance of treating each child right during the time they had them. He said they were on loan to us. Can you believe he would abuse kids, kill kids?"

Richard turned toward the cluster of young people. When his expression faded to blank, Beth knew she had failed to convince him. "Richard, we have to find out what's going on. We can't just believe the worst about him."

"The investigation is over. Look, I'll make a deal with you. You want him to be innocent; I want to uncover his past. Let's join forces and seek the truth."

Beth held her breath. Richard's tone told her he was confident he had already won. What he didn't know was that she would play by his rules or any others to get to the truth. She would help him search, but while she was doing it, she would find the proof she needed to clear Chuck.

"How do we find the truth?"

Richard answered too quickly to be improvising. Beth remembered how he'd always had a plan when they worked together on a story. He had a uniquely warped talent for sniffing out long shots that paid off. "If I'm right, Chuck has a history of sex offences. He was what, forty-five? Therefore, statistics say that as an offender, he would have been caught with kids before now. The police will run a check through criminal records, but most of those cases don't get reported or if they do, some court seals them to protect the kid's identity, so it will be a fruitless search. Also, he's taken care to keep his past a secret. After all, if he didn't tell you all about his childhood, he didn't tell anyone."

Beth flicked a wrinkle from her linen skirt. She wasn't sure whether to be pleased with his analysis, but decided to let his comment pass.

"So we do what," she asked.

"Well, we're left with civil cases and internal hearings. We can try accessing those records. Maybe we can contact kid-friendly associations in other provinces and ask them to check their files for Chuck's name, or someone of his description."

Beth stopped his words by raising her hand. "The police will do all that and better than we can. I've got an idea though, but if we don't come up with positive proof that Chuck was an offender, will you agree to do a story retracting what you've said?"

"Sure, if we find nothing and the cops get nothing, we must be wrong, right? Now, what's your plan?"

"I'm going to put a message on the Internet. I'll send a description of him to various sites including those listing known sexual offenders. By describing him as a photographer who volunteered to work with kids, we might get a response."

"Go to the people? It's a long shot."

"Why? We know he lived in Edmonton for five years. If you're right and he offended during the twenty or more years before that, his victims would be thirty or younger. Some would be male. You're assuming two of his current victims are male, so the pattern would hold. Males between fifteen and thirty make up a large percentage of Internet users."

"If he didn't kill them all, who's going to admit he was sexually assaulted?"

"They can remain anonymous if they want. Do you have an old picture of Chuck?"

"His personnel file includes one, but why an old photo? Oh, I get it, he might look different now."

Richard stretched his arm around her silk clad shoulder and hugged her close. He smiled his enamoured-suitor-smile and said, "It's good to have you back, Beth."

She shrugged his arm away and stood.

"Richard, I know all your moves so don't waste your time. When can you get that picture? I'll scan it and send it to anyone who asks for it."

"Who will you send the initial letter to?"

"A few appropriate sites come to mind, like the Scouts and the Criminal Lawyer's Association and a couple of victim support groups, but I'll do some research to identify as many sites as possible. Walk me to my car and I'll start composing the message tonight."

"Still nervous about the parkade? Don't worry, I parked close to your sexy little car and I borrowed Chuck's personnel file hoping you would help me."

CHAPTER 14

"Detective Ceretzke."

Mike listened to the twanging voice coming through the receiver and tried to attach a name to it. Before he could, the man identified himself.

"Lyle Lamont here. From the River Belle."

"The steward from the boat. I remember. What can I do for you," Mike asked.

"Jennifer's disappeared."

"Yes, Mr. Lamont, we know she wasn't at work Saturday night."

"No, I mean she's really disappeared. No one's seen her since Saturday. I checked the club where she works out and her favourite bike trails too. No one from the Belle has seen her and none of her friends have either. Do you think she's been hurt? Maybe she walked in on the murder of that man and was killed?"

"Have you checked the hospitals?"

"No. I mean, if she was hurt and dumped in the river, wouldn't she be dead? If a man couldn't make it because the river was too swift, it'd be impossible for her to survive."

"We found only the one body, Mr. Lamont."

"What if she was washed down river? Detective, we have to look for her."

"Have you checked with her family?"

"I don't know where they are. She didn't say where she was from, but I know she hasn't been in Edmonton all that long. I'm about the only friend she has here."

"Do you know where Jennifer lives?"

"I was just there again and her landlady said she ain't been back since Saturday morning. It's Wednesday, now."

"Listen, I'll meet you at her apartment and speak to the landlady. What's the address?"

After he wrote down the south side address and hung up the phone, Mike ran his hand through his hair then down his neck and rubbed at his tense shoulder muscles.

He had told the kid's parents that the police were certain they had stumbled onto the murderer of their children. Their disgust was easier to cope with than their angry reaction to his question about their whereabouts on Saturday night. Jim Paterson had been the most vocal.

Mike pushed away from his desk and walked toward the door.

"Mike," Sam called out as he passed her office. "How did the families take the news?"

"Mr. Paterson blew up and started yelling that he was tired of being interrogated every time someone was killed. It seems he didn't appreciate being hounded and suspected of murdering his own daughter. Now he thinks we're persecuting him because, and I quote, we think he did our job for us by killing a monster."

"I expected as much. Does he have an alibi?"

"They all do. They were gathered at the Jamieson's to give comfort and support, and a joint press conference. From seven to eight, they recorded a program pleading with the public to call Crime Stoppers if they knew or suspected anything. Half a dozen reporters and a couple of cameramen are witnesses. With all the media floating around the house, someone would have missed them as soon as they walked out the door."

"Still it's a motive, the only good one we've got."

"I'm on my way to meet a kid from the boat who's worried about his girlfriend. She's the one Evan mentioned, the one who should have been working on the boat Saturday night. Apparently she missed more than work because no one's seen her since then."

"Is there a tie-in?"

"The kid thinks she got in the assailant's way, but maybe she was the target and Chuck was the one who was at the wrong place."

"What do you know about her?"

"Lyle Lamont, the kid who phoned, says she's new in town. He doesn't know much about her himself."

"Could she be Tanner's snitch? Maybe she got cold feet and took off without making contact?"

Mike shrugged. "If she was the contact, she could have been hurt too. This Lyle kid sounded pretty worried so maybe he knows she was in danger."

Mike drove through the downtown traffic then crossed the river to the south side of the city. The apartment building was a three-storey walk-up backing onto a ravine. A wide, grassed area extended downhill to the beginning of the city's trail system. Picnic tables were scattered around the lawn, but only one was occupied. A woman had spread a blanket on the ground and gently rocked her baby in its portable chair as she watched a toddler follow a scruffy poodle across the dandelion-speckled field.

The sun was at its blinding best and not a single puff of cloud marred the cornflower blue expanse of sky. The rancorous clamour of nesting robins sounded from a tree on Mike's left and the bushy tail of a squirrel disappeared into one of several spruce trees on his right.

Lyle stood at attention watching the mother and her children with an intense and unwavering stare. With his cropped blond hair, broad shoulders, and six-foot height, he looked like a poster boy for the Aryan Nation. Mike noted his frown and look of forlorn abandonment. The frown faded when he crossed into Lyle's line of vision.

"Detective, I'm glad you came. I'm really worried about her."

"If you're so worried why didn't you phone me earlier?"

Lyle's massive shoulders rose, pulling up the straps of his sleeveless tee shirt. Mike tightened his abdominal muscles. Did the boy work out or had that muscleman physique grown naturally? As Lyle stepped toward Mike, sunlight glittered from the blond hair coating his tanned tree-trunk legs. Mike shivered slightly. To cultivate a tan so early in the year, this kid must expose his body to the sun while snow still covered the ground.

"I didn't want to cause trouble."

"What trouble?"

"Well, you know, getting everybody in a tizzy over her being gone, just to have her come waltzing in, wondering at the commotion."

"She disappears regularly then?"

"Can't say as I know. Only just met her a couple of months ago when she started working on the Belle. Ain't missed work before now though and with this murder and all, I figured it best to phone you."

"Will someone let us into her suite?"

"Yes, sir. The caretaker said if a police officer asked, she'd let us in."

"Which apartment is hers?"

"One-fourteen. It's the ground floor one under the balcony with all them baskets of geraniums."

He pointed and Mike let his gaze drift upward to an array of red bedding plants, delicate spears of dracaena, and tiny sprigs of midnight lobelia. Another month and the curtain of fragrant colour would completely hide the railings.

Mike strode across the grass to the shaded ground level window. He tried looking inside, but the lined curtains were tightly closed. He backtracked to the building's front door and stepped into the small alcove where mailboxes and buzzers lined one wall. No one answered when he pressed the buzzer labelled one-fourteen.

"I told you she weren't here. The caretaker's in one-ten, she'll let us in."

Mike took his time searching each buzzer until he found the one that was labelled caretaker. The name McPherson was printed underneath. Before he buzzed her, the detective turned back to the mailboxes and peered inside Jennifer's to see if any mail waited pickup. It was empty.

"There's nothing in there. I already checked."

Lyle reached out to press the caretaker's buzzer. Mike grabbed his muscular arm and held it motionless.

"Slow down, son. I'll handle this my way."

Mike released his arm. So, the kid got rattled easily. Did he have a temper too?

"I'm just worried about her."

Taking pity on young love, or lust, Mike called the caretaker, who assured him she'd be right there to check his identification. However, when she surged into view and opened the inner glass door she waved his badge aside.

"Only a cop would wait for me to open the door, not like this youngster who was wandering the halls, all ready to break into that girl's apartment. If it hadn't been I'd seen him with her, I'd have called the police myself."

"Has Ms. Rivers lived here long," Mike asked.

"Since the beginning of February. She's a nice girl. I hope nothing has happened to her."

"She hasn't been back since Saturday," Mike asked.

"I didn't worry about not seeing her until Lyle here mentioned it. Being the weekend, if I'd missed her I'd have thought she was off on a bike trip or something. She's always on her bike. I was out of town myself, visiting my son and that no-good wife of his on the farm. My farm. They moved right in after my husband died and suggested I'd be more comfortable in town. That idiot husband of mine had signed over the whole place to the boy, some kind of a tax-planning thing, so I didn't have much to say about it. Damn lawyer fought it but . . . ."

"The apartment, could we see it," Mike interjected into the stream of verbiage.

"Sure, it's just down this way. I know you don't want to hear about my troubles. It's not like it's a crime to dispossess an old woman of her home. How was I supposed to know that they would kick me out? My husband figured I'd be a welcome part of the household . . . here we are. I checked already. She's not in there dead or anything. I'm just down the hall. That's why I could keep an eye open so he couldn't sneak back in. The owners really should change all these locks, they open just one, two, three."

"Thank you, ma'am. I'll let you know when we leave."

"You keep an eye on that boy, too. I don't want Jennifer saying anything is missing. Those grandkids of mine do that. Especially the boy. Come to visit and when they leave you're ten dollars short in . . . ." She sailed through the door of her suite and closed it, silencing her monologue.

Lyle raced into the apartment and down the hall, while Mike took a moment to absorb the feel of the room. It was tidy. Only the faintest covering of dust lay on the top of the laminate coffee table, easily three days' worth. The furniture was old, perhaps family discards or things she had discovered at garage sales. He walked to the window and opened the curtains. They fit well and matched the room's beige and blue colour scheme. Mike decided they must have come with the suite.

No TV or stereo, just a clock radio sitting on the kitchen counter. The cupboards held four place settings and the bare minimum of utensils lay in the silverware drawer. The bedroom was equally bare, just a single bed and a chest of drawers.

Lyle was crouched in front of the chest, looking up at the underside of the top drawer.

"What do you expect to find under there?"

"Letters and stuff. You know, taped to the bottom of the drawer."

Mike felt his face crack into a grin. He ran his hand through his hair and savoured a moment of humour at the young man's expense.

Then he asked, "Did you check inside the drawers?"

"What kind of hiding place would that be?"

"Why do you think she was hiding anything?"

"Well, she disappeared didn't she?"

"I thought you were afraid she'd been hurt."

"Maybe she were, but maybe she weren't."

"Let's assume she wasn't hiding anything and just look inside the drawers for an address book so we can contact her family."

He was about to reach inside the drawer when a loud bang and clatter led him back to the apartment door. The door handle rattled and he heard swearing through the wood panel. Mike pulled the door open. A young woman, wearing a look of panic on her stricken face, stood in the hall. Hers was a long face, framed with brown hair.

Her waif eyes opened wide as she looked at him then swung her head from side to side, as if searching for an escape route. She was literally frozen where she stood, because moving with the aid of a crutch seemed to be a new experience for her.

"Jen." Lyle's outburst came from behind Mike's shoulder and ended in a garbled stutter as he stepped toward her. "What happened? You look like a truck ran you over."

"Lyle, why are you in my apartment and who is this man?" As she spoke, her gaze darted from Lyle to Mike and back again.

Mrs. McPherson called from her doorway. "Jennifer, these two said you were missing, so I let them into your apartment. I hope you aren't too upset."

"I'm Detective Ceretzke, Ms. Rivers. I'm sorry if we startled you, but Lyle thought you might have been hurt Saturday evening. It looks as though he was right."

"Can you help me in? I have to get some money to pay the cab." She tilted her head in the direction of a burley, bearded man standing in the hall. "I've lost my purse and keys. Do you have a spare apartment key, Mrs. McPherson?"

"I'll pay," Lyle said. After taking a moment to realize he wasn't getting around Jennifer's crutch, he reached over her shoulder and handed some bills to the man.

"Let's get you inside and comfy, then you can tell us what happened. I've been worried. When they found the blood and the man dead and you were gone . . . ."

"Lyle, get out of my way. It's taken me hours to learn how to manoeuvre with this crutch, but I still can't manage corners very well."

Lyle jumped backward, nearly falling over his feet as he plastered his husky frame against the wall. Mike found himself admiring the way she handled herself with only one workable foot and a cast on her wrist. With a smile at the caretaker, Lyle closed the door and dogged Jennifer's painfully slow progress to the sofa. Then he reached out to help her turn and seat herself.

"A stool, do you have a stool for your foot? No, then here, I'll put it up on the sofa for you."

She swore at his attempted kindness, then through gritted teeth said, "Make me some tea, please."

The sound of cupboards being opened and closed and then

the rush of water filled the silence that followed his departure. Mike pondered the stick thin woman before him, then he went to the table and brought back two wooden chairs, the only other seating in the apartment.

"Can you tell me how that happened?" He motioned in the direction of her cast.

"Fell off my bike. Broke my wrist; sprained my ankle. The doctor wouldn't let me out of the hospital until I could get around some."

"Did you have a head injury, too?" He pointed at the tape plastered to her forehead.

"That's just a cut, but the doctor said I was unconscious for too long to leave the hospital right away."

"This accident happened when?"

She looked at the cast on her arm and started drawing circles on its surface with the index finger of her uninjured hand.

"Saturday night."

"According to the employee schedule, you should have been working on Saturday night. Why weren't you?"

"I felt sick."

"Did you tell anyone you were leaving?"

"No."

"When did you get off the boat, Ms. Rivers?"

"It was about ready to leave for the dinner cruise. There wasn't anyone around to tell, so I just left."

"That wasn't very thoughtful of you. People were worried when you disappeared."

"I thought I could phone them later and explain. I'm sorry if I caused a problem."

"You left the boat and then what did you do?"

"I got my bike and headed for home, but I got dizzy and fell."

"Where do you keep your bike when you're working on the boat?"

She stared at him, then after a long pause she said, "Usually I keep it in a shed by the parking lot."

"Was it there Saturday evening?"

Another pause, then she said, "No. Saturday I chained it up near the park shelter building."

"Why did you do that?"

She shrugged her thin shoulders and kept her head bowed as she answered, "It was a nice day. Why? Was there some problem about where I left it?"

"You're lucky it didn't get really cold Saturday night."

Mike watched her gaze dart toward the kitchen and back again.

"I—it was cold, but I was unconscious. I don't remember anything else until the hospital."

"Which hospital did they take you to?"

"The University, it was the closest."

"And the doctor you saw, what was his name?"

She paused before answering. "Raj something. But he'll tell you the same as I just did, so you don't have to bother him. After all, I'm not really missing." She raised her head and flashed a smile at Mike. "Lyle didn't have to call the police."

Lyle returned to the room with the teapot in one large hand and three mugs suspended from the fingers of the other.

"But Jen, someone murdered a man. When you were missing, I was worried you'd been killed too."

"That's something we should discuss, Ms. Rivers. Did you notice anything unusual on the boat that evening," Mike asked.

"I wasn't on the boat. I told you I was sick and left before we sailed."

"Were you on board when the two men from Channel Six arrived?"

"I don't remember seeing them." She rubbed at a rough ridge on her cast.

"Did you know a woman named Linda Olsson was looking for you?"

Frightened doe eyes looked at the detective. "She was on the Belle?"

"You know her then?"

"She's my mother. I don't want to see her. It's my right not to see her."

"But Jen, you can't shun your own mother."

Mike flipped his notebook closed. "I'll leave you now, but I'd like to get a formal statement from you in a couple of days."

"I told you all I can," she whispered as he left the room.

Mike detoured to the hospital before he returned to the station. The doctor introduced himself as Dr. Rajaratanam, but he told the officer to call him Raj because he was weary of hearing people mangle the pronunciation of his name.

Mike refrained from mentioning how badly the doctor had mispronounced his own Ceretzke, but said, "You've treated a young woman, Jennifer Rivers, over the past few days. What can you tell me about her case?"

The doctor took Mike by the arm and moved them closer to the wall opposite the nursing station.

"She has a sprained ankle and a broken wrist, plus a sufficiently severe concussion that I insisted she remain for observation. Then, I found out she had no one to look after her, so she stayed longer. It should have been longer yet, but I am no miracle worker."

"Bed shortages," Mike said, nodding his understanding of the problem.

"No, that I could have managed. The young lady refused to stay. If she could have walked to the elevator without assistance, she would have left yesterday."

"Some people don't like hospitals." Mike sympathized with Jennifer, because he was also a person who loathed the smell that clung to everything in the place.

"I fear it was more, Detective."

"Meaning?"

The doctor shrugged his ignorance, but Mike waited until he replied, "She is bruised on nearly every part of her body. It is not possible she was so injured from falling off her bike. More likely the bruises and scrapes resulted from being beaten."

"Did you report this to the police?"

"She insisted her injuries came from the fall."

"But, you don't believe her."

"No, Detective I don't believe her, partially because she is a very scared lady and partially because she is a very bad liar."

******

"Gloria here, sorry I missed your call. Leave a message after the beep or check with my office."

Mike left a message while looking across his cluttered desk at Evan. He hadn't been himself since attending the Jamieson autopsy, in fact since the abduction.

"I'll try her at work," Mike said, choosing to let Evan deal with the demands of the job in his own way.

Gloria Azzara's secretary said she was in a meeting, but promised him a return call the minute she was available.

"Any luck with your list," Mike asked.

Evan looked up from the page he'd been studying for at least five minutes. "Ten robberies out of the hundred people I've contacted, but I've left lots of messages. A few have fraudulent credit charges, though most haven't received this month's bills yet so I'm suggesting they check with their credit card companies."

The phone on Mike's desk rang. Ms. Gloria Azzara was returning his call.

"Detective, what can I help you with?"

"It's about the robbery."

"You found my laptop?" She sounded surprised.

"Not yet. Do you remember what you did with your keys Saturday evening?"

"I should have had them in my purse."

"Did you?"

"I don't remember."

"Is that where you usually keep them?"

"Of course, well, sometimes I slip them in my jacket pocket. We did leave our coats with the hostess when she checked our dinner reservation. Do you think they copied my keys? How would they know where I lived? Damn. I gave them that information so they could mail out my tickets. How many others have they hit?"

"We're not certain. At this point in our investigation we don't even know if the robberies are connected, but it is beginning to look that way."

"That's one person I'll never defend at trial."

"Pardon?"

"I'm a criminal lawyer, but I don't defend people who rob me."

"Of course not. I'll let you know who not to represent when we catch them."

"Great," she said, disconnecting the call.

Evan's serious look made Mike feel his banter had been frivolous and he explained the joke.

"You better hope she doesn't change her mind, she's got some real scum off."

"You know her?"

"By reputation. She moved from Calgary last fall and she's made the cops in fraud and robbery pay close attention to details ever since she arrived."

"No wonder she was so angry about getting ripped off. She probably figured it was the work one of her clients."

******

Cara looked up from the column of figures she was inputting into the computer system. The sun, now low in the sky blinded her until Lap stepped into its path, cutting the glare.

"Have you shut down the operation," she asked.

He pushed a pile of paper back from the edge of her desk and leaned toward her. "I think you're over reacting."

"We don't know what if anything, Jennifer told that reporter and I don't want to disgrace the family. Just tell me your people won't be robbing any of the customers."

"I couldn't stop one because the guys moved too fast, but I collected all the other keys. Cousin Tom will hide them in his shop until things cool down."

Her disapproving glare made him add, "Destroying them is overkill. Even if the cops learn about Cousin Tom, they'd expect to find keys at a locksmith shop. Besides, he hid them and the key codes in his high security safe. We're in the clear."

"And the reservation forms?"

He pulled a knife from the pocket of his jacket and started drilling a hole in the top of her desk. "The card numbers are on their way to our foreign partners. I was too late to stop them, but I have called and told them to shred the batch from Saturday night. As you requested."

"We had to take the precautions." She watched him carve the hole deeper and wider. Why did he have to destroy things?

"We're losing a lot of money because you think she talked. If she didn't, we're out of pocket for no reason."

Cara extended her hand cautiously, hoping she could stop his nervous gouging. He flicked the knife out of the hole and pointed it at her.

Relieved that the damage was minor, she said, "Lyle found Jennifer. She's hurt, but alive."

"Damn." He flipped the knife in his hand and without taking aim, plunged it into the corkboard behind her head, pinning a notice securely to the surface. "She'll talk."

"Maybe not. She told Lyle she left the boat before we sailed and was hurt biking home."

Tiny wrinkles appeared at the corners of Lap's eyes. "An interesting story." After a pause he added, "But she could change it."

"I told Lyle to get her out of town."

"Can you trust him?"

Cara pushed her chair back, pulled the knife from the board and handed it to Lap.

"When I caught him stealing from the cash drawer, I thought he was ours forever but since he's become enamoured with Jennifer he seems to have rediscovered his conscience. Keeps talking about how his father would be ashamed of what he's doing."

"Families."

Cara clasped her fingers to stop them from fiddling and said, "Family is the only important thing in life. Where would we be if not for family?"

"I don't know about you, but if Father hadn't died I wouldn't be stuck trying to scrap together enough money to keep food on the table. If the old lady wasn't so proud, she would go on welfare."

"We agreed it was important to maintain our dignity and not become dependent on charity."

"You think our mother wouldn't disown us if she knew what we were doing?"

"That's why she doesn't know. Anyway, I have a good job now and you are working again. Perhaps we will be able to stop soon."

"You weren't the one who had to quit school and work minimum wage jobs. I could have been finished university by now, had a career, a life."

"I've helped. It was my ideas that got us started in this business. I take the risk of fixing the records. I have taken many risks since the day I started working in that dress shop."

"Sure, except you got greedy and old Hatfield almost caught you. If he hadn't died before he told the cops how you were skimming, you'd be in jail now."

"Don't say that. It was a tragic accident the way his car was sideswiped."

"And just luck that he died of heart failure right after the doctor announced him out of danger."

"Don't say it like that. Cousin Anna was his nurse, she watched over him. She said it was something that happens sometimes."

He met her stare and returned it calmly. "No one is going to jinx our set-up. Cousin Yu worked hard to get you this job."

"He gets his cut from what his trick accounting program skims, plus 10 percent of our take."

"Consider it an overhead cost. We have to decide what to do about Jennifer. We can't give her the chance to talk to the cops."

"Lyle said he would look after her. Keep her from talking. He's taken tonight off so he can stay with her."

Lap ran his thumb over the thin knife blade before returning it to his jacket pocket.

"You can't take on Lyle with a knife. He'd hold you off with one hand."

"He can't stay at her side forever. Just make sure he works tomorrow night. I'll convince her where her continuing good health lies."

"You're risking too much."

"I'm helping support my family. Didn't you say family was important?"

He turned and with a leisurely stride left the office. Cara opened the centre drawer of her desk. Far in a back corner, she felt the handle of a gun that she had taken from an overcoat the previous winter. When no one reported it missing, she'd left it in the drawer. Now her instinct was paying off. If Lap started acting crazy, she could use the gun to make him listen to commonsense.

CHAPTER 15

Tuesday afternoon and all of Wednesday, had been spent reassigning officers from the task force to other investigations and clearing up administrative details. Super Sam had used the evidence pointing to Chuck's guilt to disband the task force and reassign Norman. Now the once crowded room felt empty, but Mike perused the four desks that remained staffed with officers prepared to solve Chuck's murder and to document his guilt in the abduction and murder of the children.

The entire mess was now his responsibility and his first job was sorting through the piles of evidence. This time they would be searching for anything linking Chuck to the victims.

The boxes taken from Chuck's studio sat beside investigative files dating from the four child murders. Their contents had been examined, but now they demanded further attention and a different perspective. Mike watched as the detectives cast furtive glances in their direction. Two of the boxes contained homemade videotapes of little children being physically abused and emotionally destroyed. Mike had watched a few and couldn't bring himself to watch more.

In one, Tommy Jamieson asked where his hat was. He had come to the studio to find the hat his mother was so concerned about him losing. Mike felt sick. He hoped there was a special hell for child abusers.

"Gold," Mike addressed a tall, thin officer. "Check with the kid's parents. I want to know if any of the other kids lost something important to them just before they were abducted. Something like Tommy's baseball cap. It might give us a handle on how he lured them away so quietly."

"You figure he promised to return some item if they came with him? It might work, especially if the parents were mad at them."

"Also, take Chuck's photo, see if they recognize him as someone who was involved with their kids."

Mike then addressed Rose Byron, their computer whiz. "Any progress searching the violent incident database?"

"No mention of a Chuck or Charles Albright and no luck yet on his fingerprints. However, if we do find a match we may discover a new name."

"You think he was using an alias?"

"There's just too little history on the guy. It's as if he was born shortly before he applied for work at the TV station. All I find is his driver's license and he got that using a birth certificate that belonged to a kid who died at age two. The Mounties said they would help, but they won't promise speed or results, though they are sending bulletins out to all their offices."

"Well, keep searching. Try working with descriptions of the crimes instead of his name. Okay," he held up his hands in response to her venomous look, "I won't tell you how to do the job."

Mike turned to the next officer, a fifteen-year veteran and all-round bulldog for details. "Liu, check his work records. Find out if he has an alibi for when those kids were taken."

That left Evan and Detective Howard. Mike chose Howard, a married man with no kids, to go through the photos and videos.

"Evan, you keep on the crew and passengers. If Chuck's murder wasn't related to those kids, I want to know what the motive was. I'm heading back to the boat tonight. It's another theatre night and I want an idea of how events flowed on Saturday. If any of you want me today, I'll be going over the abduction scenes first hand."

Mike had studied photos taken at the scene of each abduction and read the reports, but now he wanted to get a first-hand feel. Maybe by adding the identity of the offender to the mix, he could understand why Chuck had chosen those particular kids.

The files noted a few similarities in the scenes such as convenient access to major roads and parking nearby. Had Chuck used the station's van to take the kids? He would know soon enough, because the lab was it checking for hairs and fibres.

When Mike pulled to a stop in the parking lot of the community school, he looked left toward the playground where Sally Paterson had been last seen alive. She'd been taken on May 14, four years previous. Sally's picture showed a cute, cuddly six-year-old, with carrot-red hair and green eyes. Reports said her friends were teasing her and she walked away, angry with them.

Her friends last saw her heading toward the swing set in the playground. Two teachers saw her there when they left the school at four-ten. A third left the school around four-twenty and had not seen Sally. The girl's mother arrived home from work at five o'clock to find an empty house.

Two days later, the custodian had discovered Sally's body propped against the door he routinely used when arriving at work. Sally had been bathed, her hair washed with a generic shampoo and combed, and her clothes laundered with a common detergent. They had found no trace evidence or anything suitable for a DNA analysis.

Mike looked at the small hill that partially hid the playground from the parking lot. A few houses faced the schoolyard, but no school windows overlooked the area. No witness to the abduction had ever come forward.

He stepped out of the truck and walked toward the school. When he reached the main door, he stopped and turned toward the playground. The line of vision was clear. If Sally had been on the swings, the third teacher would have seen her.

A large philodendron flanked by a Norfolk pine sat inside the front entrance of the school. Mike looked around and after a moment found the office. It contained two desks. The school secretary's empty desk was hidden behind a high counter. A multi-line phone sat on the empty desk closest to the door. Two photocopy machines occupied the wall space on his right and a room filled with supplies was visible on his left. The office of the school principal was directly ahead, but it was also deserted. Mike listened, however no sounds of human habitation came from the office area or from the coffee room that he saw beyond the photocopiers.

Unwilling to roam the school, he sat on an uncomfortable chair and waited. Five minutes dragged by before a well-dressed, middle-aged woman entered the room.

"Can I help you with something?"

Her tone was wary.

"Are you the school secretary?"

"Yes."

"I'm with the city police. I have a few questions to ask you about Sally Paterson's death."

"I wasn't here then."

"Perhaps the principal can help."

"He came the following year. The only staff member left from then is Joe Phillips, the janitor. Do you want me to call him to the office?"

"Just point me in the right direction. I'll find him."

"We don't allow people to wander around the school."

Not up to a contest of wills, Mike asked her to page the janitor. She disappeared behind her counter and after a brief moment of whispering, the silence in the office grew deeper. Several minutes later, a slim man with stringy hair and ground-in dirt marking his knuckles walked through the door.

"You the cop wanted to talk to me? Every year it's the same. Don't you guys keep records?"

"It's more than routine now. Can we go outside to talk?"

"Sure, I need a smoke anyway."

Mike followed him through corridors decorated with pictures of spring painted by a grade two class, cut-outs of flowers came from grade three, and poems were written by a grade five class. They walked to the rear of the school and out a door to the staff parking lot.

The janitor pulled four inches of cigar from his pocket. He took his time examining it and picking a couple of bits of lint off before lighting and puffing on the malodorous stub.

Satisfied, he removed the cigar from his mouth and asked, "So what's happened to make it not routine this time?"

Mike held out a picture of Chuck Albright and asked, "Do you recall seeing this man?"

"Chuck. Sure I know him. Too bad someone killed him. I heard that slimy TV reporter claiming he hurt kids, but I don't believe it for a minute."

"So he wasn't around here on May 14, four years ago?"

"How would I remember that?"

"You said we've asked you about that day every year since the murder. You must have told several officers who you saw."

"Seems like I've talked to hundreds of them, but that was about people who could be guilty. Chuck helped with the Scout troop that met here Tuesdays. I think he volunteered to teach some grade six kids how to take pictures too. He belonged, he wasn't some stranger you had to watch."

"So, he could have been here that day?"

"Sure, but he wouldn't hurt a little kid. That reporter is crazy, he figures if he can change Chuck into the villain, it will stop people accusing him of murdering a nice fellow. Hell, everybody knows Chuck was one of the good people."

"What was the name of the teacher he helped by giving photography lessons?"

"A first year teacher. I don't remember her name, but she left that June for another school. It was a shame, I seem to remember the kids liked her." He ran his sleeve across his damp brow. "Hot already. I hope we don't have a drought this year."

When the cigar shrunk to three inches the caretaker stubbed it out on the school's brick wall, then lovingly put it back into his pocket.

"Time I got back to work."

After leaving the school, Mike walked to the playground and surveyed the swings and climbing tubes. Children's footprints had churned the sand and forced patches of it onto the broad, paved walkways leading toward an ice arena and sports field. Mike noted several approaches to the playground. Chuck wouldn't necessarily have parked close to the school, however if his van was a common sight it might have been the safest spot.

He checked his watch, plenty of time to check with Sally's teacher before lunch. The file was up-to-date and showed she now worked at a nearby school. He wanted to find out if Sally had known Chuck and if she had lost anything around the time of her disappearance.

When he parked in front of the school, he saw it was an older style, with lots of windows and a pill box shape. The playground was hidden behind it, in full sight of the office and staff room. Another grey-haired woman manned the desk in the school office and she greeted him with a smile that he couldn't help returning and a friendly inquiry into his business.

After paging Sally's grade one teacher, the secretary led him to the empty staff room and handed him a cup of coffee.

"She'll be just a few minutes. It'll take that long to get her class busy and alert the teacher across the hall to keep an eye on them."

She returned to her desk and the click of computer keys and occasional student voices drifted to Mike.

Mrs. Staples, Sally's teacher, marched into the room from the direction of the office.

"I saw you caught someone, officer. What can I do to help?"

"Did you recognize his picture, or the name Albright, Chuck Albright?"

She pulled a cloth from the pocket of her full skirt then removed her glasses from her square face and held them up to the light that was streaming through the window. She rubbed the lenses in a circular motion.

"No. I saw his picture on TV, but he wasn't familiar."

"The janitor, Joe Phillips, said he helped the grade six teacher with a photography unit."

She rubbed her lenses harder then replaced them on her large, flat nose.

"I never met him. I'm sure of that."

"Was Sally upset about anything just before she was abducted?"

The glasses came off again, the pale eyes stared somewhere only part way to where he stood, and the cleaning began again.

"The kids were teasing her, that's why she didn't walk home with them."

"Do you recall why they were teasing her?"

"We'd had a few days of rain and Sally had wore a new pair of rubber boots to school. They had some movie character on them. I forget which one but when she went to leave the school that day they were gone and she had to wear her indoor shoes home. The kids, being what they are, tormented her about the grief she was going to get when her mother found out. It was probably just a mistake because they showed up a couple of days later. They'd been pushed out of sight behind a garbage tin. We sent them to a charity at her mother's request. Do you think that had some bearing on the case?"

Mike thanked her for her assistance and left. It was a link, but by putting the boots back, Chuck had ensured they would never prove he'd taken them.

Climbing into his truck, Mike wondered if Tommy's hat would have reappeared in a few days.

By two o'clock, Mike had talked to the teachers of the other kids and was back at headquarters briefing Sam and the detectives.

"Chuck volunteered at each school until within a month of the abductions. Each of those schools has a playground with several access points so it is possible he watched the kids and waited to get them alone. Security at the schools is a joke. Even the best of them would be easy to walk into and because Chuck's face was familiar, no one would question him being around."

Mike held up the plastic evidence bag containing Tommy's baseball cap. "I'm guessing he took something from each kid, then waited until they were alone to tell them he had found the item and to ask if they knew who it belonged to. Of course, it would be in his vehicle and they would have cheerfully gone with him to retrieve their belongings."

"Good theory, Mike, but can you prove it," Sam asked.

Mike pushed at an unruly lock of hair. "Only that he volunteered to help with the kids and that each kid had lost a personal item within days of being taken."

Sam slammed her pencil down on the cluttered desktop. "Why didn't we know this before now?"

"No one connected Chuck to the crimes. He was familiar and everyone liked him, they just didn't think of him when we questioned them about possible suspects."

"And the missing items?"

"Insignificant. Kids are always losing things so no one thought to report it."

The room's occupants fell silent; Mike looked around at their discouraged faces.

"Okay, we have a link. Liu, was he working at the TV station on the days of the abductions? Could he have killed them?"

"They can't tell. Chuck sometimes worked overtime without signing in, so they took his word for his hours. The most his supervisor would say was that he was on call at those times."

"Check with Tanner, maybe he'll remember if Chuck was working with him when the kids went missing."

"The killings started more than four years ago, do you think he'll remember?"

Mike shrugged. "It's worth a try. Anything in the photos linking him to the families?"

"Just the pictures of the kids."

"Gold." Mike looked across to the lanky, aging detective. "Did the families recognize Chuck's photo?"

"No one is admitting it if they did."

"Do you believe them?"

"Jim Paterson is so consumed with anger he's not hiding anything."

"So, he didn't know Chuck?"

"He recognized Chuck's picture from Tanner's news report."

"The others?"

"They said the same. Once they're confident Chuck killed their kids, they might start to heal, but they aren't convinced of that yet."

"But they didn't know him?"

"They don't remember ever seeing or meeting him, not even at the schools. Nevertheless, if their kids knew him as someone associated with school, they might see no reason to fear him."

Mike stared at the group, wondering what more they could do. "Gold, visit the Scouts and the Little League office. See if someone made a complaint against him, anything minor that they didn't pass on to us."

"Where are you off to Mike," Sam asked.

"Tracking the editors of those sleazy magazines. Maybe he submitted pictures of our victims to one of them."

Rose Byron interrupted, "There's another market."

He met her myopic stare.

"The Internet. Kiddie porn sites are growing in number. I've started checking them out."

CHAPTER 16

Richard tossed Chuck's file onto the Little League Director's desk.

"Look. You're legally responsible for reporting suspected child abuse. You can't just file this in a drawer marked ancient history and pretend it never happened."

"The kid's mother was incoherent and making sweeping accusations about the harm done to her poor little son, but the boy was vague and his father refused to let us push him for details. The board members decided it was a case of the kid seeking revenge. Chuck told us he'd benched the kid after a couple of bad games. We all know kids make these kinds of accusations to get back at coaches, but Chuck didn't hold a grudge. He understood and assured us the kid was just misguided, not malicious."

"Yet the letter stayed in his file."

"Sure, just in case other incidents ever cropped up. You can never be too careful. We would have acted immediately if another complaint was filed, but you can't expect us to jeopardize a man's reputation on the word of a kid who was mad at him, can you?"

"Why wasn't he coaching this year?"

"That was his choice. We may have been relieved to accept his resignation in light of this letter, but we didn't force it. No one can say we treated him unfairly."

Richard opened the door, catching Anita Philips straining to hear more. He wondered if finding that file on her desk hadn't been too easy. He left without acknowledging her smug grin.

Richard knew the story was begging to be told, but he wanted to give it an unusual slant, not the routine malicious garbage other reporters were aiming for. He would start digging for it at the home of the kid who had made the complaint.

It took more than an hour to gather Christy from her gym class and get across town, but the early evening was still hot when Richard smiled his apologetic-but-sincere-smile into the face of the woman who opened the door. She was one of those women who turned dumpy the day they hit forty.

"You're Richard Tanner," she sputtered as her wary expression changed to wonder and even hero worship.

He revved his smile up a few volts. Giving fans, even chubby ones, full value for their worship was good PR.

"Mrs. Markham, I apologize for disturbing your evening but I would like to speak with your family for a few minutes. It concerns Chuck Albright and the complaint you made to the Little League Association last summer."

Her enraptured expression changed to a frown, then a scowl. "We aren't to talk about that." She darted a look over his shoulder to where Christy stood holding the camera. "My husband doesn't want Mark Jr. on television. My husband says it would make him a laughing stock. That's why we didn't pursue legal action in the first place. My husband will be mad if I talk to you."

"Where is Mr. Markham now?"

"In the living room, watching the hockey playoffs."

"Is your son home as well?"

"Like I said, you can't talk to him."

"Who's there?" a coarse voice bellowed from the depths of the dark hall.

With a reproachful glare, she called over her shoulder, "Richard Tanner, from Station Six."

"What does he want?"

"To talk to Mark, Jr."

"Tell him to go away."

"Mr. Markham," Richard interjected in a loud voice as he held the door to prevent the heavy-breasted woman from closing it. "Let me talk to you for a minute. I am certain we can come to an agreement."

"Shit."

The single word hailed the arrival of a lumbering form. Hair sparsely covered his round head and his tee shirt stretched over his bulging stomach. He held the TV remote control like a weapon.

"I'm in the middle of watching the game." His voice held a reproachful glower.

Richard was not sure which teams were playing but knew better than to admit his ignorance to an avid fan. He extended his hand. How was he going to get this flaccid lump to agree to an interview? "Yes, sorry to interrupt. What's the score?"

The man motioned toward Christy. "Don't want my son on television talking about that pervert attacking him."

"We don't have to tape this. Just let your son tell me what happened, I won't even mention his name."

"The whole team would know who you were talking about. They'd just laugh at us for trying to pretend it was a secret."

"But Mark . . . ." Mrs. Markham began then stopped speaking, silenced by her husband's look.

"You caused enough trouble writing that letter. A boy can't hide behind his mother's skirts all the time. He has to learn to cope with that kind of thing."

"Mr. Markham, how can I persuade you it is important that your son to tell his story? It might help other children spot abusers and learn to deal with them."

"They can learn on their own, not from my boy."

"Maybe some form of compensation." Richard let the words hang in the air.

Eventually, with the words escaping one by one, Mr. Markham said, "Can you make the interview general—not say anything about the team or mention any names?"

"Sure, I could work around those details."

A throat-clearing cough from Christy interrupted them. He would strangle her if she made Markham realize the story was too weak to report without all the scandalously titillating details. If he got the basic facts, he could manipulate them to create a great story and deal with the family's complaints later.

"Does your station get hockey tickets," Mr. Markham asked.

"I'm sure the station has a few play-off tickets lying around. I can certainly arrange for you to have them."

"It would have to be two tickets to the last home game, so I can take my partner."

"No problem. Now, can we come in and talk?"

"Not her." He pointed the TV controller at Christy. "I don't want this on film."

"If we tape the interview, you would be sure I don't misinterpret what you say. We will obscure your faces."

"You'll change my voice too? No one will know it's me."

"Whatever you want."

"Okay. It's intermission anyway. Just make sure it doesn't take long."

Richard followed him down the narrow hall, through a fussy sitting room and a large kitchen, to the family room. Floral slipcovers, with a predominance of orange and brown flowers, covered the long sofa and two armchairs. A small boy sat crossed-legged in front of the large screen television. His long, thin hair and vacant expression gave him the look of a meditating yogi.

Mark Markham Sr. headed for a recliner. His attention darted to the television screen where another commercial was beginning. With an impatient look, he said, "Okay, let's do it now, but be quick."

Richard looked out of the corner of his eye at Christy and spotted the telltale record light. Good girl.

"Just tell me what led up to your complaint."

"You know, those people at the League office said the letter was confidential. How did you find out about Mark Jr. anyway?"

"With Mr. Albright being murdered, we looked at several things very closely and the staff at the Little League office was kind enough to share that information."

"Oh," Mr. Markham grunted. "They should've told us before handing out that letter. Without getting our permission, what they did was an invasion of our privacy."

Mrs. Markham moved a pile of folded clothes from the sofa so they could sit. Richard complied, but motioned to Christy to stay in the doorway where she was inconspicuous and could film without anyone noticing. One day the Markhams would thank him for airing this incident.

"When did the incident with Mr. Albright occur?"

"Last year the team went off for a tournament at the end of May. Hockey playoffs ran late, so I couldn't go with them. Sometimes I go with them. Besides, they were going to camp out and that plays havoc with my bad back."

The commercial ended and two sports reporters, debating the merits of the game, filled the screen. Mr. Markham kicked at the boy who sat quietly on the carpet.

"Mark, you tell him the rest."

Richard was surprised this was the kid in question instead of some younger sibling because he looked too scrawny to be much of a ball player. He focused his kindly-uncle-look on the little boy.

The boy stared at the television, ignoring his father and Richard. Richard knelt close to him and putting as much sincerity as he could muster into his voice, said, "Just tell me what he did that upset you."

The boy twisted to look at his mother, who nodded encouragement. Finally, in a tiny whisper, he said, "I liked Mr. Albright a lot. All the guys did."

Richard leaned closer so he could hear him over the excited tones of the announcer.

"He said I had to share his tent cause the others were full and I was the smallest kid."

He was staring at the screen, though Richard doubted the boy saw anything but the events of that night.

Richard nodded his most encouraging nod.

"When I woke up, he was naked and unzipping my sleeping bag." The kid turned back to the TV.

"Mark, did he touch you? What did he say?"

"He won't say more. He never does," Mrs. Markham whispered. She cast a furtive look at her husband who was now deeply engrossed in the words of a young man garbed in a team uniform.

"You can guess the rest. Those stories you've been doing about him killing kids prove that he would have hurt Mark Jr."

"Please, Mark, can you tell me any more at all?"

The child stared vacantly at the screen, giving no indication that he heard Richard.

Richard turned his attention back to the mother. "What happened to stop him?"

"The other parent on the trip heard Mark Jr. scream and he went running. Mr. Albright said he'd had a bad dream, but Mark Jr. didn't used to have dreams, at least not ones that scared him. He does now though."

"Have you taken him for counselling?"

"My husband doesn't believe counsellors help. He says they put ideas in kids' heads, lead them into thinking strange things. My husband says they would have Mark Jr. digging up memories of all kinds of abuse that never happened. He says the next thing you know social workers would be pounding at our door threatening to take our son away because of something some counsellor told him to remember."

"Shut up, Martha. Mr. Tanner doesn't want to hear you ramble. Anyway, he's been told what happened so it's time he left. The game is starting again."

The man's attention returned to the screen where the teams were flowing onto the ice. He put the remote control down for just long enough to grab a handful of popcorn, shove it in his mouth, then reach for his beer to wash it down.

Through his mouthful he said, "Send those tickets over by courier."

As Mrs. Markham led them to the front door, Richard heard the crowd roar its approval.

"You have to understand about my husband. He isn't always so abrupt, just when he's watching sports. That's how he relaxes."

"A lot of people get caught up in the playoffs."

"It's not just the playoffs. He watches sports all the time. Not golf or bowling, he says they're too boring. Just team sports. Mark played football in high school. Mark Jr. is a disappointment to him, being so little. He takes after my family. You won't let people recognize us, will you? My husband would be really mad if the people he works with tease him about being on TV. And Mark Jr., well, he's had enough trouble over this."

"Like I told your husband, we'll obscure your faces and change the voices." Richard stepped onto the porch, wondering what the point of the interview was. The story was too weak to use—unless he added a few lurid details and maybe shots of the dead kids to satisfy the audience's need for blood, sex, and violence.

"I never did trust that man."

"Chuck?"

She nodded. "Mr. Albright was just too good to the kids. You know taking the team for burgers and letting them ride in his van. He even took team pictures and individual ones if the kids wanted them. When we complained about that incident, the other kids stuck by him. Their parents did too. They're only too glad to have someone look after their kids. This year's coach insists parents come to at least half the games and he makes the parents chaperone during tournaments. Mr. Albright's way was easier, but what if he's done this to other kids?"

"Can you give me the name of any other team member you think he might have molested?"

She pulled back at the word molested. The startled look on her face told Richard he had accidentally brought reality into her world.

"That's such a hard word." She was whispering again. "I think you better go now, before my husband realizes you're still here."

She glanced over her shoulder then grasped Richard's hand. After a quick squeeze, she released it, and shut the door in his face.

Christy was already at the van packing the camera away when he arrived.

He climbed into the passenger seat and said, "With parents like that, it's no wonder the kid turned to Chuck. At least he noticed the kid was alive."

"Tanner, shut up. The kid's parents might not come up to your ideal, but that kid doesn't deserve more grief."

CHAPTER 17

The level of the river had dropped and the current had slowed since Saturday evening. A beaver expertly manoeuvred the current its head creating an apex as it skimmed the quiet water near shore.

Mike leaned against the rail of the River Belle studying the forested riverbanks. A mist of barely opened green leaves hung over the hills, promising summer's imminent arrival. The air was filled with the pungent perfume of damp leaves recently freed from the grip of ice and snow, and slowly turning into rich loam. He could almost forget a city lurked behind the green belt.

Mike estimated they were at the point where Chuck had been thrown into the river. The boat dock was a mile downstream and the landing at Fort Edmonton was too far upstream to reach by swimming against the current. Even if Chuck had been alive and conscious when he landed in the river, his chances of reaching shore safely would have been slim.

"Is this where it happened," Beth asked, addressing her question to Mike's back.

Mike nodded, then turned to face her. "According to the times supplied by witnesses, we're near where his body went over. The Ident Unit found traces of his blood on this portion of the railing, confirming that Chuck hit his forehead when he was struck from behind and fell forward."

"Or he might have slipped and hit his head on the rail by accident. You said he had a number of cuts on his body, so he could have got that one while in the river."

"How did he end up in the water?" Mike kept his tone noncommittal.

"You just will not admit it could have been an accident, will you?"

"The evidence says he had help going over the rail."

"Maybe he tried to jump and hit his head on the way down." Beth laughed uncomfortably. "Okay, that doesn't make sense. But even if someone did kill him, it doesn't follow that he was a killer."

"Sometimes people fool us, Beth." Mike spoke softly, not wanting to re-ignite the furore with which Beth had earlier defended Chuck.

Before she could start reciting Chuck's virtues again, Lyle Lamont shuffled into sight. After a quick look at the boy, Beth stepped into the shadow of the snack bar.

"I've got time to talk to you now. The second intermission is over and we've served dessert. Nothing to do now but wait until the boat is ready to dock."

"Are you usually finished your duties around this time?"

"Yeah."

"We won't dock for over an hour."

"Not to worry, I help with the cleanup and paperwork. First, I like to take a break and pretend I'm back home. This isn't the ocean, but at least it's a boat on water. Not many jobs with those qualities in Alberta."

"Did you come up here Saturday night?"

"Not around this side. I saw Mr. Tanner on the other side of the boat, though."

The young man's voice seemed tight.

"Did you see anyone else?"

The blond giant examined his shoes and rocked back and forth, swaying gently with the motion of the boat and sneaking looks at Beth.

"Don't recall seeing nobody else, but I didn't stay out long."

"How long would you say you were on deck?"

"Five, ten minutes tops that time. Of course, I was up here on and off all night."

"And you saw no one but Richard Tanner? Was he acting strangely?"

"Strange, you mean like breathing hard or what?"

"What was he doing?"

"Just standing near the rail, smoking. He did look sort of anxious when I came up the stairs, but when I kept my distance he just went back to river gazing."

Mike noticed Lyle staring intently at Beth again.

"Is something wrong, Lyle," Mike asked.

As though the question finally gave him permission to ask, Lyle said, "I know you, don't I?" A flush spread into his tanned cheeks.

"You were in the library a couple of weeks ago. I gave you a list of research sources."

The flush deepened and a sheepish grin spread across his face. "Oh that. It was for a friend, like I said before."

"Of course, Mr. Lamont. I hope the information was helpful." Beth's voice contained the cool professional tone that Mike knew she used when masking intense emotion.

"Yes. Really helpful. My friend said it was just what she was looking to find."

"That's good."

"Why are you here," Lyle asked, as he jabbed his hands in his pockets and studied the deck.

"The man who died was my friend. Did you know him?"

"Me? No. No, I didn't even see him Saturday night."

"Still, you must have seen pictures of him since then? They've been all over the media."

What was she probing to uncover? Mike held himself motionless curious at how the conversation would develop.

Lyle shrugged his shoulders, but kept his head down. He looked like a child who didn't want to answer, but who felt compelled to say something.

"Sure, I saw it plastered on the front page of both papers and the detectives showed us a picture too. But I didn't know him."

"Did you read the news articles?"

"No." The word exploded from him. "Look, Detective." He turned toward Mike. "I've got to get back. Nice seeing you again."

He addressed the latter comment to Beth, turned on his heel, and fled toward the stairs. With a final look over his shoulder, he clamoured down the steps and out of sight.

Mike waited for Beth to say something, but she continued staring into the night.

He cleared his throat to draw her attention. "What was that about?"

"Nothing."

"The way he reacted, it wasn't nothing. He practically ran away from you. Why were you probing so hard about whether he knew Chuck?"

She chewed her lower lip, working it through her teeth several times before she walked to the rail and pulled Mike close.

"Maybe I was wrong about Chuck."

Mike stopped himself from making a cryptic comment and waited for her to continue. He slid his arm around her waist, but remained silent. Whatever had made her see the light was still sifting through her thoughts.

"You saw how scared he was," she said in a tiny voice. "Do you think he recognized Chuck?"

"He said no, but he did get upset when you asked him."

"Mike, he was researching material about child abuse, specifically information concerning adult survivors of child sexual abuse."

Mike released her and clutched the rail with both hands. Damn. Had Lyle been one of Chuck's victims? Tossing Chuck overboard would have been easy for someone with Lyle's strength.

"I'll get a background check going on him."

She paused, then drew Mike's arm around her shoulders. She turned and hugged him tight.

"If Chuck hurt Lyle as a kid and he retaliated, what would happen to Lyle? Would there be some kind of extenuating circumstance when the case went to court?"

Mike inhaled the fragrant scent of her short, curly hair. He pulled her closer.

"Don't jump to conclusions. He said he didn't know Chuck and that the research was for someone else. It is possible he's telling the truth."

"Then why did he look so embarrassed?"

"Most young fellows wouldn't admit an interest in such a sensitive topic, people might think it was personal."

"Like I am doing?"

"Just like that."

The deck lights burst on, the shadows turned back into objects and their mood of intimacy was dispelled. Beth pulled away and tugged at her sweater.

"Am I betraying Chuck by doubting him?"

"Nothing's changed yet. Hold onto your faith until we do some more checking."

Then Mike kicked himself. He should have taken the opportunity to encourage her change of viewpoint, but at least she had let a small doubt penetrate. Maybe it would grow into belief on its own.

******

Richard preferred staying at work or hanging around any bar, so that he didn't have to spend the evening in the quiet of his thrown-together abode.

When Beth banished him from her life, he had rebelled against her organized, sanitized lifestyle and had rented a furnished apartment. It might have the class of a petting zoo and the same feeling of permanence as a room in an airport motel, but it was his. Being tied-down bothered him. It always had, even before Beth. Besides, now he was free to leave town at a moment's notice. You never knew when a better job offer would pound on your door.

He gulped his beer and put his feet on the coffee table. Running his finger down the damp bottle, he admitted that if the station brass started questioning his methods, he wouldn't be looking for a better job, just a job. Discrediting Chuck had diverted disaster before his allegations of unprofessional behaviour made an impression, now he was counting on an exposé of Chuck's warped life to solidify his reputation. Maybe it was the story that would lead him out of this blue-collar town.

Tonight he had actively sought solitude and privacy so that he could look through Chuck's files. He had to decide if they were filled with junk that he could turn over to the cops or if they contained the clue he need to point him toward the real Chuck Albright.

He held his beer bottle up to the light of a ceramic lamp, then sipped the amber liquid, savouring its flavour as it flooded his throat.

The two library books were drivel. Sad stories about people too weak to fight back, but who were ready to capitalize on their own misery. Well, he could skim them later if it proved necessary. They might hold the key that would help him bluff his way into running a full scale series on the issue.

Fortified by his drink, he opened the top folder of the pile. It contained copies of articles pulled from magazines and newspapers. Stuff about repressed memories, about survivors of child abuse, about boys who had been sexually abused, and about the trials and tribulations of being the partner of an abused adult. Each article had its publication details neatly printed on the bottom of the sheet.

He closed the folder. What was Chuck collecting this garbage for? He had to be an expert on abusing kids. He didn't need a victim or worse yet, some author, to tell him how it was done.

Richard tossed the file aside and turned to the next. It was stapled closed on three sides forming an envelope and showed signs of prolonged wear. Opening the unstapled end, Richard peered inside at scraps of paper, serviettes, restaurant place mats, and three coil-bound notebooks.

He upended the folder, spreading the contents across the table. A sketch on one of the serviettes looked like a roughly drawn map. Another showed a list of numbers that could be times or dates. Richard straightened the folds and looked at both sides of the scraps of paper, then he sorted them into piles.

This stuff couldn't be important, it was just jotted notes and comments. Why had Chuck collected these scraps of ideas? Richard pushed them aside and turned his attention to the notebooks.

Work assignments from the station were recorded in the red-covered book. Richard understood the numbers listed because he kept a similar book as the basis for his timesheets and expense claims.

A yellow-covered book contained the names of magazines with each entry including contact names, phone numbers, e-mail addresses and cryptic notes about payment policies and rates. Other names were followed by the scrawled phrase Home Video. These entries provided only e-mail addresses. The last few pages listed websites. One to five stars were drawn next to each name. A rating system?

The final book had a green cover. Richard flipped it open halfway through, then thumbed the pages slowly back to the beginning. The names in this book were foreign and the short notes it held were written in a form of code. Richard had seen books like this before, rating prostitutes on performance and specialty, but he had never seen one list the ages of nine and ten next to the names. The pages at the beginning of the book had a line drawn through them. The dates at the top of those entries showed that eight years had passed since the names were added.

Richard drained the bottle and walked to the fridge for another. Had the boys become too old for Chuck's taste?

The dates in the book were all in April; the month Chuck supposedly visited Hawaii on his vacation. However, the entries gave addresses in Thailand and the Philippines. Was that why Chuck never talked about his vacation?

Richard returned the scraps and books to the folder. For a long moment, he held the green-covered book. Could the nucleus of his story be how respectable men spent their vacations in tropical countries abusing child prostitutes? He could detail how they traded kids and information like baseball cards. It had potential.

He slid the contents of another folder onto the table. The articles it contained told the stories of abandoned and abused children. The clippings had been torn from magazines and newspapers. Some were old and grubby; some seemed recent. Still, they all told the same story of unwanted, unloved children, of parents full of remorse when they had finally damaged their child beyond repair.

The final folder also contained clippings concerning Edmonton's child abductions and murders. Chuck had kept a complete collection of not only news articles, but also editorials and features on the repercussions of his actions.

Richard sat back and pondered the materials arrayed before him. What was the connection between the files? Why collect such a wide range of information? Had Chuck intended writing about the whole spectrum, the child abuse and pedophilia? Did he plan to tell how he had exposed his hidden memories of being abused as a child? Maybe he was going to claim his story was that of an abused child who became an abuser and finally a murderer.

Richard picked a smoldering cigarette stub from the crowded ashtray and inhaled deeply, enjoying the surge of well being that hit his lungs. Damn, the abuse cycle was a good angle. Maybe searching for more info on Chuck's life would be worth his time. This could be sappy enough for a movie of the week.

He turned back to the folder of scraps. If he applied a little imagination to those sketches maybe filled in a few applicable times, he could recreate the scenario surrounding the abductions and murders of the kids.

This was meant to be. Chances like this didn't fall into your hands every day. The cops weren't going to get hold of this stuff until he culled every bit of information and photocopied the entire contents and maybe they wouldn't get it even then.

******

The row of solar lights glowed softly along the path that guided them toward the brightly-lit parking lot. Mike felt the evening had been partially successful. He and Evan had watched as the staff of the River Belle checked the guests' reservations and took their coats, and Beth assured them procedures hadn't been altered since the Saturday evening cruise.

While Evan continued watching the financial procedures, he and Beth had questioned staff members in an effort to trace the movements of both Richard and Chuck. The only new tidbit they learned was that the cook was missing a fry pan. She used a heavy cast iron pan for frying the onions she served on hot dogs. She remembered putting it away Saturday afternoon, but it was gone Monday when the boat reopened. Mike felt certain they had discovered the murder weapon.

As they followed the crew toward the parking lot, Mike asked Evan what he had learned about the money handling procedures.

"It's a pretty routine set-up that works if you hire honest staff," Evan answered. "But someone in the crew is siphoning off information. Too many of the people I've called have had unauthorized purchases recorded on their credit cards for it to be a coincidence."

"Any prime candidates?"

"It's not just credit cards. Seven people I contacted had their vehicles stolen within a month of being on the boat. That's an incredible coincidence that points to an organized group, not just one person on staff."

"You've been doing the background checks, any criminal records popping up," Mike asked.

"Nothing. One curious item though. Maybe it's a coincidence, but the bookkeeper, the parking lot attendant, and two waiters are related."

"Helping a family member find a job is almost the norm these days."

"I just thought I'd mention it. I'm heading home now," he said as he veered off the path toward his sedan.

"So apparently Richard's contact was right about the theft ring," Beth said as she slipped her hand into Mike's and moved closer to him.

"There's no doubt something is going on. We'll inform the owners of the boat so they can do an audit. We will also keep surveillance on this parking lot to discover whether the attendant is part of the ring that's stealing cars or if he's just careless with the keys."

"He didn't keep the car keys when we parked. I suppose he could break in while they were empty, but Evan didn't say the cars were stolen from the lot."

"This group is being careful not to have the thefts traced back to them. My guess would be the attendant checks for unsecured cars, open windows, or doors left unlocked, and then takes the registration information. If a request comes in for a specific model of car his gang can check their list for a match and steal it from the owner's home."

"Wouldn't someone see him rummaging through the cars?"

"The area is isolated and he can be sure that once the boat sails for the evening no one will be returning to their vehicle. The window of opportunity is several hours and in that time an experienced thief could break into all the vehicles parked here."

"So they would know where I live if they broke into my car last Saturday?"

Mike didn't like the fear he heard in her voice. They had reached his truck and he stopped and placed his hands on her shoulders.

"You know being careful is the only way to be safe. Besides, with your full house who could get near you?"

"Jim's moving into his own place now that he has a permanent job. Mom and Dad are talking about converting part of their new fitness centre into an apartment. I don't know what happened, but suddenly Mom's all ready to start her business. They can't open for at least six months after they find a place but they want to move out as quickly as they can. Soon I'll be alone again."

"Say the word and we can set a date." Mike squeezed her shoulder, willing her to agree.

She shook her head. "I'm not asking for a protector. I just have to overcome this fear that my house isn't safe. I hate feeling like this."

"You can't have someone saunter into your well-protected house and try to kill you without some reaction." He fought his impulse to use her unease to his advantage and push her for a commitment. They were both happy with their relationship the way it stood, weren't they? Why mess things up by changing the rules?

It must be Evan and his nagging that made him do it. He studied Beth's frown and hoped their friendship would survive. Then he leaned ever so slightly and covered her frown with his lips.

CHAPTER 18

Jennifer flicked off the television that Lyle had lent her to help hold boredom at bay. She hated the dramas with their make believe problems and ready solutions as much as the comedies that were full of sexual innuendo and humour bordering on farce.

She half-stumbled, half-hopped to the patio door, opened it, and stepped into the fragrant evening air. A wall sheltered her patio, separating her from her neighbour and with the sun now set, it was a cool refuge from the stifling heat in her apartment.

Lyle had offered to stop by after work, but she had told him not to, in case she was sleeping; however, the throbbing in her arm wouldn't let her sleep. That doctor had given her a prescription for painkillers that she hadn't bothered filling because she didn't want the temptation of having the pills around. She would rather deal with the discomfort. It wasn't as if she was unfamiliar with pain.

Then ever-helpful Lyle had filled the prescription. She looked at the full bottle sitting on her coffee table. If she took enough of the pills, she could stop the pain forever. When had she begun thinking that way? After Eric died.

But she didn't want to die and she wouldn't if she got far away as soon as she could.

A week ago, she had considered Edmonton her home. She had planned on working and going to university. She had thought she could make a good life for herself and put the remnants of her old life behind her. Her brother was dead; her mother was buried under the weight of guilt, of no use to anyone. Now though she had nowhere to run to, she was afraid to stay.

Maybe Lyle would take her away, but where would they go? Could she trust him to stand by her? Men were untrustworthy by nature. They took without asking and left without saying goodbye. Even Eric, who she had thought infallible, had left her to fend for herself.

Jennifer sought out the Big Dipper, the only constellation she could identify. One of her mother's friends had showed it to her. Why was her mother here? Was she seeking forgiveness? Not a hope, she would receive that. Jennifer had spent too many years hiding from her mother and her mother's boyfriends to ever forgive. She hated remembering her mother cooking breakfast for yet another stranger who usually became a temporary part of the household. Most of them had been brutal men who hated kids and who lashed out violently.

Her mother never cared; she never protected them. She let her kids do anything, as long as they didn't interfere with her life. The kids at school had called her mother a drunk, a whore, a fat pig. Jennifer never defended her against any of the names. How do you fight the truth?

She cradled her throbbing arm. Her mother wasn't her biggest problem right now. She shivered at the memory of Lap's fierce glare. So much had happened since her call to Richard Tanner, but she not heard a word about the scam on the news. Had he forgotten about the story after his friend died? Unlikely. Maybe he had investigated and discovered Cara had an innocent reason for passing the information to her brother? Was she being paranoid, worrying about retribution that would never come?

Jennifer shivered and stepped from the cooling night air into the overly warm apartment. Perhaps she should have encouraged Lyle's visit. He was kind and she wanted to trust him. He had never touched her aggressively and she thought he might even ask permission before kissing her. That would allow her time to get used to the idea. The last few weeks had been fun because of Lyle. He could easily tease a smile or a laugh from her. In that way, he was just like Eric.

Jennifer sagged against the wall beside the patio door and looked around the room. What would she take when she left? The sofa was impossible; the dishes could be easily replaced. She would start fresh with only the clothes she could carry in a backpack. She let her gaze rest on each item, mourning its loss, until she noticed the doorknob move.

When it stopped moving, she exhaled. Then the door began to slide inward. She shifted her weight. Did she have time to slip onto the patio? Before she could adjust her crutch to move, Lap stepped inside and closed the apartment door.

His dark hair was pulled back and tied into a ponytail. A black leather jacket hung loose on his shoulders. His hands were empty, but he held them tensed and she feared a weapon would appear if she made a wrong move.

Jennifer felt a sense of release, as if she had been anxiously awaiting his arrival. Resignation to her fate cloaked her fear. She could not run, she would not beg for mercy, she would try to talk to him. If unsuccessful, she would suffer his rage with dignity.

"So, you are hurt. I thought Lyle might be lying."

She would not let fear grow and overwhelm her. "Get out Lap or I'll scream."

He shrugged. "You scream. You die."

His hand disappeared into the pocket of his jacket. It re-emerged holding a knife. With a touch of his thumb, a shiny blade appeared.

Jennifer dragged her stare from the blade to his eyes. She felt panic rise in her throat. She froze as he took a measured step toward her. The light of the desk lamp glinted off the blade. A whimper escaped her lips. She stumbled over her crutch when she tried to move toward the patio door.

"I didn't tell him anything," she said fighting the waver in her voice.

"That's how it's going to stay. I must protect my family business from attacks by outsiders."

"I promise I'll keep quiet."

He shrugged again. The soft leather of his jacket sighed with the movement. "You promised that before but you lied and now the cops are sniffing around."

Jennifer gathered her breath to yell for help, but the squeak of fear that escaped her throat was barely above normal conversational level.

Lap laughed and shook his head.

The door burst open and before Lap could turn, Lyle was beside him. One blow from Lyle's large fist and Lap lay crumpled on her carpet. Lyle stood over him, legs spread, balancing his weight on his toes. He stooped and grabbed the knife from Lap and held it loosely.

"Get out and leave her alone!"

Lap pulled himself onto his elbows, shook his head, and scooted toward the sofa. When he regained his footing, he crouched ready to defend himself.

Jennifer cringed and struggled to move away from the patio door; Lap took a shaky step in her direction.

"Get away from Jennifer!" Lyle ordered.

Lap edged toward the centre of the room. Lyle circled away from the door, freeing up an escape route. Jennifer hoped Lap would take the hint and leave.

"Lyle, you can quit playing games now that I see whose side you're really on. Toss the knife over to Lap," Cara said, as she stepped inside the patio door. She gripped a pistol in her finely boned hand. "Help her walk. We're getting out of here," Cara ordered.

"Cara, let us go. I'll take Jen and leave town tonight."

"Sorry, pal. It's too late to bargain. You've demonstrated where your loyalty lies."

"You can't kill us."

Cara looked toward Lap, who shrugged, and then back to Lyle who moved to stand beside Jennifer.

"We will think of something."

"No." Jennifer hobbled to the sofa and sat down. She plucked at the cast that encased her arm and stared at Cara. "If you're going to kill me, do it here. I'm not going to make it easier for you."

"I'm not bluffing. I will shoot you if you don't walk out that door."

"Give me that knife," Lap said and started toward Lyle with his hand extended.

"No way." Lyle stepped in front of Jennifer, shielding her from Lap's advance.

The four of them remained motionless. Jennifer, hampered by her cast and sling, felt her heart pump faster. She didn't want anyone hurt. Why had she started this? What twisted sense of justice had made her call Richard? Now Lyle would die defending her. She just wasn't worth it.

Lap hesitated, then cautiously moved nearer the patio door where Cara skulked.

"What's all the commotion? Don't you realize it's midnight? I can't have you disturbing the rest of my tenants."

The four young people turned toward the door where Mrs. McPherson stood with a double-barrelled shotgun resting on her forearm. She was dressed in a floor-length, pink velour robe that she'd cinched around her waist, cutting her abdomen into two rolls. She looked like a grandmother, not a mad protector. Still something in the casual way she held the shotgun told Jennifer it was a trusty old friend.

"Better put that tiny little pistol down, miss, before you shoot something. A little thing like that is not going to stop anyone, it'll just make them mad. This darling however will make it necessary to scrape you off the walls. I saw my husband splatter a rabid fox all over a granary with this girl. It was probably just about as far away as you are. Yes sir, this old shotgun has put many critters out of their misery. No human animals yet, but this could be my chance."

Cara cast a helpless look at her brother then they turned and raced through the open patio door into the night.

Mrs. McPherson rested the shotgun against the sofa as she bent to check Jennifer. "Damn. Sorry Jennifer. I thought I could hold them with a threat, but I guess they could tell I wouldn't shoot."

Lyle reached out to help her from the sofa. "Jen, we have to leave before they come back."

She looked blankly at his hand, then up to his tense face. "I've run far enough. Call the police and tell them to arrest the two of them."

"We can't do that."

"Then don't call them." She rested her head against the back of the sofa. "I'm too tired to go anywhere."

"I can't leave you alone. What if they come back?"

"You run after them, boy. I'll watch over her until the police get here." Mrs. McPherson patted her gun.

Jennifer reclined on the sofa, only half relieved to be alive. She wished everyone would leave her alone. She was tired and she hurt.

"Jen, did he hurt you?"

Jennifer opened her eyes and smiled at Lyle. He was still with her and he cared about her. She knew he was a good person; now she had to send him away.

"He just scared me. It's over."

"Don't worry Mrs. McPherson." Lyle rose and ushered the woman toward the door. "We'll call the police. You go back to your apartment. I'll make sure Jen is safe."

He pushed her through the door, closing it behind the heavy woman's velour-clad back. He then turned toward Jennifer and knelt on the floor in front of her.

"Will they come back," she asked.

"Probably."

"We should call the police," she said, thinking that maybe he could stay with her until they arrived.

"And testify against Cara and Lap? How many friends do they have who are willing to finish us off?"

"I can give the police some details about their set up. Then we can go to another city." She reached out and grasped his hand, dreading sending him away.

"I was involved in their operation."

"Oh, Lyle, no." She squeezed his fingers. He was too good to be hurt because of her actions.

"I didn't want to be part of it but Cara forced me to help."

"You have to go to the police."

"If I'm in jail, I can't protect you." He held her hands tight. "What will happen if I'm arrested? How will my parents survive the shame of what I've done?"

"Don't call. Just leave." Jennifer heard the words and knew she meant them this time. She knew you couldn't trust the police to understand. Besides, did it really matter if Cara came back and killed her?

"No. I'm not going anywhere," Lyle insisted.

Jennifer closed her eyes to block out his wonderful smile. Somehow, she had to force him to go.

******

It was late when Beth let herself into her two-storey home. The house was dark and quiet, but the security lights flared to life as her car approached the garage. A murmur of voices came through the screen door leading to the patio and Beth followed them into the cool night air. The senior McKinneys were huddled over the picnic table where a battery-operated lantern spread light on the sketches lying before them. They looked up, excitement glowing in their eyes.

"That crazy idea of Jim's might just work. I talked to a couple of old friends today and they're interested in renting some of the space. They're keen to hold their classes in a facility that's designed as a gym, not just a room in a church basement or community hall. If we keep our prices low, they can make a profit. And if we handle their registrations . . . ."

Beth interrupted her mother. "If you do that, charge a straight percentage of the fees."

"That's what I was going to say. I've already lined up three aerobic instructors and two personal trainers who have been operating out of their basements and want to expand. Sara Benton, my friend who teaches yoga, is super keen on having a hardwood floor for her class. With the response I'm getting, I don't know if we can wait six months to open. These people want to start their classes in September."

"You're in a rush to get going so you can sit back and rake in the rental money," Beth teased.

"That's all you know. We need just the right location and then an architect to design the renovations. I want a laundry, and a sauna, and steam rooms. We should check to see if we will qualify for government retraining subsidies to help pay employees. We're planning the apartment right now. Having our own place again will be wonderful. We'll empty your basement of boxes."

"Are you sure about the apartment? You can stay here. I don't understand why you want to live at the gym."

"Why you need your privacy. I've seen the way you look at the detective and I don't plan to stand in the way of whatever is going to develop."

"We're friends and that's as far as it's going."

"Whatever you say dear, but moving to an apartment close to our gym is also a business decision. You taught us that with your computer consulting service. People just cannot fit everything into nine to five days anymore. We must respond to our customer's demands. Maybe we will even open twenty-four hours a day."

Beth left them to their plans and headed for her den via the kitchen where she grabbed a cup of coffee. She had to check her computer for E-mail replies to her request for information about Chuck. Eighteen hours had passed since she sent the inquiry off to fifty-seven sites. Some were long shots, but she had wanted to be thorough enough that she could tell Richard he was wrong to think badly of Chuck.

Now, after talking to Lyle, she dreaded the answers. What if she received messages from people Chuck had hurt? She inhaled deeply, hoping to calm her fears. She would think positively. Perhaps no one had replied.

One hundred and fifteen responses awaited her. Sipping her coffee, Beth looked through the messages. Most were expressions of sympathy for the victims and promises to keep an eye open for the man she was seeking. A few people chastised her for trying to prevent children from choosing to have sex with adults. Others accused her of persecuting a respectable citizen.

Beth read fifty messages before her mother popped her head around the door. She held Splatter in her arms and was stroking the little cat's multi-hued head.

"It's after one. We've locked up the house and set the alarm. Are you going to bed soon? Didn't you say you had an early client?"

Aware of Dominike's six o'clock lesson in stock market investment, Beth grudgingly signed off the computer. Maybe getting out from under her parents' watchful eyes wouldn't be so bad. But her mother's assumption that she was ready for a permanent relationship with Mike was presumptuous.

Even with her mother's assurance that the house was secure, Beth physically rechecked the windows and doors. Her nightly ritual complete, she made her way upstairs. The counsellor had encouraged her diligence in checking the security precautions, assuring her that after a life-threatening scare, a little anxiety was normal.

Still Beth couldn't fall asleep. Mike's mention of marriage taunted her. She was not comfortable with the idea. Other people got married, not her. She loved Mike. She had ever since they met in the fall, but committing to a lifelong relationship was premature. How did she know she wasn't using marriage as a way to keep from being alone? What really terrified her was that since Richard had reappeared, feelings she thought she had resolved long ago were stirring.

CHAPTER 19

Mike's phone buzzed as he pulled into the parkade of his apartment building.

"Detective Ceretzke," a woman's voice asked.

Before Mike could confirm his identity, the woman continued breathlessly, "I'm Mrs. McPherson, the manager of Jennifer River's apartment building. A couple of people were here about half an hour ago. They were trying to hurt Jennifer but that young man of hers came along and we sent them packing. He told me not to call the police, he said they would do it, but no one has arrived and I'm worried about them coming back. Can you come over and talk to Jennifer? Find out what's going on."

Mike backed his vehicle out of the parking spot and onto the street. "I'll check it out. Mrs. McPherson what can you tell me about the assailants, did you recognize them?"

"They were Chinese or Filipino, or something like that. Black hair, dark clothes. The man had a knife, the woman a gun."

By the time Mike arrived at the apartment building, deep night had settled over the city. Pools of light gave the street an eerie air of half illumination, but in the area near the neighbouring ravine, the darkness remained unbroken.

Mrs. McPherson let him into the building and surged at full speed down the hall toward Jennifer's apartment.

"Took off running they did. I should have blasted them with my shotgun, just like my late husband always said, 'Protect your property. The more bad guys dead, the lower the crime rate.' He believed in capital punishment too, he did. Said it was the answer to all of society's woes. But I couldn't do it. He'll be turning in his grave. Of course, I wasn't really protecting myself was I? I'd never have hauled that old gun out if they hadn't been making such a fuss. Stuck my head out the door and heard all sorts of threats, so I figured that was the best way to go. Meet danger with a big weapon. I mean, it wasn't like I was in danger, just poor Jennifer and that young man of hers, but it was danger anyway, right? He's gone now. Took off right after those other two left."

"Was he chasing them?"

"I don't think so. He said he would look after Jennifer, then the next thing you know I see him heading off down the street on his bike. He's guilty of something, that's for certain."

"Can you describe the people you saw?"

"Black hair, dark eyes, high cheek bones. A man and a woman. I told you that on the phone, right? My son says I either forget that I told him something and repeat myself or think I told him and forget to say anything."

"You said they had weapons?"

"The man must have had the knife, but by the time I loaded my gun and got there, Lyle had hold of it and was trying to protect Jennifer from the girl with her little gun. A knife against a gun. Of course, her gun was a joke. Little peashooter-sized toy. My late husband would have laughed at such a weapon."

"What did the gun look like?"

"It was grey, a short little barrel. Not a derringer, bigger than that, but not as big as the guns the television police shows use. Somewhere in between, but closer to the derringer in size. Her being so small, a big gun would have knocked her over. She didn't hold it like they do on TV either. I don't know much about pistols, but if you held a shotgun in one hand like that, you'd end up shooting a hole in the ceiling."

"Can you identify them? We can arrange for you to look at some pictures."

"Sure can."

"Can you pick out the type of gun?"

"That's tougher, but I'll try."

"Was there anything else you noticed?"

"Well, they all knew each other. It wasn't one of them home invasions I hear about."

"Okay. You go back to your apartment and wait for the Ident unit to get here. I'll talk to Ms. Rivers."

"I'll make some coffee. If any of you want some, just come on over. I've got some chocolate chip cookies too. Baked them for my grandkids. They're supposed to visit this coming weekend, but I can . . . ." She closed the door on her words.

Mike ran his fingers through his hair then scrubbed his face with his hands. Someone had been watching over them. With a knife, pistol, and shotgun in the room, and in the hands of amateurs, it was a miracle no one was hurt.

He knocked and identified himself. At the answering murmur, he pushed the door open. Jennifer sat on the sofa with her foot propped on the coffee table. He moved a chair close to her. Mike detected watchful resignation rather than hysteria or panic in her eyes.

******

Jennifer had cringed when the detective called his name through the door but realized there was no avoiding this interview. She had known Mrs. McPherson would phone the police and was relieved Lyle was far away by now. Perhaps she could keep him out of it.

She remembered the cop who walked into her apartment looking concerned and official at the same time. He had seemed okay when he was with Lyle, but you could never tell with men. Why had he moved the chair so near to her, was it just a cop thing, or was he blocking her escape route? She looked at the closed apartment door and wondered if she could ask him to open it.

Jennifer stared at the patio doors. Could she move fast enough to escape through them? Lyle had closed and locked them, but then he was so naïve that he still believed strangers were the biggest threat.

Jennifer studied the detective. His fingers were long, his hands broad. He hitched his trouser legs and then smoothed them as he sat on the wooden chair. He reached into his inside jacket pocket and pulled out a notebook with a pen clipped to one edge.

He frowned as he flipped to an empty page, then leaned forward. Jennifer pushed away from him, leaning back into the cushions lining the sofa. The creases highlighting his eyes deepened as he stared at her. She saw him analyzing her, taking in every detail of her helplessness. She couldn't escape.

"Just some questions, Jenny. What happened here tonight?"

"It's Jennifer. Don't ever call me Jenny."

"Okay, Jennifer. What happened?"

"Didn't she tell you?" Jennifer motioned toward Mrs. McPherson's apartment. "She must have called you."

"I'd like you to tell me."

How much could she tell him? She couldn't say Lyle was involved in a crime ring. She owed him silence for saving her life. Cara would have shot her dead with that huge gun. Jennifer shivered at the memory of the evil looking weapon.

"Did you know the intruders?"

She nodded and forced her fingers to relax their grip on her thigh. "Cara Poiter works on the River Belle. The man is her brother."

"Mrs. McPherson said they were Chinese."

"No. Their mother is Vietnamese, their father was French."

The detective nodded and wrote in his book. Then he asked the question that she didn't know how to answer. "Why were they trying to hurt you?"

She shrugged. The police wouldn't help anyway. They never stopped people from hurting you. You couldn't even trust that they wouldn't hurt you themselves.

"Mrs. McPherson said the woman had a gun."

The detective leaned toward her. His eyes pierced her soul. The room closed in around her. Jennifer shifted on the sofa, trying to move away from him.

"Can you describe the gun," he asked, looking up from his notebook.

Why wasn't he angry at being hauled over here in the middle of the night? What did he want from her?

"Was it a small gun?"

Jennifer shook her head, then watched his reaction carefully. Did he want her to say it was a small gun? Was that important? She shook her head again, refusing to lie to please him. "It looked huge and deadly when she pointed it at me."

He nodded again. Then he said, "I understand Lyle was with you."

She had to force Lyle to leave. He wasn't like other men who ran away when they felt trapped. She would protect him, like he'd protected her. "Lyle was brave, shielding me like that. He shouldn't have done it though. If she had killed me it would be over."

"What would be over, Jennifer?"

She was quiet for a long minute, then turned her head to look out the dark window, but the black night had turned the glass into a mirror that reflected the room's interior.

In the reflection, she saw him resting his forearms on his legs, a predator waiting for her to make a mistake. Waiting for her to give him a reason to hurt her. Charlie used to do that too. When her mother was out of the house, he would sit and watch her and Eric. Sometimes it was all right and he went away, alone. Other times he took one of them into the back room.

The detective spoke into the silence that filled the room.

"Let's talk about why Cara threatened you. Did it concern what happened on the boat?"

She ran her finger across the rough surface of her cast. It was solid and she could put almost all of her weight on her ankle, but could she move fast enough to escape after she hit him?

"Jennifer, you were scheduled to work Saturday night. You signed in but never signed out. Is that correct?"

She stared at the black of night and the reflection of the room and the man. His voice was pleasing, but he wanted answers. What answers did he want? She had already told him all she wanted to reveal about Saturday. Maybe he would go away if she told him again.

Her words broke into the stifling silence. "I felt sick. The boat was leaving so I got off and biked home."

"What time was that, Jennifer?"

"Just before the boat left the dock."

She shifted her leg on the pillows. Why was he looking at her like that? Men never believed you. Well, maybe not all men. Now, she knew she could trust Lyle, though if he hadn't called the cops when she was in the hospital this wouldn't be happening.

"No one remembers seeing you leave."

"Why would they? I haven't worked on the boat for long and I'm just a hostess. No one would remember me."

"You're a very attractive woman. I'm sure lots of people noticed you."

Jennifer felt the blackness engulf her. Men were all alike. She used her good hand to pull herself forward and applied some weight to her sprained ankle. She struggled to stand, using the crutch as a lever, but gave up in frustration. She was at his mercy.

"Let's go a little further into your evening. After you left the boat, what did you do?"

"I started home but I felt sick, like I said, and I got dizzy and the bike skidded and I fell. I woke up in the hospital."

"No one saw you on the trail. Surely someone would have seen you lying near a trail in the hours before sunset."

"That trail isn't busy. Sometimes it's so quiet it's scary."

"Do you always take such a quiet path home?"

"No, mostly I use the main bike paths."

"The path you used was lonely and scary, but still you took it on a night when you weren't feeling well?"

"It's a shortcut and I was sick."

"You parked your bike near the shelter, right?"

"Yes."

"But you usually parked it in the shed by the parking lot?"

"Not always."

"Someone broke into that shed Saturday night."

"I was lucky I didn't put it in there then, wasn't I?"

"You must have a key to the shed. Where is it?"

Jennifer poured water into the glass sitting on her table. The key was in the river. Or was it? Had he found the key? Was he guessing? What would he do to her if he discovered her lie?

"I lost it Friday, that's why I didn't put my bike in the shed."

"Why didn't you tell me that earlier?"

A loud knock on the apartment door gave her time to think of a reply. It opened to admit another cop. This one was younger and shorter. He seemed harmless, not like the first one who was so big he crowded her apartment.

The detective asking the questions said, "Jennifer, Detective Collins is going to sit in for a few minutes. He wants to know about the rest of the crew, particularly Cara."

It was better with two of them present. Charlie had never hurt them when another adult was around.

"Jennifer, Richard Tanner said he received a tip about crimes being committed on the boat. He says someone phoned him, wanting to meet him during the dinner cruise. Do you know anything about that phone call? Did you know that someone on board was stealing credit card numbers and key codes?" Detective Collins used her full name; she liked that. Her mother and all her mother's friends had called her Jenny. She had outgrown that helpless little girl name.

"What's a key code," she asked.

"The alphanumeric code that's engraved on some keys. With those codes a locksmith can make a duplicate."

"I didn't know that. Is that what was happening on the Belle?"

"That's what Richard Tanner believes."

"Why are you asking me?"

"I could tell you that we're asking all the crew members, but that wouldn't be true. Right now, we're just asking you because Mr. Tanner looked over the passenger list and crew manifest and recognized your name. He said you might have worked at the television station as an office temp."

Jennifer smiled at the thought of that job. It had been the turning point in her life. Most of the temp jobs she took were in offices where she spent days photocopying and doing other mundane tasks. At the television station, she had been thrown into the fray that very first morning, just a list of names and extension numbers and then she was on her own. It had been exhilarating. The people at the station accepted her on the merit of her work. They were casual when they asked her to run errands or do jobs, and as she earned their respect the requests increased in complexity. Seeing how they worked convinced her that becoming a broadcaster was a worthy goal. Not that she wanted to be on television, but doing background research was fun and you never knew where it might lead.

Of all the reporters, Richard Tanner had been the one she most admired, but he had rarely talked to her except to ask her to do work for him. Jennifer savoured the words of encouragement he'd offered when she approached him asking what education she would need to become a reporter.

"He remembered? I didn't think he would remember me."

"Were you the one who phoned him?"

"Mr. Tanner really remembered me?" She waited for the officer's nod.

"Why wouldn't he remember you?"

"I was just the temporary receptionist. Mr. Tanner hardly spoke to me."

The officers looked at each other. Their stupid grins told her all she needed to know. She couldn't trust either of them. Better to make them leave while she could. She traced a cloverleaf on the sofa cushion with her index finger, around and around, faster and faster.

"Jennifer."

The older one was talking again.

"Did you ask Richard Tanner to meet you on board the River Belle?"

"It was a mistake. I made a mistake. That's all."

"So you phoned because of something you thought was happening, then found out you were mistaken?" The young one asked.

"That's what I said."

"What did you think was happening?"

Now it was the older one again. She turned her gaze toward him.

Why did they both keep talking? How could she watch them both? How could she know what they wanted her to say?

The young detective asked, "You've only been with the riverboat a short time, did some of their procedures confuse you?"

She shook her head.

"We spoke to the Captain. He said you were being promoted so that you could work in the office with Cara. I assume that means he thinks highly of your work. It must also mean you were learning the procedures for handling client information and the daily receipts. Was it something about those procedures that made you call?"

She looked at the men leaning toward her. Their eyes were bright like predator eyes. She had to stop their questions. Would it be faster to lie or tell the truth? Maybe she needed a lawyer? No, that would drag it out.

What she said would have to be based on the truth because she didn't have the energy to fabricate a detailed story.

"I thought I saw Cara Poiter give a man some registration forms, but it was a mistake," she said in one quick exhalation of words.

"She gave them to someone? Was it her brother, the man who was here tonight?"

"Those forms have lots of information on them, addresses, credit card numbers and stuff. I'm just starting to learn the procedures on handling them. I read somewhere about credit card thieves and jumped to the wrong conclusion."

"Did she give the man keys, too?"

"No, no keys. Just a stack of paper that she was photocopying. It was probably nothing."

The older officer started speaking. She looked toward him.

"Passengers have had their cars stolen, houses broken into, and their credit cards used fraudulently, so we believe Cara did pass on some information."

Jennifer pushed her long, straight hair from her eyes. "Maybe it's a coincidence?" Damn, her voice was too tentative. She had to be forceful if they were going to believe her.

"Jennifer, you saw something you thought was important and

you tried to do the right thing," the younger one said. "I'm sorry you didn't come to us or go to the captain of the boat with the information. We would have investigated. But at least, you alerted Richard Tanner."

She held her anger close. They didn't believe her story. The young detective was good at pretending to believe her, especially when he put lots of sincerity into his voice. The older one just nodded his head, as if he agreed with everything. They did not believe a word she said.

She knew the signs, the blank smile, the stupid nodding, the little looks at each other. Her mother hadn't believed her either, not until Charlie lived with them for months.

"I'm sorry I wasted Mr. Tanner's time, but as I said I made a mistake."

"Jennifer, why didn't you talk to Richard Tanner before you left the boat?"

A shudder of fear shook her. They had to go away. "You have to go now. I don't want you in my apartment anymore. Mrs. McPherson shouldn't have called you."

"How is Lyle involved in this?"

"He's not. He just came by to make sure I was all right and got caught up in Cara's scheme to hurt me. He's not involved."

"Why did he leave? He should have stayed until we arrived."

"Why? We didn't call you. Mrs. McPherson did."

"But they were trying to kill you."

"They didn't say they were going to kill me. They just wanted me to go with them."

"Where do you think they were going to take you?"

"I don't know."

"If you make a statement, it will be too late to stop you from talking about their scam so there won't be any reason for them to hurt you. If you don't help us, they might go unpunished. More people will have their homes robbed and their cars stolen. You can help stop the harm they're causing."

Jennifer raised her good hand to her face. Her head hurt. Why didn't they just leave her alone? She knew people shouldn't be allowed to hurt others, but they always did and they always would. They hurt you if you were too little to defend yourself, or if you were different from them, or if they detected a weakness. Weakness was what drew the worst of them, the ones who knew best how to hurt you to death. Sometimes the hurt that didn't show killed people. Like Eric.

Now Lyle was in danger because he'd tried to protect her. If Cara and her brother stayed free, they would try to shut him up. She couldn't let that happen. She wouldn't be like her mother. She wouldn't let the hurting continue. Maybe these officers would stop Cara. Maybe they would make that nightmare disappear, even if they couldn't stop the other dream, the one that had returned to haunt her.

She didn't have to tell them about Lyle.

"They do have a scam going and I did phone Richard Tanner," she said.

The detectives sat back, notebooks in hand. The younger one placed a tape recorder on the coffee table.

******

Mike felt the intensity of Evan's questioning stare, but kept his concentration on his notebook.

"What has her so scared," Evan asked.

They had left her in her apartment, visibly relieved at their departure and looking unhappy with Mrs. McPherson's guardianship. She'd been more upset yet when Mike assured her an officer would be posted outside the building until Cara was in custody.

"She is scared, isn't she. The doctor mentioned that, too. Still, having your life threatened is scary. Beth is still dealing with it."

"No, I think it goes deeper."

Mike thought back over the interview. Something nagged at him, something about the look in her eyes. The way she had huddled in the corner of the sofa hugging herself and pulling her uninjured leg under her buttocks. Was she always that closed to scrutiny? Did she deny access to anyone seeking more than the most casual of relationships?

Mike stared at the notes he had made. He was missing something. He remembered seeing that kind of body language before, but where? Did it matter?

Mike pushed the thought away. He would deal with it later. "We have to find Cara and her brother. I'll feel better knowing those two are in a good old-fashioned jail cell."

"Why do you think she was so scared," Evan asked again, refusing to let the topic die.

"It was partially the attack. However, it was interesting that she seemed unconcerned for herself and so determined that we not discuss Lyle. What do you think she's protecting him from?"

"He could be involved with Cara. That would give him a reason to run."

"Or maybe she suspects he went after that pair himself. If that's the case, we better pick them up before he gets close."

"Do you think Cara Poiter was responsible for Chuck's death? Maybe he learned what they were up to?"

Mike shook his head. "We couldn't find hard evidence when we were looking for it, so I doubt Chuck stumbled onto some clue, especially if he stayed on the deck all night."

"They might be more cautious now."

"With Tanner on board investigating, they would have been careful then."

Mike flipped his notebook closed and slid it into his jacket pocket. Something nagged him about her body language and he knew it was important. Perhaps Evan could help decipher it. "Something about Ms. Rivers is familiar. Did you pick up on anything when you ran her background check?"

Evan slowed his pace, then pulled on his upper lip. "We didn't run a check on her because she wasn't on the boat at the time of the murder."

Mike stopped walking and stared at him. Evan rarely made elementary mistakes.

"I'll set it in motion," Evan mumbled.

CHAPTER 20

Light from the street lamp illuminated the gleaming brass of the night latch. Cara regretted her delay in replacing it with a secure deadbolt. With both Lap and herself gone, their family would need more security. A high wooden fence surrounded the backyard and Cara reminded herself to leave a note telling her younger brother Chim, to paint it this summer.

She rested her head against the door, absorbing the memories that filled her home. How would her family manage? How many months would they have to stay away to be certain the police search was ended?

Her brother and sisters would need to work very hard to earn scholarships. Am would excel, as would Thuy, but Chim would have a very hard time because studying did not come easily to him.

She turned to survey the dark kitchen and the table where she had often supervised her siblings while completing her homework. Perhaps Jennifer had not called the police? Perhaps even now they were safe and could continue living here amongst their friends and family. At least their mother would have the comfort of being surrounded by familiar things after they left.

A darker shadow moved in the doorway leading to the stairs and the second floor of the small house. Cara caught a whiff of her mother's lavender talcum powder.

"Are you planning to run off?"

"We tried not to wake you."

"I have expected Lap to leave, but not you Cara."

Lap entered the room from the basement carrying his bulging rucksack over one shoulder. "I have no choice but to run. The police will lock me up if I don't."

"That is an excuse. You are like your father and have found the responsibilities you shouldered these past years uncomfortably heavy."

"Father died, he had no choice about leaving."

She pulled a chair away from the table and sat, resting her chin in her hand. "That was a story for children. He did not die when he travelled to his home in France, except in my heart. Your father left us on a pretext then had his friend write that lie that he had succumbed to a heart attack. The detective I engaged sent me pictures of him and his new family."

"Oh, no Mama, this cannot be true," Cara said, thinking back over the years she had spent worshipping her father's memory. He had been gone for more than six years now. She had struggled to accept his loss and to fill the void created by his absence. She had blamed her mother for allowing him to travel so far away, for letting him die alone and be buried where they could not visit.

She had also censored her mother for abruptly ending her grieving and for rarely speaking his name. However, if he had run away from them she could understand her mother's behaviour.

Lap dropped his bag onto the floor and leaned against the counter. When he spoke, his voice mixed disbelief and venom. "You're lying. How could you know he's alive? Why would you check? When did you find out?"

"Long ago, when the investments we had made were cashed and the government refused to give me a widow's pension."

"You never told us. You should have told us."

"It was my wish that you not think harshly of him. Now however, it is something you need to know so you will understand and not become a coward like your father."

Cara flinched. How could her mother think so poorly of them? Had she discovered their method of adding to the family's income?

"Come on, Cara. Don't listen to her. She's lying to make us stay and we've got to get out of here before the cops come."

The floor squeaked as Lap shifted his weight from foot to foot, impatient to run. Cara fingered the webbed strap of her back pack, it was ready for her to pick up and walk out the door, but she knew with a sudden certainty that the women in her family did not run from trouble, regardless of their men's actions.

Cara didn't pause to question the truth of her mother's words. Deep in her unconscious mind, she had questioned many details of her father's death. Her mother's words made sense of so much. Cara felt an ice damn melt in the pit of her stomach as stray details grew and merged.

The memory of the years she had believed her mother to be uncaring flowed away as the truth answered questions Cara had longed to ask. She now understood the sacrifices her mother had made to keep them fed and clothed. She saw how the discipline, so strictly enforced, had kept their minds active and their bodies drug free. How much scorn her mother must have accepted to let them continue believing in a father who had cowardly forsaken his family?

Perhaps she and Lap were also cowards for running from the results of their actions?

"No," Cara said.

"What do you mean, no?" Lap demanded. "Are you going to let her make you feel guilty enough to stay? Do you want to be thrown in jail? Think of the disgrace you will bring to the family."

"We've already caused the disgrace. I don't want to lose Mother's respect as well. You go run and hide, but I will stay and take whatever punishment is required. Then I will return home and help Mother raise our sisters."

"With a criminal record you'll never get a decent job."

"And being on the run, you will?"

"Have it your way, but I'm out of here."

Cara listened to the muffled rustle of his backpack as he hefted its weight.

"Give me your gun. I'll need it more than you."

"I dropped it down the sewer outside Jennifer's apartment. I was crazy to have taken it."

"You didn't have to follow me; I would have handled the situation."

"Oh, so you were just playing with Lyle when I walked in? I don't think so."

"Well, you wouldn't be in trouble now if you'd stayed out of it."

"If Jennifer told the reporter about our operation, we would still have trouble."

"She doesn't know anything so keep your mouth shut and let them try proving what was going on," Lap said. "Worry more that they'll find out what really happened to Mr. Hatfield."

"He had a car accident. People who drive in treacherous conditions have accidents."

"If the cops trace the link to Cousin Anna, just remember he was cremated and they can't prove anything."

"What do you mean about him? Did you do something to him?"

"All they've got is the thing tonight and I'll get my friends to persuade Jennifer not to testify."

"Then why run away," she asked.

Cara felt her brother's embarrassment. Was he so frightened of going to jail? Then a more terrifying thought entered her mind. Was their mother right? Did he want to run away from his responsibilities? She felt his hand squeeze her shoulder briefly.

The latch clicked softly as he opened the door. The hum of traffic, a baby's cry, and the ringing of a telephone drifted into the dark kitchen. Cara waited until the door closed once more.

Darkness filled the room. Perhaps she was foolish to stay, but Cara couldn't abandon her mother. She could handle the public shame but not her mother's scorn.

She sat across from her mother and reached for her hand. When would the police come for her? Perhaps she should turn herself in? Still, if Jennifer had not reported them that would be foolish. But of course that old woman would.

Cara heard a muffled sob coming from her mother. The words that followed it were harsh.

"He is gone. I raised a coward, just like his father. I am proud that you chose not to run but to face your troubles."

Cara knew what she was doing was right and squeezed her mother's hand. A tiny clatter came through the window. "Someone is in the backyard."

Cara pushed the wooden chair away from the table. Stepping with care, hoping the creaking joists under the cracked linoleum would not betray her location, she tiptoed to the back door and slid the night latch into place with a quiet click. Then she turned toward the living room and glided across the polished hardwood to the front window. Cara pushed the curtain open far enough to peer into the night. Everything was still. Then she shifted to look south, toward 107 Avenue where she caught the pulse of an emergency light.

A distant shadow blocked her view of the hypnotic beam, then as it entered the pool of light beneath a street lamp it separated into several dark figures. Their neighbours were being rushed down the street. Each adult carried a child and police officers hurried the grandparents along behind. Cara let the curtain drop and turned to her mother.

"They have come for me. I will do whatever I can to return to you quickly."

Her mother's arms encircled Cara's shoulders and during the feather-like touch of their cheeks, Cara felt her mother's tears.

"I will call a lawyer. You are doing what is right."

The buzz of the telephone broke into the darkness, startling the women apart.

Cara cleared her throat as she picked up the receiver and said, "Hello."

"Cara Poiter?"

"Yes."

"Detective Ceretzke, Edmonton Police Service, here. Throw the gun out, then exit the house with your hands visible."

"I threw the gun away."

The slight pause was followed by his repeated request for her to exit the house.

"You didn't have to make such a big deal out of this. Why did you make the neighbours leave, now they'll all know what happened."

"Standard procedure when firearms are involved, Cara. We can't risk innocent lives."

"How many people did you tell?"

"We cleared the houses near yours. Cara, it's time you came out of the house."

"You won't hurt my family?"

"We don't want anyone getting hurt."

"All right, I'm coming out now."

She replaced the receiver, walked to the front door, and unfastened the night latch. She stood for a moment behind the metal peacock that decorated the screen door, looking into the still night. The street was empty of people and cars.

She reached for the door handle and with one hand held high, she pushed the screen door open. As she stepped outside someone grabbed her arm and pulled her off the porch and onto her stomach on their small patch of grass. The grass was decorated with dew and she felt moisture soak into her cotton blouse.

Cara lay still for a long time, suffering the hands that touched her body. She forced herself not to flinch at the pull in her shoulder muscles when her arms were forced behind her, or at the pinch of the handcuffs on her wrists.

She listened to the police questioning her mother who seemed to have forgotten that she spoke English fluently. Boots thundered into the house, tracking across the polished hardwood. Cara squeezed her eyes tight as the porch light flared to life. Opening them again, she saw light shining behind the curtains of the upstairs bedrooms. Her brother and sisters were awake.

"All right, Cara, you can stand up."

She recognized Detective Ceretzke's voice. He bent down and with a hand on her elbow helped her to her feet.

When she looked into his face, he asked, "Where's the gun?"

"Down the sewer in front of Jennifer's apartment."

The detective nodded at an officer, who turned and strode toward a police vehicle.

"You admit you threatened Jennifer Rivers and Lyle Lamont?"

"Would it help if I denied it?"

Her mother called out, "Cara, don't talk to them until I get you a lawyer."

Though the words were probably incomprehensible to him, the detective seemed to catch the meaning because he shrugged and led her toward a police car. From the car window, she watched people standing behind barricades, staring at her as the car drove by.

A news crew tried photographing her through the closed car window. She turned her face away. Where had all the people come from? The police cars that blocked the traffic at 107th Avenue backed out of their way.

"So many policemen just to capture me. If you had knocked on the door, I would have gone quietly."

"We can't count on that."

"You haven't asked yet about Lap."

"Your brother was arrested trying to escape from your yard."

"What happens now?"

"You tell me how you assaulted Jennifer Rivers, how you stole from the passengers of the River Belle, and name the others involved. You are then processed into the system and the Crown Prosecutor takes over."

CHAPTER 21

The alarm jolted Beth awake at five o'clock. Her first appointment was scheduled for six so she took time for a quick series of stretches, a shower, and a breakfast of a bagel, orange juice, and coffee. Since her parents' return from their winter in the south, Beth had changed her more strenuous workout and run until ten o'clock, so her mother would accompany her.

Somehow, her father had managed to restrict his exertion to an occasional stroll through the neighbourhood. And during those walks, he spent more time admiring gardens than increasing his heart rate.

Beth checked her watch and saw she still had fifteen minutes until Dominike's session. She set her timer for ten minutes, then signed onto the Internet to cull a few more messages. Magpie jumped onto the computer desk and with a loud cry protested this use of time that Beth would ordinarily have lavished on him. Splatter was still curled at the foot of her parent's bed. Never an early riser, she now bed-hopped until the last warm body had risen.

With one hand on the cat's shiny, black coat and the other on the mouse scrolling through messages, Beth quickly trashed most as having no value to her search. Then the words 'little league' caught her attention, making her reread a rambling note from someone using the pseudonym 'Newfoundlander'.

'Newfoundlander' had been on a baseball team where the coach had singled out boys and promised them a fabulous future in modelling. He then took them to his photo studio and asked them to pose in the nude. The message ended without providing other details.

Beth typed a reply asking for more information. Could the coach have been Chuck Albright? Did the caller know where the coach was now? When had this happened? She attached Chuck's picture to her message and sent it speeding through the network. Then she printed out the letter.

Her alarm beeped. Still lots more replies to read, but work came first.

Just over an hour later, her lesson completed, she phoned Richard. It was after seven and she was confident he would be awake. He was, but barely. Newfoundlander's message woke him up.

"I'll be right over to collect it."

Beth remembered Jim's reaction to Richard's presence and hedged. "I'll E-mail it to you instead."

"Computers are the spawn of the devil. If you use them more than necessary they steal your soul and rot your brain. Besides I know people who know computers so I will never need to own one."

"Then I'll fax the note to the station."

"No!" he said, too quickly for Beth's liking. She stroked Magpie's head. What was Richard up to now?

"Meet me for lunch, maybe by then you will have his reply."

"By then I'll have read more of these messages and maybe have some answers."

"You haven't told Mikey about doing this, have you?"

"Don't call him that."

"Well, have you?"

"No. It hasn't come up in our conversation." She perused another message, then discarded it. She knew she should have spoken with Mike about her collaboration with Richard. She wasn't actually hiding anything from him. Not really.

"Good. Be a pal and keep quiet about it. At least until we get real results."

Beth pushed Magpie to the floor and phone in one hand and empty mug in the other, went in search of the fresh coffee she smelled brewing. What was Richard hiding? She'd heard that scheming tone in his voice before. It usually led to trouble.

"Why hasn't he moved in with you yet," Richard asked, his tone of voice close to a taunt. "Do your parents object or are you waiting for my return?"

"Don't push your luck Richard," she said as she cut off the call.

******

The early morning sun streamed through Mike's window rousing him from a disturbed rest. He reached for his phone and punched Beth's number. Sometime in the night, he had remembered why Jennifer was so familiar and he wanted to ask Beth to help him check his hunch out.

Her welcome seemed strained and she sounded embarrassed when she explained that she couldn't see him until her evening shift was over. Her reason bothered him more than it should. Why should he care that she was meeting Tanner for lunch? Mike prided himself on not being the jealous type.

His gloom deepened when he arrived at the station and surveyed the piles of work remaining for his group to plod through. The sense of urgency that usually surrounded a murder investigation didn't exist with Chuck's death. The guys were doing a job they didn't enjoy. They were digging through filth to track down someone who had permanently removed a criminal from the city.

The first thing Mike had planned for the morning was interrogating Cara, hoping to find proof that she and her brother were involved in Chuck's death. It made sense and would tie up loose ends.

Last night Lap had confessed to threatening Jennifer but denied being part of any theft ring on the riverboat. Cara had flatly refused to talk to them until her lawyer arrived. Instead, she went to her cell neither confirming, nor denying the charges.

Mike was working on his strategy for the interrogation when his phone rang. Cara was anxious to speak with him and the crown prosecutor. With a shrug, Mike replaced the phone and trudged to the interview room where the group waited.

Cara's lawyer, a burly oriental man, sat at her side. He spoke first. "We want to deal, gentlemen."

Mike looked from one closed face to the other. They thought they had something to trade, but what?

"If my client helps you find Chuck Albright's murderer, what's in it for her?"

"What does she know about it?"

"She would have to be guaranteed protection. The person she can tell you about is in a position to harm her."

"We'll protect her. Now, what's your information?"

At her lawyer's tiny nod, Cara spoke for the first time. "What would it be worth to know the name of the man who followed Mr. Albright onto the River Belle?"

Mike held his breath. It might be worth a lot, but how little could they offer to obtain the name?

"You told me you didn't know him. What changed that or were you lying?"

"It was no lie, but since Sunday I have learned who he is."

"Surely learning his name is worth letting my client go free. After all no one was injured in the misunderstanding that occurred last evening."

"It was hardly a misunderstanding."

"But, Detective, the woman you claim was in danger has told me that she will not lay charges."

"Her landlady won't be so easily intimidated."

"I believe the landlady entered the apartment uninvited and prevented my client from leaving by threatening to shoot her. Perhaps Miss Poiter should be the one who is laying charges?"

Mike looked sideways at the prosecutor. It was his call.

"Give us the name. If it proves helpful, your client gets her charges reduced."

"Clear her on all counts and you have a deal."

"If the name leads to a conviction."

"No. We just supply the name. We don't guarantee results that depend on the criminal justice system working correctly."

The prosecutor stood and motioned to Mike.

"We'll discuss your offer."

When the door closed behind them, Mike said, "We're checking the backgrounds of staff and passengers for possible links to Chuck, but right now we have nothing concrete. This guy's identity might open a fruitful line of questioning."

"Your case against the girl?"

"Mrs. McPherson will testify to what she saw in the apartment. But, Jennifer doesn't know much about their operation and if the lawyer is right and she won't testify about last night, we have nothing." Mike ran his fingers through his hair, stifling a yawn and fighting the fatigue clouding his mind.

"So we won't have the victim screaming if we make a deal?"

Cara and her lawyer stopped whispering as they re-entered the room. At the prosecutor's nod, her lawyer said, "Tell them."

"I saw his picture in the paper. They were interviewing him about solving the murders of those kids. The caption said his name was Detective Carswell."

******

Mike combed his fingers through his hair, then bit his lip as he walked into Sam's office. Being the bearer of bad news was an unsavoury task he would rather shift to someone else.

"Any more on your mysterious passengers," Sam asked while rearranging the files on her desk.

"The woman, Linda Olsson, is our missing crewmember's mother. The crewmember's name is Jennifer Rivers and she's the person who tipped Tanner. We haven't confirmed whether the mother is still in the city or if she returned to her home in Saskatchewan."

"And?"

"We apprehended Cara and Lap Poiter early this morning on charges of assaulting Jennifer. He confessed, but we just made a deal to drop the charges against Cara in exchange for the name of the man who followed Chuck onto the boat. She identified him as Norman Carswell."

Sam stopped shuffling files and looked at him. Her expression shifted into neutral. "Do you believe her?"

Mike felt Sam studying him as she awaited his answer. He asked her the question he'd been asking himself. "Why would she lie?"

Sam leaned back and turned her chair to face the sunshine streaming through her office window.

"Why was he on the boat," she asked.

When Mike didn't reply, she continued speaking in a slow, controlled tone. "Norman handed me his request for retirement yesterday said he'd been hanging around until the child murder cases were solved. He seemed delighted with the solution, which surprised me because I thought he would be upset that you were the one who uncovered the evidence."

"He's right, how we solved the case is irrelevant, though I still hope to discover Chuck's motive. Why those kids? Why only one per year?"

"I talked to the profiler about that," Sam replied. "They're working on it." Her voice became confidential. "Mike, find out where Norman was Saturday evening."

"So you believe her?"

One side of her mouth rose along with her shoulder.

"When I asked why he was out of the office Saturday, he said he was following a lead in the industrial park. He showed me an old Crime Stopper's tip from the second murder. It was a report about suspicious activity in a building in the area and he claimed he just wanted to check if anyone had been around lately."

"It could be legitimate."

"Or, it could be a lie."

"You want to know if he was on the River Belle?"

Sam raised both eyebrows and pursed her lips, but said nothing.

"After all these years you think he figured out that Chuck was the killer and what, acted as judge, jury, and executioner? That's crazy."

"You didn't see his eyes when he talked about finally being able to retire knowing the killer was punished and those kids were at rest." She straightened her chair and shuffled the pile of papers on her desktop, signaling the end of the interview. "Besides, you have to justify the deal you made with Miss Poiter."

******

Beth was late. Richard ordered another drink and flirted with the waitress. This was going to be his day.

Evan Collins had phoned to thank him for mentioning Jennifer Rivers and to tell him that she had admitted being the tipster. It was fortunate that he had passed that crew list onto the personnel office because he hadn't recognized her name. Who could expect him to remember the name of someone who had covered the reception desk for less than a month?

Of course, if she had been his type there might have been a chance of him remembering her. Though if he had known she was moving in criminal circles, he would have taken the time to cultivate her. He vaguely remembered her talking to him about becoming a researcher and how she had some story idea for the anniversary of the kid killings.

He shrugged and turned his attention back to the busty waitress who suggested he might like an appetizer while waiting. Richard grinned. Was she insinuating a different kind of appetizer? One price of his fame was that pretty women and even not-so-pretty women, sought him out.

He wouldn't respond now though because Beth would be along soon. Anticipating her findings gave him lots to think about, like the respect he would earn if the story developed into the big splash he thought it might and the awards he could win, and the job offers that would overwhelm him.

A couple of minutes later he spotted Beth following the manager through the dimly lit restaurant.

"Well, did you get an answer," he asked as the manager pulled out her chair and placed a menu in front of her.

"Have you ordered," Beth asked.

"Not yet. Do you want a drink," he asked as the waitress approached.

When she refused, he turned his most lecherous smile on the waitress and asked her to return in a few minutes for their orders.

"I have a staff meeting at the library in an hour."

"You're the one who's late. For good reason, I hope."

She seemed unaware of the worshipful look on the waitress' face. Why couldn't she be just a bit jealous?

"I waited until the last minute and was printing off relevant messages when our boy 'Newfoundlander' replied."

She handed him a sheaf of paper, then picked up her menu. "Now can I order? I haven't eaten since five-thirty and the French onion soup here is the best on the continent."

"Damn. Beth, the way you eat you should be the size of a horse."

"Such flattery. You know I exercise every day so that I can eat what I want."

"And I miss watching you do both. Okay," he added as she sent him a frozen look. "We will keep this lunch strictly business. Bottom line, did your guy recognize Chuck?"

"He knew him as Charles Altman who lived in St. John's, Newfoundland for at least three years. That was between nine and twelve years ago. The kid was a target for Chuck's abuse while he was on the baseball team but he didn't report the assault on himself. It wasn't until two years later when he saw Chuck working on his younger brother that he told his parents what was happening. Soon afterward, Chuck vanished from town. They never laid charges and as far as the kid knows it never became public knowledge that a problem existed with Coach Altman."

"Will he confirm this information?"

"He won't even give me his name, so you might not want to believe him."

"I believe him but I need confirmation before I can put it on the air. Just think of it, our Chuck, a countrywide abuser! Did anyone else answer?"

Beth gestured to the pile of papers she'd placed near his plate.

"Lots of answers, most are cranks, but the ones I brought with me have merit. I've sent a copy of Chuck's photo to each of them with a request for more details."

She skimmed the menu, then put it back on the table saying, "I don't think I'm hungry after all."

CHAPTER 22

Mike had returned to the station after tracking the cook to her second job and was now faced with giving Super Sam bad news. "The cook at the snack bar identified Norman from a photo array. Damn it, what do we do now?"

Sam's reply held a little-used note of authority. "We ask him why he was on the boat and why he didn't tell me he was there when I asked."

"I realize you and he don't get along, but you can't think he went that far. "

"I'll just ask him to come in and clear this up."

Mike looked out the window at a column of clouds advancing across the mirrored surface of a distant tower. He didn't want to be here, but his uneasy silence was his only way to protest her suspicions. Still, what the hell had Norman been doing on the boat Saturday night?

The greying detective opened the door and after a quick look that enveloped the others, shut it. "What's the disaster," he asked.

Sam made a steeple of her fingers then clasped them tightly. Her gaze moved across Norman's creased face a laser-width at a time. "Tell me about Saturday."

"We've had this conversation before."

Mike watched the long-time adversaries try to out-stare and out-macho each other. After a minute of tense silence, Sam slammed her hand on the top of her desk. "Cut the games. Norman, why were you on that boat? And, for God's sake, why didn't you say anything?"

Norman Carswell turned toward Mike, then looked back to their superior officer. "I had a hunch about the assailant. We had checked out all the cops so often that I couldn't see how any of them could be under suspicion. Still, the same type of person kept coming to mind. I figured him to be someone in authority, a person in uniform, or someone the kids knew. Then, while I was watching the news broadcast it dawned on me that reporters were always hanging around and could overhear details that they shouldn't. Like where we were putting surveillance. Watching Tanner made me think that a kid might go with him because he was a celebrity, someone they recognized, someone with authority, someone who could promise them fame.

"I was following Tanner, not his cameraman. When I heard them arguing about Tanner doing a story exposing abusers, I realized he couldn't be my man so I got off the boat at the Fort Edmonton landing. When you told me about Albright drowning, I didn't connect the events. To me it was just a dead-end hunch."

"Can you prove you left the boat?"

"I took a cab back to the main parking lot." He pulled his wallet from his back pocket. After a brief search, he retrieved the receipt.

Sam studied it closely. "Why did you lie to me?"

He shrugged. "To keep in practice?"

"So you left the boat about two hours before he was killed. You should have told us, we gave Cara Poiter a walk for your name."

"You could have told me you were investigating me." He turned on one foot and wrenched open the office door. "I'll be glad to retire and escape this bureaucratic quicksand."

✶✶✶✶✶✶

Beth looked at Mike in disbelief, but he took her hands and held them firmly in his own.

"Jennifer is insecure and afraid. I've seen the symptoms before, especially the way she seems to fade into the background."

"I'm not a social worker or a psychiatrist."

"All I want you to do is talk to her, nothing official or scary, just a casual conversation. See if you can get her to talk to you about what happened to her."

Beth took a deep breath, enjoying the taste of gently scented air and looked down the long incline. The slope was a ski hill in the winter, gliding toward an array of four glass pyramids that housed the city's conservatory. City workers had recently planted the flowerbeds dotting the landscape and they held a faint promise of the lush beauty soon to dominate the view.

Black clouds hovered on the horizon, threatening much needed rain. A week remained until the end of May when the hazard of a late frost or snowstorm would be gone, until late August—unless nature decided to play a nasty joke on people who complacently planted their flowers before the first full moon in June. Tonight, no hint of frost lingered on the evening air.

"Why do you think she was abused," Beth asked as she turned away from the view and directed her attention toward Mike.

"She reminds me of a ten-year-old I once taught. A tiny, skinny little girl with big eyes, who jumped every time someone moved quickly and who made herself disappear if you looked at her."

"She'd been abused?"

"That's what she told me. She had attacked a boy in the class because he was teasing her. Small as she was, she'd gone after him with a baseball bat. After my lecture on proper behaviour toward others, she started crying. It took some time, but finally she told me her parents had hired a math tutor. She claimed he abused her in her own home, while her parents were in the living room watching television.

"I reported the abuse to the principal, who told me to forget her excuses and punish her for hitting the boy. Then I talked to the police who said the same thing. The parents refused to believe it had happened. The teacher packed up his bags and disappeared. I suppose he moved to another school district and preyed on other kids."

"And you quit teaching and became a police officer."

"If you can't fight the system, you work to change it. At least being a cop, I had a chance to deal with the creeps when someone pointed them out to me."

"So now you want to help Jennifer Rivers?"

"Just talk to her. Find out if I'm right and if I am, direct her to a support group."

"Do you suspect she was one of Chuck's victims?"

"It's possible."

"And you think she killed him?"

"Someone did."

"You might be wrong."

Beth pulled a manila envelope from her shoulder bag.

"About ten years ago Chuck was in Newfoundland."

"How did you learn that?"

She stood with her back to Mike, watching the traffic flow over the bridge to the downtown core.

"Richard asked me to investigate Chuck's history."

"And you felt obligated to help? He still has a hold over you, doesn't he?"

"No. It wasn't like that. Richard said he would retract his story about Chuck if nothing turned up to confirm it. I wanted to prove Chuck's innocence. I refused to believe we would turn up anything that would show guilt, until the night you talked to Lyle."

"You believed that low life Richard would let a little thing like innocence stop a story? Why didn't you talk to me?"

"You were adamant that Chuck was guilty. At least Richard agreed to research the matter with an open mind."

"Right. Now you've given him a lead that should have come to us first. You have given him the information, haven't you?"

Beth clenched her hands. Damn, Mike was too upset.

"At lunch," she admitted in a whisper.

"It wasn't on the six o'clock news, why is he holding back?"

"The information came through the Internet and the guy who sent it won't reveal his identity. Maybe Richard's station won't let him broadcast the story without confirmation. How would I know?"

"Are you two getting cozy again? Is he the reason you won't agree to marry me?"

"Mike, no." She touched his arm, stopping him from turning away. "I thought I could use him, but as usual he turned the tables.

Would you want me to break my promise to help him, or more important, to abandon Chuck to his brand of reporting?"

"Then why won't you commit to marrying me?"

"I will, eventually. Taking this time is not about us, it's about proving to myself that I'm a whole person again, with all the wounds healed and fears banished. When I've done that, I'll meet you at the altar."

"You mean it?"

She reached a hand behind his neck and stretched up slightly. "Scouts' honour."

After several moments they pulled apart, suddenly self-conscious, and held hands as they strolled toward the conservatory parking lot.

"Do you want a big wedding," Mike asked as they wandered downhill.

"I want to solve Chuck's murder. Look over the messages in that envelope. The caller from Newfoundland identifies Chuck as Charles Altman, so you should run that name through your database, though I doubt any of his victims' families laid charges. Some of the other messages are vague, just possible leads, but if they represent even part of Chuck's past, he has blazed a trail of traumatized lives."

Mike shifted the envelope in his hand. "Any others you think are particularly relevant," he asked.

"One from Saskatchewan where the victims were a girl and a boy. The person who sent the message is acting on behalf of a member of her support group. Apparently, this woman lived with an offender named Charlie Anderson until she found out what he was doing to her kids. He left her six years ago. Since then the woman's son killed himself and she lost track of her daughter."

Beth watched the sunset send red highlights into the clouds. "Also, I have one from B.C. That one happened fifteen years ago, the same scenario, except the man's name was Carl Appleman. The offender moved in with a single mother and abused the kids. A son sent that message. He said his sister had just undergone therapy and dug up hidden memories."

"Any cases of abduction and murder?"

"That's police territory. Have you found anything?"

"Cases like that pop up all the time, it's linking the modus operandi that's the hard part. Maybe we can check for the initials because he seems to stay with a version of Charles and a last name starting with the letter A. I'll get this to the Analysis Unit. Maybe using your data, they can find a pattern of murders in specific areas at the right times."

When they reached their vehicles, Beth turned to Mike and drank in his profile. He cared about people. How could she do less than help him reach out to someone in need?

"I will stop by and talk to Jennifer on my way to work tomorrow. Can you phone to let her know I'm coming?"

He pulled her close, captured her lips, and ended all talk of business.

When she was free to speak, Beth said, "An informal, intimate wedding is more to my taste."

That won her another embrace and a lull in the conversation.

Releasing her, Mike said, "I'll call Jennifer as soon as I get back to the station. Keep in contact with the people who send you messages. Try to get names, addresses, and dates from them if you can and forward their replies to me at the station."

He held her hands tight. She felt his reluctance to let her leave. "How does a ceremony in your backyard sound," he asked, prolonging their departure.

Beth smiled and with a shake of her head, pushed him toward his vehicle. "Let's get this business wrapped up before we start making plans."

******

Mike found Constable Rose Byron still at her computer when he returned to the station. He pulled the sheaf of messages from the envelope Beth had given him and said, "See what you can find on these names, or any other version of Charles and a last name beginning with an A. Also, search the relevant cities for any unsolved child abductions or murders during the years given. Then send a copy of everything to the Crime Analysis Unit. Beth promised to fax any new messages directly here, so check them as they come in."

"Detective." Mike looked toward the doorway where a constable was ushering Lyle Lamont into the room. "He asked to speak with you personally."

Mike motioned him toward a desk in the corner, then pulled out his notebook, and asked, "Why did you take off last night?"

Lyle was unshaven and his clothing rumpled as if he'd been roaming the streets since he left Jennifer the previous night. "Have you caught them yet," he asked, his words coming out slowly, exaggerating his Newfoundlander drawl.

"Yes, we caught them and then we let Cara go, but her brother's still in custody."

"You let her out? Why would you do that! She's dangerous, she might hurt Jennifer."

"Why did you leave Jennifer alone? She could have been in danger."

Lyle shrugged his hefty shoulders, then turned his attention to chewing the cuticle of his thumbnail.

"Were you trying to follow them," Mike probed.

Lyle shook his head.

"Well, why are you here now? Is it about Chuck Albright?"

"I've come to turn myself in."

"For killing Chuck Albright," Mike asked.

Lyle's head pivoted upward and his frightened stare met Mike's. "No! Not that. I helped Cara and her brother sell credit card numbers. She caught me taking twenty dollars from the till and threatened to have me fired. I groveled and she said that I was thinking small time and that if I helped with their scam I'd do better, plus she wouldn't report me to the captain. I couldn't afford to lose my job."

Mike closed his eyes, then rubbed at them. "So you allowed them to steal from people."

"No one got hurt. Those credit card companies just write-off the losses."

"You're rationalizing your behaviour."

"I couldn't let my parents find out. They're good, churchgoing people."

"Lyle, that theft ring is low on my list of crimes right now. Chuck Albright is my concern and I think you knew him. Do you remember someone called Charles Altman? Was he your baseball coach about ten years ago?"

"No."

"Did you play baseball?"

"Yes."

"Ten years ago? You would have been about ten or eleven."

"Yes."

"In Newfoundland?"

"Yes."

"St. John's?"

"No. In Bay de Verde, in the north. It's a fishing village a long way from St. John's."

"Were you ever abused as a child?"

"My dad was free with his belt, but that ain't abuse."

"Why were you researching child sexual abuse and adult survivors of abuse?"

"I told Ms. McKinney it was for a friend."

"What is your friend's name?"

"Hey, it's not like you think. Jen was gathering some background information for that reporter, Tanner. She wants to get into reporting and talked to him about it. He encouraged her to develop an idea. She figured that with the anniversary of those little kids being kidnapped coming around, it would be a good story. I just asked your friend for some sources, Jen did the work. I saw her leave the stuff on Tanner's desk myself. It was the day she finished working at the station. She hoped he would call her about it, in fact she called a couple of times and left messages, but he never called back."

"Did you know that she phoned to tell him about the thefts on the River Belle?"

"She told me."

"Why didn't she identify herself to Tanner?"

"Jen said he was avoiding her and she was afraid he wouldn't follow up on the tip if he knew it came from her."

"So she had a grudge against Tanner. What about Chuck? Was she upset with him too?"

"Hey, don't try to hang this on her. She wasn't even on the boat."

"Did you see her leave?"

"She was sick."

"Did you see her leave the boat?"

"I didn't see her on it after we sailed."

"Could she have hidden anywhere on the boat?"

"Look, she didn't even know the guy, he was on holidays all the time she worked at the station. She even covered part of his job while she was working the reception desk."

"And she worked on the River Belle during the same time?"

"Sure, one was an eight to five job, the other seven to midnight, three nights a week and Saturdays."

"She worked part of Saturday?"

"Of course. She didn't get sick until the dinner theatre cruise. Look, she didn't know the guy and she wasn't on the boat. No one can hide on a boat, they're set up to use every inch of available space."

Mike nodded, distracted by his thoughts.

"How much trouble am I in with this theft ring thing?"

The boy's forlorn look made Mike angry. "A lot more than if you had stopped with that first twenty dollars."

CHAPTER 23

Jennifer woke crying and terrified. She longed for time to reverse itself. She longed to be on her mountain bike, free from casts and crutches, riding through the narrow, twisting paths with branches speeding by inches from her face. Tearing up and down hills that were both steep and treacherous was how she usually outran her devils.

Jennifer visualized the bike trails as they wound between the spruce, pine, and aspen. They ran for miles, some wide and paved, full of seniors, baby carriages, and wheelchairs. Others were gravelled and safe for the half-hearty hikers and timid bikers. But Jennifer craved the freedom of the wind, the silence of the dawn, and the awakening cries of the blue jay and robin.

A predawn chill seeped through the open window and she pulled the afghan closer to her chin. The pain in her ankle wasn't too bad. Soon she would be able to—what? Go back to work? Leave the city? Was there a need for that now?

For two days, Mrs. McPherson had fussed over her. She had insisted that Jennifer take her painkillers and had left the childproof cap off the bottle. She kept the two thermal carafes on the coffee table full, one with milk, the other with water. A basket of fruit and a plate of chocolate chip cookies sat next to her latest offering, a plastic wrapped cheese sandwich.

Last night Jennifer had had enough of her well-meaning attention and sent her away. She didn't want food and she didn't want to dull the pain. It reminded her that she was still alive, although her life lay in ruins and her dreams had crashed to earth. Now they were like her beautiful bike, all twisted and bent. Why had she called Richard Tanner about the thefts? How many people had she hurt with that one call?

Cara and her brother, though they deserved punishment. Still, she had repaid Lyle for his kindness, for all she owed him, by hurting him. That was unforgivable.

And her mother. Jennifer knew she would have to face her soon. She couldn't run anymore. Maybe it was time to tell her how Eric had died. How he had been depressed about losing his lousy minimum wage job, how he feared his future held nothing more fulfilling.

Jennifer worried she was tied to that same downward spiral. If she lost her job, she wouldn't be able to save the money she needed for college and she wouldn't become a reporter. Would she lose Lyle too? Would he go to jail? She was too tired to try putting her life back together.

Dawn peeped between the black needles of a towering spruce. The picnic table became a shadow against the brightening backdrop of the grassy field.

Another day. She didn't want to face the pain of another day. The pain of knowing she had hurt people. The pain of memories that haunted her nights and overshadowed her days. Physical pain was like a pinprick compared to that other pain.

The first ray of sun darted through the open curtain and landed on the bottle of pills. They could make the pain go away. If she took enough, she would never have to deal with the pain again.

Maybe Eric had been right after all. Life was too hard.

******

"Late night, my love?"

Beth hadn't booked any clients for Saturday morning and was enjoying a leisurely sleep-in. She smiled dreamily at the tenderness in Mike's voice.

"Did you get the messages I faxed over?"

"Yes. We've spent the night checking out names and dates, a definite cross-country pattern exists."

Beth heard a hard edge in his voice and felt her hope of proving Chuck innocent drift far away. "How extensive a pattern?"

"We've tracked Chuck to six provinces and Rose found a correlation with ten unsolved homicides."

Barely able to comprehend the enormity of his crimes, Beth said nothing.

"Lyle came to see me last night," Mike continued. "He admits he was part of the operation on the boat."

"Did you question Lyle about Chuck's murder?"

"He claims the child abuse research was for Jennifer, who was researching the story for Richard. I'm on my way to confirm that with him now."

"It's only seven. You're not going to wake him are you?"

"Police business knows no regular hours. Besides, I want to get his story before I head home."

"And, you will love waking him up."

"Are you busy tonight," Mike asked.

******

Richard glared into Ceretzke's steady blue eyes.

"Ceretzke, don't you ever sleep? Beth must really hate your hours."

"Put on some coffee, we've got a few things to talk about."

"Put the coffee on yourself, I'm getting dressed."

Richard stomped down the hall. What did the cop want now?

"What is this about, Ceretzke," Richard called from his bedroom as he pulled on a shirt and socks to go with his hastily donned slacks.

"Jennifer Rivers. Why did you say you hardly remembered her when she was researching a story for you?"

Richard walked into the kitchen where the detective was scooping fresh grounds into the coffee machine.

"She was a dumb kid who wanted to be an ace reporter. I might have made encouraging noises. Nothing more."

"What about the research she gave you?"

"She didn't give me any research."

"We have a witness who says differently."

"What is this? Even if she did give me some stuff, which she didn't, why does it warrant an early morning call?"

"I'm trying to lock down a motive."

"Okay, I'll play your game. What was the research about?"

"Sexual abuse and adult survivors of abuse."

"That was hers?" Richard regretted the words as soon as he spoke them. He lit a cigarette and inhaled deeply while trying to ignore the detective's triumphant expression and the folders stacked at the end of his kitchen table.

"So it's not such a surprise?"

The harder Richard ignored the folders, the more Ceretzke's gaze swung in their direction.

Gathering them with a quick sweep of his arm, Richard moved toward the hall. He had to hide the folders. "I'll clear this stuff so we have room for coffee."

"Hold it Tanner. Let me see that."

Richard debated evoking his rights and kicking Ceretzke out. Finally, he returned to the table and dropped the stack of materials. Damn, he should have realized two people had gathered the clippings in those files. That one with the tidy citations had to be information that that Jennifer kid had collected. Still, the important ones were in Chuck's handwriting.

"This is just research for an unrelated story," Richard said. Could he hold back the prize winning material and bluff Ceretzke into accepting the dull stuff?

"Why don't I believe you," Ceretzke asked.

"Hey, I found them. If she meant them for me, why didn't she give them to me?"

"If she didn't give them to you, how did you get them?"

"It's basic, first draft research stuff." Richard ignored the detective's question as he tossed the library books at him, then slapped the meticulously compiled file on the table.

"What about those?" Ceretzke pointed at the stapled folders.

"They're not hers."

Richard felt Ceretzke delving into his mind, pulling his secrets into the light. Ceretzke extended his hand, his eyes never leaving Richard.

"I want them back." Richard thrust the files at Ceretzke.

Ceretzke started with the last folder, rifling through the scraps of paper.

"Do you know what you have here?"

Richard shrugged. He knew all right. He had a major story that he was probably going to lose to the cops. Still, if he played his cards right perhaps he could salvage enough to present to the network moguls. He pulled a cigarette pack toward him. He should never have let Ceretzke in before enjoying a pot of coffee and a pack of cigarettes. If he'd been thinking properly, he would have photocopied the stuff before letting it out of his hands.

"These are Chuck's plans to abduct the kids. Maps, time lines, details. When did you get this stuff?"

"I found it in his locker the morning after he died. I figured he'd stolen my idea. I didn't even look at it until a couple of nights ago and then I couldn't make sense of most of it."

"So Jennifer gave her notes to Chuck to pass on to you but instead he kept them."

"That can't be right. She left on Friday and he was back at work the following Monday. They never met."

"Did you get to work before him?"

"I try not to rise before nine ordinarily and I rarely arrive at the station before eleven."

"Why would Chuck take the research?"

"Chuck wasn't happy when I mentioned doing a similar story. That's what our argument on the River Belle was about. Perhaps he thought I asked for the research material and took it, hoping to delay my progress."

Richard inhaled more nicotine then poured a cup of coffee from the still dripping machine. "Since I've co-operated, you can reciprocate and leave me that material."

"Sorry Tanner," Ceretzke said, tucking the files under his arm.

"These deserve a thorough analysis. They're my absolute proof in our case against Chuck."

******

Magpie had decided Beth should stay awake and paced the full length of her body to emphasize his decision. She gave up with good grace and hugged the large black and white cat, then headed for the shower.

Now, with her coffee mug in hand, she faced her computer where the volume of incoming messages had slowed. This morning only three new ones waited, one from Montana, a second from Germany. The last was a follow-up message from the woman in Saskatchewan.

Beth forwarded the first two to the police station. The third said the woman wanted to talk to her and gave a phone number.

Beth reached for the phone. The time on the message was seven, more than an hour earlier, and it asked her to call as soon as she could.

The woman's hesitant greeting was followed by an excited exclamation when Beth identified herself.

"I'm so glad you called me back. When my son showed me your message I knew it was important to speak to you, but I don't like those machines. You don't know who is looking at what you send."

"What did you want to talk to me about?"

"Linda's in Edmonton and so are you, so you can talk to her yourself."

"Linda is the friend you wrote me about?"

"Yes. Linda Olsson. I told her I saw Jenny working on the River Belle and she hopped right into her car and took off. Barely had enough time to ask me to water her plants and feed the dog."

"Jenny is Linda's daughter?"

"She ran away with her brother. Then he killed himself and she wouldn't let the police tell Linda where she was. That's why Linda is in our support group."

"What kind of support group?"

"One for parents with troubled kids."

"You say this woman is in Edmonton?"

"Yes. We always stay at a motel near West Edmonton Mall during our semi-annual shopping trips."

"Why is it important that I speak to her?"

"Well, I saw the picture of the man who was killed on the boat. The newsman said he's a suspect in the murders of those little kids. He's Linda's Charlie all right and that boat was where she was headed to meet Jenny. That kind of connection needs exploring."

"I think you better tell the police about this."

"No way. And don't set the police on Linda neither. I thought long and hard before I called you. One person talking to her will be bad enough, but if you bring in a truckload of cops, well, she don't like them, not since the way they treated her after Eric killed himself."

Beth contemplated passing the information onto Mike, but he would probably treat the woman like a murder suspect. Richard could deal with her, but he would pull up to the motel with a camera, trying for an exclusive interview.

No, she would check it out on her own. She would just talk to the woman in a non-threatening way and find out how much of what her friend had said was the truth.

It was nearly nine-thirty when Beth reached the motel. It was a one-storey building built in an L-shape, with a small coffee shop and office at the foot of the L. It was only three blocks from West Edmonton Mall so its parking lot was full of tour buses from neighbouring provinces and the closer states. Beth couldn't understand what drew people to the world's largest shopping mall. That promise of magnitude alone had kept her away from its stores for years.

The manager pointed her toward the room registered to Linda Olsson. A car with Saskatchewan plates was parked in front of the unit and Beth knocked, then waited for so long that she wondered of she should have phoned first.

Eventually the door opened, revealing a middle-aged woman. She was thin, scrawny Beth's grandfather would have said. Her hair hung limp around her face and her voice contained a fatigue that told Beth she hadn't slept well in a long time. She held the door wide and waited for Beth to explain her presence.

"Mrs. Olsson, my name is Beth McKinney. I was a friend of Chuck Albright, the man who was murdered last Saturday evening."

The woman remained motionless.

"I've been told you knew him under a different name. Look, could we go to the coffee shop and talk for a minute?"

"Charlie fooled me into thinking he was heaven sent, but he was the devil. Because of him, I lost my kids." Linda stepped backward into the room. "We can talk in here."

"I don't want to impose, the cafe will be fine."

Linda shrugged and started closing the door.

"Okay," Beth said as she held the door ajar, then followed her into the well-worn room. The bed covers looked as if they had been hastily straightened. The furniture was standard, mid-range motel. A print of a prairie landscape was fastened tight to one wall.

Beth left the door open and perched on the edge of the tub chair under the window. Linda Olsson sat on the edge of the bed, her hands clasped, her ankles crossed.

"What happened, Mrs. Olsson. Can you tell me?"

"It seemed perfect. Charlie was a pleasant person. A good man, you know. He wasn't like some of the guys you meet who like to hit women. He just had a problem with kids."

"I know. He had me fooled too."

"Do you have children? I'm so sorry for them."

"No, nothing like that. He was a friend. You said you lost your kids, how did that happen?"

"He didn't kill them, if that's what you think. I still don't believe he killed those kids like the television says he did. He was always so adamant that parents had to watch over their kids. Going on about how valuable they were and how people should learn to appreciate them because you never knew when you would lose them. He never beat my kids."

She sat very still. "What he did was worse. I figured Jenny was just being spiteful. You know how kids can be, all active imaginations. Then my boy said he was being hurt too, so I kicked Charlie out. Eric seemed to come around, but Jenny was never the same."

"I understand your daughter works on the River Belle. You were on the boat Saturday night, weren't you?"

The thin, little woman pushed herself off the bed and advanced on Beth.

"Are you accusing me of killing him?"

Beth stood and edged toward the door. "I'm just trying to find out what happened."

"To your friend." She spat out the words. "I heard you the first time. Leave me and mine out of your questions. He was a pig who deserved to die."

Beth hesitated, then plunged ahead. "Mrs. Olssen, I didn't mean to imply you would hurt anyone. When your friend phoned, she was so concerned that I thought I should talk to you before I went to see Jennifer."

"You know where Jenny is? She hasn't been back to work and those people on the boat won't give me her address. I've spent days looking for her." The hope in her voice changed, as did her anxious expression. "Why are you going to talk to her?"

"To suggest some agencies that might help her deal with the abuse she suffered. Perhaps an agency that will help recover any repressed memories or that can teach her to cope with how she was hurt."

"You know why she hasn't been to work? Was it because of me?"

"She was hurt in a bike accident Saturday evening. You didn't know?"

"I said I've been looking for her. Where does she live?"

Beth hesitated, aware she didn't know all the facts. "Maybe I can ask her to phone you?"

"No, she wouldn't do it. Tell me where to find her. After I've talked to her, I can go home. I have to get back home soon or I'll lose my job."

Beth thought for a moment but was unable to see any reason not to pass on the information. Finally, resolving to be at Jennifer's side when her mother arrived, she recited the address Mike had given her.

As Beth left, Linda said, "If I'd have recognized him that night,

I might have done it, but I was so busy thinking about Jennifer I didn't notice anyone else."

******

Linda watched Beth McKinney drive away. Maybe she should have left on Monday as she had planned, but she found she couldn't desert her child without talking to her just once more. Even if Jenny refused to talk to her, she had to know her mother cared enough to try to make contact. This might be her only chance to beg for forgiveness.

Linda started emptying drawers, folding the clothes neatly before she placed them in her suitcase. It was time to go home, but first she was going to drive to Jenny's and talk to her. Maybe they would go home together.

Charlie's death had already been paid for in the pain and misery of his victims, surely that was enough.

******

"Mike, I forgot to ask, did you tell Jennifer Rivers I would be around to see her?"

Beth's voice came through the telephone receiver, penetrating his sleep-filled mind. After logging in the files he'd taken from Tanner, he had signed out and gone home for a few hours sleep.

"Sorry, I forgot. Too much has happened since we talked last night. I'll call her now."

"I talked to her mother, she's in Edmonton. Mike, she wants to talk to Jennifer, too. I gave her the address. Look, I'm on my way to her apartment now. I'll call you after I speak to her."

Beth hung up before Mike had time to reply. He dialled Jennifer's apartment. When no one answered after numerous rings, he rolled out of bed and out the door to his truck.

CHAPTER 24

Beth rang Jennifer's buzzer. There was no response. She scanned the nameplates and rang the manager.

A breathless voice boomed from the speaker. "You here about the one bedroom for rent? It's got a good view of the ravine."

"I want to talk to Jennifer Rivers. Is she in? She doesn't answer her bell."

"How am I supposed to know why she's not answering? She didn't answer for the other reporter either and I chased him and his camera crew off pretty quick."

"I'm not a reporter, but I'm afraid she might be hurt. Can you let me in to check?"

"I'm not her mother, besides she's made it plain she doesn't want my attentions."

Beth waited, debating whether to call Mike for assistance. The manager continued speaking, "Who are you anyway? Why should I let you in?"

"Detective Ceretzke asked me to drop by to talk with Ms. Rivers. Would you let me in so I can make sure she is all right?"

"If that handsome detective is a friend of yours, I guess it's okay. Just a minute."

"You can just buzz me in."

"Nope. I like to see who people are. You can never be too careful."

"Please hurry."

"Always in such a rush. Don't see it helps . . . ."

The voice cut off in mid-sentence leaving Beth staring at the speaker. Moments later a heavyset woman strolled down the hall toward the glass door.

" . . . life on the farm meant you were always busy, but . . . ."

She continued her monologue as Beth followed her down the hall.

"... never rushing. Just did what had to be done to keep everything ... here we are. This is Ms. Rivers' apartment." She raised a fist that was covered in age-spots, and pounded on the door.

"Jennifer, you in there?"

They stood listening for any faint sound until the manager turned to Beth.

"I better open it. Just to see if she is all right."

She pulled a ring of keys from the pocket of her polka dotted housedress and sorted through them at a speed that displayed her contempt of rushing. Blocking the room from Beth's view, she pushed the door open.

"She's sleeping. Poor dear is in such pain and then all that ruckus with the gun the other night and those people trying to kill her. I'm just glad she's finally resting."

The woman started closing the door, but Beth pushed by her and stepped into the room.

"Wait a minute. I want to check her."

Moving swiftly out of the woman's reach, Beth crossed the carpet to the sofa, uncertain of what she would find. A bottle for prescription painkillers lay on its side, empty. A thermos jug sat in a small puddle of white liquid.

Beth shook the girl's thin shoulder. Her breathing was shallow and rapid.

"Jennifer."

She shook her again, but got no response.

"Phone for an ambulance," Beth ordered.

No words came from the woman who now moved with a speed and economy of movement that surprised Beth. The door buzzer sounded too quickly to be an ambulance. A moment later Mike rushed into the room.

"Is she alive?"

Beth looked up at him and nodded. "But she took a lot of pills. An ambulance is on the way."

On cue, the sound of a siren penetrated the room.

******

Linda rushed toward the attendants as they wheeled the gurney to the waiting ambulance.

"Jenny," she whispered, trying to catch some sign of life in the pale face. "Why?"

The attendants pushed her aside. She felt a strong hand grab her forearm. It belonged to the reporter who had first said Charlie was a killer. He was pushing a microphone at her, crowding the medical people who were trying to help Jenny.

"Mrs. Olsson."

She shook her head, denying his plea. She had to help her Jenny.

Then the woman from the motel stood beside her and a tall man, who looked like a cop, pushed the microphone away. His words confirmed her guess.

"I have to ask you some questions."

"I must go to the hospital with Jenny. She needs me."

"Not right now. You can see her later."

******

Again, Jennifer woke to the sounds and smells of a hospital. She opened her eyes, not surprised to see Dr. Raj.

"You come to harm too often, miss. Please take better care of yourself." His smile seemed plastered on, good bedside manners by the textbook.

She groaned aloud when she realized that she was still alive. "I shouldn't be here. Should have died."

"Ms. Rivers."

She turned her head. The deep voice belonged to Detective Ceretzke.

"Why did you take those pills?"

"Trying to stop the pain."

"What pain?"

"All the pain that ever was or that ever will be."

"Your mother is here."

"She shouldn't have come. Now she will be in pain too."

"Tell us about the pain."

She kept her eyes closed as words, barely louder than a whisper, rushed from her.

"His voice brought back the pain, the blackness, the fears. The nightmare started, although I was awake. All the therapists said to forgive him, that he was sick. Even the police said I was mistaken about him. He was a good man, they said."

She remembered the pats on her head, the visits to a therapist who accused her of lying out of jealously.

"He said it was just a game, but he hurt me. My mom kicked him out of the house, but sometimes after he left I imagined I heard him telling her he would read me a story. I hated going to bed. I still do. Mom wouldn't believe me, but after my brother said the same things, she started watching. Why wouldn't she believe me?"

Jennifer remembered the horror she had seen on her mother's face when Eric finally confirmed her stories. She had acted then, kicking Charlie out of the house, but it was too little and too late to stop the pain.

"The police didn't do anything to him. He just left town. I always hoped he was dead. When the counsellors asked, I told them I would forgive him but I knew it was a lie. When I heard his voice on the boat, I knew who he was. Then, when the words they were yelling forced their way past my fear, I got angry. He was telling the reporter that pedophiles couldn't infiltrate the city's programs for kids. He said they would be screened out. I wondered if he meant himself, too."

The detective sat there like a frozen statute. Did he believe her? Why should he be different than the rest?

"All those years of handling the fear and still I was so angry I couldn't speak or think. I just watched him and his fake anger as he stalked to the back of the boat. Then the captain announced the dinner buffet and everyone went inside. I forgot about Richard Tanner and Cara. All I could think of was Charlie standing at the back of the boat. I hid in a stall in the women's room so no one would wonder why I wasn't working."

She remembered stifling the claustrophobia that haunted her. She had savoured the knowledge that she was going to exterminate vermin and had only to figure out the best way to do it.

"The anger I felt as a kid had grown huge. It makes you crazy when people won't listen, except for the stupid counsellors with their platitudes. That anger grew until I heard his voice on the boat and then it exploded. I didn't know he'd hurt other kids but I did know I could end my pain. Not that I really thought about it, it was just something I knew.

"I waited until it was almost dark and everyone was in the dining room. Then I took the fry pan and hit him. My brother's voice told me to roll him into the river, to make him fish food. I tried pushing him over the railing, but he weighed twice what I do. I got his blood on me. I hadn't counted on the blood. I wanted to wipe it up and hide until I could get away but then I heard someone coming. I could have hidden in the snack bar I guess, but I didn't think of that. I just slid over the rail and pulled him in after me."

She studied the detective's face. It held some pity, but mostly she saw scorn.

"The river was high and I didn't think I'd survive, but I did. I got swept about a mile down the river before I got back to shore. I scrambled through the bush, hiding when anyone passed. After the Belle docked, I got to my bike and headed home.

"I figured if I could get home, I would get out of town. I rode the trail like a maniac. Then I skidded. When I woke up here, I didn't remember what had happened right away. Then it all came back and I couldn't even run away."

She closed her eyes, blocking the judgment she read in his expression.

"You know the rest. Lyle was waiting when I got home. He looked so pathetically happy to see me. He told me he was scared because they'd found Chuck's body and the blood on the boat, and he thought I'd been killed. That's when I realized no one suspected me and decided to bluff it out. I guess no one saw me after the boat sailed because they were busy watching that argument."

She opened her eyes and looked around the room. "When you see Lyle, tell him I'm sorry. I didn't mean for him to be involved with all of this."

"Jennifer, I'm going to call a lawyer, someone who can help you get through this. Maybe she can make a deal, after all you did help us solve the murders of those kids."

She looked up at the detective, her eyes filling with tears. "He deserved to be killed you know. I'm not sorry I did it."

CHAPTER 25

Cool air drifted into the shade of the deck, reviving wilting bedding plants and allowing the occupants the chance to enjoy the warmth of their coffee.

Beth was angry again, a feeling she had felt too often lately, but this time the anger was directed at the justice system in general. "But why did you have to arrest her?"

"Beth," Mike turned to her parents as if looking for support. "She did kill Chuck. What kind of provocation she had doesn't matter."

"But Richard got barely a slap on the wrist for taking the files from Chuck's locker. Why don't you arrest him?"

Mike ran his hand through his hair before he answered. "How can we prove he didn't think it was research material that Chuck had gathered for him? The chief says to call it poor judgment. The television station is busy licking his boots over landing a nation-wide story they can turn into a TV movie."

"But he broke into Chuck's apartment."

"When Richard started poking around, Chuck's death still looked like an accident."

"Let it rest, Beth," her brother said, coming to Mike's rescue. Then he asked Mike, "What can we do for the girl? She shouldn't have to go to jail."

"Gloria Azzara is a good defense attorney and she's already working on a deal. Legal Aid will pay some of her legal costs, but Jennifer will need moral support and maybe a job when this is all over."

"What about the two of you," Dorothy McKinney asked.

Beth looked across to Mike and felt her anger dissipate. "We will be discussing our future."

THE END